I0618480

Green Monk of Tremn

Book II
The Rise of Plant Man
Lord of War,
Conquest and Revenge

~

NJ Bridgewater

Abergavenny, UK: Jaha Publishing

ISBN: 978-0-9957369-3-1

Dedication & Acknowledgments

To my wife, Grace, without whose support this book could not have been written.

In addition, I would like to thank my mother, Carolyn, who helped to edit this book, and to my son, Jalál, whose constant love inspires me.

I would also like to thank my father, Leslie, for inspiring me to think for myself and express my thoughts and ideas through art and writing.

Map of the Continent of Tremnad
on the Planet Tremn

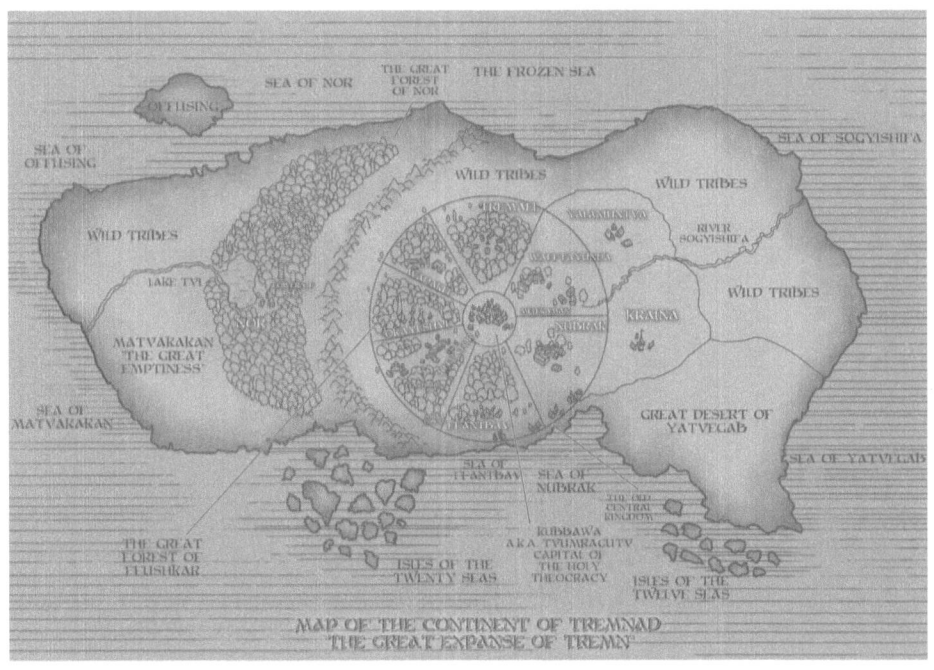

Contents

CHAPTER XIII.

The Shan

~⁃

A vast field, a never-ending plain stretched out in all directions, eternally, from endless horizon to endless horizon, rich with a verdant luxuriance the like of which no man had ever seen, radiant and effulgent with an otherworldly light which shone from an unseen source, illuminating with its splendour all created things equally, as if everything reflected that same light with perfect and complete refulgence. As he looked at his hands and his body, he found them to be as luminous as everything else.

"Where am I?" he asked aloud, but his lips did not move.

The words simply entered the air, if it could be called air, and echoed in the immensity of space. Time seemed to be still—unmoving— as the flow of time itself pertains to the physical world and Ifunka was somewhere else entirely. No time, then, could have passed between the question and answer, or perhaps it was an eternity, as stillness and motion, the immediate and the eternal, were one and the same in this place without place.

"*Tae vam* (thou knowest)," came the reply, which seemed to be in Vocatae, but whether it were utterance or thought, Ifunka could not surmise.

"*Vanitom vamso* (how do I know)?"

"*Taesiv vamediph oucau zepaic le, oucau zepai taesiv le cub* (within thee is the knowledge of all things and all things are within thee)."

"*Celphic mimra le, saup, pheum cub sipha hrhidva cel oucau siphic ademia* (this is the *mimra*, then—the universal field which embraces all of the physical universe)."

"*Hrheu cub naves* (yea and nay)."

"*Naves* (nay)?"

"*Celphic vaniut le celtemtae ucre hreudia ahrhaphelast, amenaxast–anaux-ogast* (this is a way thou canst perceive it with the senses, a symbol—a metaphor)."

"*Phel taeleso* (who art thou)?"

"*Enra levon cel enin cub eninva, tae anaux, avium methuratiph, pheum cub gehrhatiph, caquolatap, iaphasgesiamvon* (I am a being who watches, who sees, like thee created, yet wiser, stronger, dispassionate, far-reaching)."

"*Aman, saup* (a god, then)?"

"*Naves, avium sapie denor aphseiae* (nay, but a man of another kind)."

"*Vatom itiph leso* (why am I here)?"

"*Enra initov phesphatom tae naph. Caemye raquost; saquetemtae sup, temtae lisiocra–saquetemtae quost, taihrhon oninva denparum. Cacansa Vabacim ralisarum, ca taicim. Oninvathie canonarum tae Tuint exodcon arn* (I come only to warn thee. There is a treasure; if thou find it, give it away—if thou keep it, lose thy way. Trust in the Great Spirit, not in thyself. Keep to the Path or the Cursed One shall lead thee)!"

"Ifunka!" a voice seemed to intrude on this peaceful realm. It was Shem; he awoke. Morning. Shem leaned over him. The sun shone over the treetops, birds chirped, the air was crisp yet steadily warming. The smell of roast *wiro* enticed his nostrils.

"Breakfast is ready," said Shem.

"I've missed *kashroim!*"

"I couldn't wake you; anyway, in illness or situations of urgent need, we're exempt from the obligatory prayers."

As he sat up to enjoy a wonderful, hot, steaming breakfast, Ifunka's mind overflowed with images of his night-vision. Who was the speaker, that being which claimed to be a man—albeit a powerful man? He wanted to disclose every detail to Shem yet, however vivid it appeared in his mind, he could not transfer that vision into the medium of syllables and sounds. However much he tried, the words evaded him, until he felt entirely defeated and dejected. What was this impenetrable wall which stopped his tongue? He kept silent and ate with great concentration. Shem, the usually introverted one, noticed his unusual behaviour and queried him.

"What's wrong, brother?"

"What's wrong? Everything's wrong," he replied, breaking his silence. "I don't know what to say. I'm troubled. I think there's a greater purpose to what we're doing but the path is fraught with danger."

"We have faced many perils already."

"Not of that nature—I mean perils of choice—snares of the mind, moral rectitude. Shall we keep to the Path which our Lord has laid out for us, or shall we fall into the trap of Afflish, the Accursed One?"

"Do not fear, brother," Shem reassured him, placing his hand on Ifunka's shoulder. "We're in this together. We'll keep each other on the path."

"I hope so" said Ifunka, but his words were not filled with confidence.

"Ifunka... keep strong. Tvem was right. The *mimra* surrounds us, embraces us. Its energies flow through us. Indeed, we have been led along this path."

Ifunka did not respond. He lifted his gaze unto the lofty clouds above, glorious white and transcendent, which floated gently through the light-blue morning sky. His eyes looked up at a physical sky, yet his soul longed for another horizon, an unending horizon stretching on through boundless eternity. The light of the sun, ancient Vukt, brilliant and luminous as it was, paled like evanescent mist before the deathless glow which radiated from a matrix of reality that was radiant in and of its own essence. 'Yet was this not a parable, a mere representation of something which is immaterial, indescribable and unfathomable?' he wondered. But there was something even greater that this: Ganka, the realm of Paradise. So exalted must that place be, if the *mimra* be only a coil of reality binding this lesser kingdom in all its fastness! Shem observed him closely, seeming to discern an ethereal light on his cheeks and brow, as if he were, even now, reflecting light from a hidden source. He did not speak, however, and turned his attention to the more pressing matter of the ailing *ffentbaff*. As if divining his intention, Ifunka turned and asked:

"The *ffentbaff*—how is it?"

"Gadffash—he is well. The fire warmed him and he is lying by that grove of trees just there—" he pointed to a small circle of trees a few *oksha*s away. There the gargantuan beast of burden sat in contentment, on all fours, with bulbous hairy belly brushing up against the surrounding tree trunks. It flicked its ears to repel some pesky *ffug*-flies which fed on its sweat and flecks of dead skin.

"Gadffash? You gave it a name?"

"Why not? We are to rely upon it for transportation and protection. I'd rather know who or what that is which we rely upon."

"Gadffash it is then. A suitable name."

They made ready, saddled the beast and mounted it.

"Which direction?" asked Shem.

"We continue southwest. A day or two, I think, and we'll reach our goal. Then, do or die, we shall meet our fate."

They spurred Gadffash on; he moved swiftly through the forest for three hours or more, until they stopped to rest in a small clearing circled by a ring of large stones, called *keffe akffostavt* ('keeper-stones'), placed there by ancient peoples long before pen touched paper and history took its shape.

"We can wait here for a little while, but we shouldn't tarry long," said Ifunka.

"I've read about these places," said Shem. "The stones form protective circles—at least in the superstitions of the ancients. There are forest sprites, evil beings which can shape-shift or vanish at will. They lead wayfarers astray and devour their spirits."

"The *shan*? Yes, but they are mere myths and legends—figments of the imagination."

"Perhaps they refer to the *hitvah*—the clay men."

"No, those are a separate legend, and we've seen those with our very eyes. They are living men who have strayed from the path of righteousness and become like animals, shorn of reason or morality. I pity them—creatures of passion and violence that they are. The *shan* are another thing altogether, a superstition."

"Let's sit for a while."

They both rested, leaning on the large yet perfectly smooth stones until they drifted off to sleep. The *ffentbaff*, who was tied to one of these, merely rested on all fours whilst flicking *ffug*-flies with its ears and tail, occasionally grunting and snorting as he listed.

As he slept, Ifunka seemed to enter the *mimra* once more. He was in the same plain and heard the same voice which had spoken to him before.

"*Oninvathie canonarum* (keep to the path)," it said.

"*Phel tae leso* (who art thou)?" asked Ifunka.

"*Taetom isicmon* (I have told thee)," it replied. "*Enra enin cub idolad, quirb enratae naphvon cub. Enhrhon quiasra idolemcra* (I watch and listen, and now I warn thee. Heed my counsel)."

"*Ves taehrhon iedi leso* (what is thy name)?"

"*Arret banpeic cub weseictae rumiadvon, dohrhitae sueva quatoric lamavon, enu wese ca pheum cuctap aquan ca van cub* (thou clingest to the world of syllables and sounds, even when thou art standing on the plain of eternity, where sound does not exist and time has no meaning)."

"*Saup, enra liphcra dea* (let me go then)."

"*Enamcra! Cei wasiaint le* (watch out! Ye are surrounded)."

When he awoke, it was already evening and the sun had begun to set. 'How is that possible?' he wondered. 'Have we slept all day?'

"Shem!" he called.

Shem awoke with a start.

"It's evening! How have we slept so long?"

"I don't know. Even Gadffash is still sleeping."

The *ffentbaff* was, it appeared, in a deep sleep, its eyes closed fast, its great chest heaving with every intake of breath and shrinking with every mighty exhalation.

"Perhaps it is the influence of the *keffe akvostavt*. We should make haste; we've lost a lot of time."

As they got their supplies together, Shem froze. Ifunka looked at him in wonder. Shem was stiff as a stone, his eyes wide with fear. Turning,

Ifunka espied the cause—a set of eyes, glowing white, stared at them through the darkness.

"What is that?"

"Don't speak," whispered Shem. "It's one of them..."

"What shall we do?" asked Ifunka, his heart pounding fiercely. "We can't surely stay here."

"What choice do we have? This stone circle should protect us. If we leave it, those things shall surely get us. To be devoured by the *shan* is a fate worse than death."

"So, what then? Wait here? No, we can't."

He took out his dagger and aimed it at the nefarious eyes. With one, well-aimed blow, he sent the dagger squarely at the creature's temple. The dagger hummed through the night air as it spun—the eyes vanished and a thump could be discerned, as if something had fallen. Yet, what guarantee was there that this was not some trick pulled by the *shan* to appear as if it had been struck? They waited several minutes but the eyes did not rematerialize.

"What think you, Shem? Subterfuge?"

"We should stay—just to be safe."

"We're already days behind where we should be. Brother Ushwan is probably dead. But we must hope that he lives. We must go on—as fast as we can—these *shan* be damned!"

"The eyes are gone—perhaps you're right."

They poised themselves to flee.

"Now!" cried Ifunka and they sped off into the forest vastness.

They continued on for ages, bruising and cutting their hands and arms on the tree branches and twigs as they ran on, puffing and panting, thrusting their battered bodies through the pitch blackness of the night; yet there was no pursuit, at least none that either could discern, so Ifunka called for them to halt.

"Shem! Let's rest."

They fell on their knees, so exhausted were they. Their *ffentbaff,* Gadffash, whom they had forgotten, must have wandered away from the clearing by then. They had forgotten even to look for him, so terrified were they of the elusive white eyes. As they turned to look from whence they had come, two eyes became visible, bright but not radiant, as if possessed of some self-contained light, ethereal yet maleficent, fixed like jewels hanging on some ebony-black tapestry suspended by the dark forces of night and death. Ifunka and Shem froze, as if overcome by the inevitability of their own deaths—having been propelled by fate, or the Great Spirit, to the final point of their journey. The lights remained stationary—fixed—and almost lifeless. His heartbeat boomed loudly in the silence of the night as Ifunka contemplated the death that might overcome him. Shem was transfixed, as if mesmerized by the eyes' frightful duality. The standoff continued and waxed on, until Ifunka felt his nerve dissolving and hopelessness overwhelming him.

"If we turn," he whispered. "It will catch us; if we run, it will catch us. What shall we do?"

"Trust in the Great Spirit," Shem urged. "He has preserved us thus far. Why would he abandon us now?"

"Every beginning has an end—every journey has a termination. At any moment, the curtain may drop."

"Fight or flight—there are only two options. We cannot fight this thing, so let's run."

"Agreed."

They turned and ran again. This time, a palpable sense of dread surrounded them, as if all hope and light had been sucked out of them. Evil, in all its vacuous turbidity, its cold indifference, embraced them like clouds of blackest oil infusing briny depths. Like shoals of hapless fish, they drowned in its terrible progression. An ice-cold hand wrapped around the nape of Shem's neck and he froze. Ifunka turned round only to find his friend enmeshed in a swarm of pure white figures, naked yet foul in their inhuman gauntness and elongated features. They wrapped their frigid arms and legs around him, as if to ravage their foe before imbibing his innermost essence. They were silent in their slow yet unnatural movements, their terrifying earnestness. Shem could neither scream nor flee, so firmly was he locked within their overpowering embrace.

"Shem!!!" Ifunka screamed, his voice carrying far and wide throughout the forest.

Yet the *shan* were unmoving, unconcerned, save in the completion of their current act of predation. Then, in a moment of clarity, as Ifunka remembered his monastic training, a verse from the Tamitvar came to his mind—a verse renowned for its beauty as much for its potency, *Yonff Poltiffog* ('the Verse of Radiance'), which is half in Tremni and half in Vocatae:

"Roimelaffsholem roimemavtilei!
Ramtukum gel poltiffavtilei
pamshatvinitsaff Quator Vuciaeshivilei!
Ramutu ramutuvulis, vucia vuciasiv lei,
oucau zepe ramutuemvonilei!"

> ("By the dawn when it breaks!
> He is the Light which radiates
> in the midmost heart of the Fire Eternal!
> Light upon Light, Fire within Fire, indeed,
> illuminating all things!")

As he uttered these words, the *shan* untangled themselves and vanished into the darkness from which they had emerged—a darkness which formed the fabric of their own beings, the essence of their false light.

"Come, Shem! Let's get out of here!"

Shem lay on the forest floor, looking up at the tree branches and canopy above.

"Brother!" he called. "They had me—I was in their grasp. I felt the coldness of their breath, their fingers and arms."

"Get yourself together, brother. Come on! Get up!"

Ifunka pulled him up—Shem was loose-limbed, like a rag-doll, unwilling to move.

"Get up before some other beast of the night decides to make us its prey!"

"Bear with me; I have touched beings of pure terror!"

"I'm sorry, but we must go. We need to get as far as we can before daybreak. Then we have a chance of getting to our destination and saving Ushwan."

"Help me up!" Ifunka lifted him to his feet. "You read the verse well, brother. Methinks the angels heard you sing."

"Brother," Ifunka's eyes welled with tears. "I love you like my own flesh and blood. We'll make it through the night and, if not, let us die and our souls shall be as one in the Garden of Ganka."

"Your words melt my heart, brother."

"Let's go!"

They ran on, for hour after hour, taking only brief breaks, until they came to a brook, flowing with clear water over smoothly-polished pebbles. There they halted in order to perform ablutions. As they did so, a thunderous rustling of leaves and branches could be heard behind them. Turning, their faces still covered in water, they beheld the serpent from earlier. After licking its wounds, it had evidently decided to pursue its enemies, tracing them through the forest and to this point. Their swords were still embedded in the beasts' scaly hide. It hissed like a myriad whining kettles and bared its prodigious fangs. Lifting its head, it struck. Ifunka and Shem ducked, dodging its immense head which pounded the ground like a hammer. It struck, again and again, as each time they hid behind a tree or ducked for cover, avoiding the attacks. The beast was relentless—infuriated by its former attackers. Ifunka conceived an idea and whispered to Shem:

"We'll tangle it. Let's run a course around these trees, weaving in and out in a circle until it is well and truly tangled. Then you and I will both strike its head with our short knives. We'll blind it and then crack open the skull."

Shem nodded. They set about their plan, running in and out between the tree trunks until the creature was wrapped up like a bow. When it had realized its error, it tried to pull back but was locked in. It squirmed and threw its head back and forth. Ifunka and Shem each came up on one side, flanking the beast, and struck with their daggers at its eyes. Leaping on top of the head, they hacked at its skull. Its eyes poured forth a prodigious quantity of oozy green blood, while the skull spurted like a burst tin of molasses. Ifunka pushed the blade down until it had penetrated the thick, membrous brain of the creature. It gasped and then gave up its ghost, relaxing every muscle and sinew into that sleep from which there is no return—the silence of non-existence and quiet dissolution.

"Thus dies the lake-worm," said Ifunka. "Come, let us fill our water-skins and keep on moving. Who knows what else lurks in the deep forest?"

As they continued walking, Shem thought he could see a figure staring at him in the gloom. It was barely discernible but stood out from the usual background of leaves, trees, and branches. He whispered to Ifunka.

"Do you see that?"

But when Ifunka turned he could see nothing. The figure had vanished.

"Methinks you're seeing things, brother. We're weary and troubled from a long journey and have suffered much along the way. I think our eyes have started to play tricks on us."

"Perhaps," Shem replied. "But I know that I saw something. What that 'something' was is the question."

They rested by an old and sturdy *zeff*-tree of wide girth and gnarled roots. As they caught their breath, this time Ifunka saw something move between the two boles, about twenty *oksha*s off. It seemed humanoid.

"There!" he whispered in alarm. "I told you, brother, I told you."

"We're being followed, by someone or something."

"It could be the clay men."

"Perhaps. It's definitely not *shan*. It must be some kind of man."

"Or demon."

"Nonsense! There's no such thing."

"In Gahimka they dwell near the lakes of fire and brimstone."

"Yes, but we're a long way from Gahimka. This is Tremn—the world of men—fixed in the heavens between Gahimka below and Ganka above, the very centre of the universe, where salvation and damnation are both earned. Nay, we are dealing with a man."

"At this depth of the forest?"

"It could be one of the demon-worshippers, in which case we've lost the element of surprise and our cause is doomed."

"If the Great Spirit wills," Shem remarked.

They continued on until near the break of dawn when they reached a slight decline. Descending several *oksha*s, they found themselves entering an area of fewer trees and more bushes and shrubbery. *Ffig*s rolled across the mossy ground while *ffubish*es floated above their heads. They came to a small pond of pure and limpid water. They cupped their hands and drank from it—it was sweet to the taste, evidently bubbling forth from some ancient spring, its origins deep in the mineral-laden aquifers which proliferate throughout the region.

"Praise be to the Great Spirit!" rejoiced Ifunka.

"*Raffal!*" concurred Shem. "Let us do ablutions and pray, for the dawn is nigh."

"Nigh is your bane, monks!" came a voice.

They looked around. No face could be seen.

"Who speaks?" Ifunka called.

"This is my land, so I shall ask the questions."

"Why should we answer your questions?"

"There is an arrow poised to fire. The bow is taut; my aim is true."

"There are two of us. Can you kill two men with one shot?"

"I can fire two arrows in one breath. This is my home. I am its guardian. Whatever manner of man or beast ye are, do not cast away your lives for a mere trifle."

"Passage through this forest is not a trifle!" Ifunka protested. "It is a matter of life and death. What happened to generosity and hospitality? What age is this that a traveller can be so accosted and threatened for the sake of dirt and trees?"

"Thou speakest well, stranger, but common men do not travel this deep within these woods. Only demon-worshippers and unnatural phenomena—*shan*, giant worms, hideous beasts and brutish clay men wander here, intent on blood and gore; evil creatures. I am the only natural man in these parts. Ye are surely creatures of evil covered in a cloak of semblance, your powers veiling mine eyes from your true reality. Therefore, give me a reason why I should not kill you both now and be done with it?"

Ifunka did not hesitate to answer.

"Wouldst thou kill, O man, that which the Great Spirit hath quickened with a soul? Are we cattle to be so easily slaughtered? Or are we, rather, temples of the spirit made by the Hand of the Almighty, the All-Knowing, the All-Wise?"

"Praised be His name!" the man replied. "Indeed, ye speak like men and in the name of One that is all good and perfect. Therefore, I shall trust you both and lay down my bow."

He emerged from behind a tree (a bow-shot distant) and approached them. He was six-foot tall, of light-green complexion, grey eyes, wide, flat nose, large eyes, an arched brow, pointed cheeks and chin, long ears, a smooth face, and incredibly short, tightly-curled dark-green hair. His chest, rippled with muscles, was bare and covered in dried mud. He wore a brown leather loincloth and no shoes. He raised his hand in greeting.

"How now!" he said. "Peace be unto you."

"And peace be unto you," they replied.

"I am Jyoff Wagva of the Zatv, of whom I am, verily, the last scion. My house is not far distant. Ye shall stay with me as long as ye need and I shall learn your business and intentions."

"I am Brother Ifunka Kaffa and this is Brother Shem Effga. We belong to the Holy Order of the Brothers of Bishgva and come from *Preteloff Tvada Kay* (the Monastery of the Brown Owl)."

"I am pleased to meet you both. I do not know the monastery that ye speak of. I only know this forest and these woods. I have lived here all my life, save for a brief period of travelling abroad, and have witnessed the extinction of my family and clan. Come, I shall tell you of these things and more by my hearth, which is near at hand."

He pointed behind him with his bow in hand. On his back he carried a quiver replete with deadly arrows. It was made of dark-green leather, perhaps of the hide of a *ffentwash*-bison, *nimffish*-gazelle, or other forest-dwelling herbivore. The house proved to be a circular hut with a thatched roof in the midst of a small clearing. The walls were made of cob—dried mud bricks mixed with *braksh*-straw, and the entire construction was called a *tvansh* (in standard Tremni), though Jyoff pronounced it differently.

"Welcome to my *tvanj*, which is what this is called in my dialect, though I know ye call it a *tvansh*. It's not much but it's my home. Enter in peace."

They ducked and entered the small portal into the singular round chamber. Ifunka and Shem both felt that the house seemed familiar, though they had never visited it before. The story of the forest-dweller in the book which Ifunka had acquired at the *Leshka Yeishavt* inn in Habka village flashed before his mind. Were they in the same place? The hearth was situated in the middle of the hut, consisting of hot charcoals glowing softly in the peaceful surroundings. Smoke gently lifted up and rose through the porous thatch-work above them. They sat on cushions which were laid out at the circumference of the chamber, giving them just enough ease to stretch out and recline while not becoming too hot through proximity to the hearth-fire.

"I shall prepare some *yent*-leaf tea," announced Jyoff as he placed a metal frame over the coals and took a shiny brass kettle, placing it on top of the frame in order to boil some water.

He placed some *yent*-leaves, which he kept in a small woollen pouch, in a tea-strainer—also brass—which he lowered into the water. He also placed some *tviksh* sugar cubes into the pot to give it a sweet flavour.

"I've never tried *yent*-leaf tea before," said Ifunka. "It's not so common in our region."

"If it's anything like *gveg*-leaf tea, I'll like it," said Shem, referring to the tea which Brother Ushwan had prepared for them with *sheff*-cinnamon some weeks before.

"This is the only tea I know," said Jyoff. "It's the specialty of the Zatv."

"I'm afraid I don't know much about the Zatv," Shem declared, fishing for more information.

"Now no one shall, for we are a clan which has come to its end."

"Have you no wife or children?"

"We marry cousins—indeed, are entitled to our cousins for wedlock, yet there are no cousins left. Whom shall I wed?"

"You are celibate, then?" asked Shem.

"I am no monk. I amuse myself in my own way."

It did not seem appropriate for the monks to pursue that line of enquiry any further so Ifunka broached another topic.

"What do you know about the demon-worshippers of Ffushkar?"

"What do I know about them? The question is, why do ye want to know about them to begin with? What business brings you to these forest depths? And, not to be rude, but your use of 'you' instead of 'thou' is highly unorthodox. Please refrain from it."

"We apologise heartily, good sir, but our use of language is different from thine. We come from different regions and are used to different manners of speech."

"We are here to search for Brother Ushwan, who is lost."

"Lost?"

Jyoff poured the *yent*-leaf tea into three small cups, like those used by the desert Arabs to drink coffee.

"Here, drink to your health!"

"Thank you," they replied as they received the tea in their right hands.

"Here we drink in one go," explained Jyoff as he downed his tea. "Do likewise! It is the custom."

"Very well," said Ifunka.

It was hot but in such a quantity that it did not burn his tongue. *Yent*-tea invigorates the body, making one ready for good discourse and companionship.

"Very good," said Ifunka. "I enjoy its rich, earthy taste, much like *geff*-coffee."

"*Geff?* Never heard of it. That is an affectation of the city-folk."

"No, *geff*-coffee comes from the Great Desert of Yatvegab."

"Ah, well, this is Ffushkar. We prefer the leaf of the *yent*-bush."

Removing his tea implements, the enigmatic figure gathered some logs from the edge of the room and placed them on the hearth-fire.

"More heat and more friendship," he said. "The fire must needs burn bright like unto the fire within our hearts. So—" he turned to Ifunka. "*Who* is lost?"

"Brother Ushwan—from our monastery. He is a dear friend. Some days ago—I have lost track of time—he vanished completely from our monastery. We believe he was taken by the demon-worshippers, for what purpose we do not know, and we have been trying to reach their lair in order to rescue him ever since. We came with another companion, Brother Ffen Weshga, who has chosen to remain with Tem Ffash, the

Lord of Ffash Valley. If thou couldst help us to achieve our goal, we would both be eternally grateful."

Jyoff pondered this suggestion for a few moments, his brow furrowed with concentration.

"I have kept them at bay for many a long year. They came here once, a long time ago."

"I read something about a house in the forest—a story of an encounter with the demon-worshipers."

"That was my father, Jyem. He told the tale to a priest in the village of Tvon who related it to others, and he later met the writer of the book ye refer to. I was young but I was also there when the incident occurred. I still remember the light which glimmered in the darkness until a host of men appeared. I remembered their swords glimmering in the darkness and the thick woolsack which contained the body of their victim. I saw them beat that sack while the captive therein cried out. They cast scorn on the Right Religion of the Holy Tamitvar—how they glorified human sacrifice, burning flesh and flowing blood! My father travelled much after that day and settled far away in the province of Ritvator. I, however, returned to this spot and have defended my home ever since. My father told only a portion of what he knew to outsiders. The whole legend of the demon-worshippers he confided to me. Now, if the Great Spirit wills, I shall confide it in you twain, since ye are determined to face these monsters. If it change your determination, so be it. However, if it increase your desire, all the better."

"We are keen to know what we are up against."

"As well ye should be."

The hearth-fire crackled as he spoke. Smoke streamed up to the membrous roof above. His eyes lit up as his face glowed in the fire's radiance. He looked towards the entrance to his home, as if to see whether some enemy lurked in the bushes, ready to attack them.

"These men we call 'demon-worshippers' are the members of an ancient clan which has dwelt in this forest since before the Holy Tamitvar was first uttered by the great seer, Votsku, may the Great Spirit preserve him. They have always worshipped a dark creature—a demon we call him, but they see him as a deity—a divine being. This creature is called Asharru, the Evil One, who is a minion of Afflish the Accursed—or so we believe him to be. How he escaped from the fires of Gahimka, I cannot surmise. However, the legend is clear that he dwelt among the clan, which is called Shaffu, and some say he dwells among them even still. These sinful infidels worship his idol, a statue made of precious stone and adorned with gold and jewels. They kidnap and sacrifice the innocent, particularly virgin men and women, and even children, who are killed most gruesomely before their remains are defiled and burned in order to appease Asharru, who delights in the smell of burnt flesh. These brutes lust after blood and perform obscene rituals, bare-breasted and clothed in wretchedness. I cannot say whether your friend be alive, but I fear that he may already be dead."

"No!" Shem cried.

Ifunka stared into the flames, motionless.

"I cannot give up hope," he said. "Neither of us can. If we give up hope, then we have nothing. We have travelled too far to abandon our quest. Even if he is dead, shall I not look upon the face of his murderers?"

"Thou art brave, dear monk; foolish perhaps, but brave. Ye should have stayed in your monastery instead of setting out upon the wide world and getting entangled in these evil affairs."

"Tell us more about the Shaffu," Ifunka interjected, tired of Jyoff's attempts to put them off their mission.

"What more shall I tell you? Shall I tell you that I have killed a dozen of them, stealthily, as they came across my land—even as I surely would have killed you both had it not been for your good words. I have seen horrors ye would not believe, in this dark forest where evil deeds are concealed from the light of day."

"What thou hast seen is past, friend; we only wish to know our enemy and find his lair."

"That I can help thee with. The Shaffu are devils incarnate. They claim to be gods among men—the children, they say, of Asharru, who stole one of the daughters of Kyeshob—he who made the first bow."

"I have heard the story of the birth of our world and of the Seven Fathers of Tremn, but I have not heard this narration."

"It is concealed from the people by the corrupt and self-serving theocracy. Dost thou think that they will allow men to hear that which subverts their religion?"

"It is our religion, too, friend."

"The Right Religion of the Holy Tamitvar is not what those priest-crafters teach."

"We have been taught that he who seeded this world was the Him, called Cumi in Vocatae and Inta in Tremni. He it was who planted the first seeds of life at the dawn of time. He waited for an aeon and then returned to Tremnad, the middle land, carrying a white sack which he laid upon the ground. Having rolled out the contents of the sack, there lay upon the ground seven men, who were his seven sons, the fathers of our race; Kyeshob, Mael, Kven, Nub, Avis, Ril, and Itffa. He set them to work, labouring in the fields and tending livestock, but they grew frustrated. They saw that all creatures had a partner save them. Inta laughed and unrolled another white sack containing seven women, the most beautiful beings they had ever looked upon. These were the seven mothers of Tremn: Kvena, Tika, Sorumi, Tam, Ivana, Ffash, and Namffa. Kyeshob was married to Kvena and had three sons and two daughters. The daughters were Vela and Shifa. The husbands of these daughters are well-known."

"There was another—Naiva. One day, she was walking along the edge of a river when a man, handsome and resplendent, appeared before her. She was enamoured and lusted after him, and the man lay with her. In the morning, she saw that the man she had slept with was neither fair nor beautiful but, rather, his skin was dark grey and his eyes red, like a phantom. His teeth were like jagged knives. She repented and tried to flee but was captured and dragged into the depths of Ffushkar. This being was actually Asharru in physical form. From him the Shaffu were born, as well as the clay men. Some say that the *shan* were his daughters. All evil came forth through Naiva's womb and Asharru's loins. This is the origin of the Shaffu."

"What of their weapons and defences?" asked Shem.

"They carry axes and long, jagged blades. They wear black robes and chiefly move at night when they celebrate their satanic rituals and festivals. They fight in groups but are easier to defeat when isolated. The two of you must be careful to avoid being surrounded. If ye are taken captive, there is little hope that ye shall escape. Your friend may already have met his fate. If ye pursue this course, ye shall stand on a plain between life and death. One or the other shall overtake you."

CHAPTER XIV.

Worm Grove

~

"I t's time to leave," said Jyoff.

Ifunka and Shem were kitted out with food supplies, swords, throwing daggers, and other necessaries. Their host had also given them new staffs and shields, such that they could not be more prepared for their mission. Their thoughts were focused, their mettle tried, their goal distilled within the compass of their minds.

It was dawn. They had performed their ablutions and completed the *kashroim*, as well as supplementary prayers for protection and preparation for death. They donned leather gloves and *gisht*-wool head-scarves which they wrapped over their faces to conceal their identities. They pulled up their hoods—taking the appearance of bandits or brigands. Then they bade farewell to Jyoff, who had given them clear directions to the lair of the Shaffu. He gave them one final warning:

"Ye shall pass through the *maff* of the tree worms—the *ffaika* or *ffanyake-metvelatv* (i.e. 'forest-worms')—which are as tall as a man—nay, taller—and twice as long, and the forest is inhabited by all manner of beasts, including the *shan*. The worms of that forest are not as large as the *ffanyak-padku*, the lake worm, but they are quicker and fiercer. Moreover, they have deadly teeth and are seldom alone, so take heed.

If ye survive, the Great Spirit be praised; if ye die, be it on the head of Afflish the Accursed. I bid you farewell."

They turned from Jyoff, he who had prepared them so well for their journey and headed out in the depths of the forest—even unto their final destination. And what destination is truly final? The thought of death loomed more truly in Ifunka's mind than the thought of victory—if victory were a final destination. But death and victory, life and the cessation thereof, are both prongs of one fork, and neither of the two monks had any say over which would be their terminus, though both are, indeed, a destination. Finality and originality are both, in the eye of the wise, the same, for whatever begins has its pre-existence and whatever ends only changes, leading to a new beginning. The trees which surrounded them, embraced them within their living network—a conglomeration of intertwined spirits of the vegetable kingdom, breathing softly their unreasoned breaths of subtle energy, from branch to branch and root to root, as they set foot to path and paced on within the shade of their lofty boughs. How much Ifunka longed for the peaceful transcendence of the trees, their ignorance of form and meaning, of good and evil—bliss in utter abstraction from the pain of material existence.

Shem was focused on the beauty of his surroundings, the folds of bark on each sturdy bole, the warbling of *wultva*-budgies and *ffubishes* above them, the gentle rustling of *ffigs* as they rolled to and fro along the leaf-blanketed forest floor. Each footstep's crunch was like music in an eternal symphony of nature, which ever resonated within the theatre of the *mimra*, watched only by the seldom few who passed through uncivilized expanses and wilderness and the great Watcher of all, who is the Great Spirit.

They walked on for hours, until the time for *kashatvin*—the midday prayer—when they paused to perform ablutions with water from their skins, and then performed the obligatory prayer as custom and their faith demanded. They snacked on some *ragvi*-nuts, which Jyoff had packed in their rucksacks to keep their energy levels high as they progressed. After prayers, they continued on their journey and, as they marched on, the dense forest of *zeff* and *kaptitv* trees, with occasional *limbatves*, gave way to a rare and unusual variety of trees called *zasht*-willows, flaming radiant red trunks with hanging, soft-flower-bud-laden branches, thin like wisps of silk moving this way and that as the breeze listed—a vibrant display of ruddy brilliance, luminescent through some internal energy, conquering the otherwise-gloomy atmosphere of the forest of Ffushkar. The red light cast its bloody ruminescence on the green faces of the stalwart monks. Their eyes gleamed like gleeds of flame in the midst of a roaring hearth-fire.

"What magic is this?" asked Shem, his voice lowered in awe of the bursting-red surroundings.

"*Zasht*-willows!" Ifunka exclaimed. "Red like the *zasht*-willow! Didn't the poet, Hashpa, known for his vivid metaphors and similes, wax lyrical about his love's ruddy cheeks—ruddy like the *zasht*-willow?"

"Ah, yes," said Shem. "I remember: *'Eynim kont, unka tvaon ffairf-fulish envash / Zasht anaokshin patrik shoztayenghivt / Ramtiffavt kaldoge metvelatvshiv kakshuffash / Shand tvaon hoikavt gashte patrik ffairyenghivt* ('Mine eyes, they cast upon her ruddy cheek / With passion's flame like the *zasht*-willow / glowing brightly in the forest depth / Her bosom heaves with buds of ruddy fire')."

"Well-remembered," said Ifunka with cheeky grin. "Perhaps *too* well-remembered for a monk?"

"You are one to talk, Ifunka," Shem retorted. "I've seen you gaze at the imprints of Yishga in the Tale of Yishga and Yemna, the unrequited lovers."

"Perhaps you could refrain from criticizing my penchant for great literature, brother."

"If you would do the same," Shem replied.

Ifunka felt the glowing bole of a *zasht*-willow; its branches dangled down and caressed his tangled, red hair and beard.

"It's warm," asked Ifunka. "A warm tree? How is it warm?"

"I'm no scholar or physician, so I cannot say," replied Shem. "Only I think it has the element of fire within it. Perhaps the soil we tread on is rich in fire, just as some soil is rich in water, air or iron."

They continued to walk deeper and deeper into the glowing heart of Ffushkar. The ground beneath them became softer, covered as it was with discarded *zasht*-buds. When crushed, they emitted a fragrant odour, like a cross between rose-water and musk, which the monks delighted in. Screeches could be heard from the canopy, and figures could be discerned leaping from tree to tree and branch to branch. A rare species of *meish*, the red-backed, green-bellied *finda*-lemur, which feeds on the fruit of the *zasht*-willow, as well as the succulent red sap which bursts out of its many nooks and crannies. The ground became increasingly uneven; Ifunka tripped and Shem caught him, lifting him up.

"Bloody ant-hill!" Ifunka shouted.

"Ant-hills?"

Shem bent down to examine what appeared to be a muddy tube protruding from the ground.

"This doesn't look like an ant-hill."

"We're getting distracted," said Ifunka.

"But look, brother," Shem urged him. "This is a tubular obtrusion."

"A worm-hole?"

"Too small."

The tube started shaking, without warning, and expanded at the base. The bulge moved upwards while the tube glowed red at its apex.

"Get back!" Ifunka cried.

Shem fell backwards. As the bulge reached the opening, a spherical globule, dark brown like liquid mud, shot upwards and into the forest canopy, while bits of effusion splattered the two monks' faces. The end of the tube glowed and bulged again, spurting forth more globules, again and again. The ground beneath began to rumble all around them as more and more tubes became visible. A sea of globules burst forth all around them, bathing the red forest in a myriad brown, liquid spheres.

"They're some kind of globule-thrusters," said Ifunka cautiously. "Living tubular organisms which consume the earth and spit it out."

"Uh... If that's true, Ifunka," said Shem. "Then why are the spheres floating upwards and not falling downwards?"

"I don't know. They change the soil somehow, but let's continue. I think they're harmless."

"If the Great Spirit wills," added Shem.

They proceeded through the maze of jetting protrusions, deftly avoiding the globules as they were able, until they suddenly seemed to reverse themselves, gravity took hold and they rained down upon the hapless monks; yet there was no splash, no wetness, nor any explosion.

The blobs simply bounced off them and fell back into the tubes from which they had emerged.

"Most peculiar," Shem remarked. "What a wonder of nature!"

"Indeed," agreed Ifunka. "But I'm sure this is the least of our worries in this bizarre place."

They hurried on, hoping to reach their destination by nightfall, in order to avoid facing yet more *shan*. The redness of the forest was mesmerizing. The two companions felt as if they were in a dream, drifting along a landscape of eternal fire. Their senses were overwhelmed by the bleeding light which spoke to the inner essence of their hearts, like blood churning in the midst of a boiling cauldron.

A whirring sound, loud yet intermittent, woke them from their reveries, yet they could not discern whether it were real or a mere product of their invigorated imaginations. Its whirred and stopped, whirred and stopped, like a myriad fans all moving at top speed before hastily ceasing their revolution, only to start again in an endless cycle of repetition. Ifunka and Shem exchanged concerned glances as they kept walking, the noise appearing to increase relative to their approach. Whirr—pause—whirr—pause—whirr—pause, it continued. The globule thrusters had receded from view as the monks now saw a host of spinning 'things', rotating from a root fastly-fixed in the ground. When it paused, they discerned that the entire creature was a sturdy root-like vegetable, with a central hub rotating around the root which was attached to it, around which were affixed eight vanes or 'blades' which, together with the hub, formed a kind of fan or propeller.

"In all my days," Shem gasped as the fan whirred into motion.

"In all your days?" Ifunka remarked. "We're not that old, brother."

"But have you seen the like of this, Ifunka? What are these blades which move around a central point?"

"I do not know; what wonders nature produces! What mysteries the forest depths conceal! We have entered a realm beyond our feeble imaginations."

Shem placed his hand over one of the spinning roots as it spun. Air was being sucked from the forest canopy and into the fan. Insects, leaves and other detritus hit Shem's hand and bounced off into the vanes before being sucked into tiny vents at the base of the root.

"Mouths!" Shem observed. "It's sucking insects into these openings at the base of the root. Look, brother!"

"Fascinating," said Ifunka. "But we have no time for scholarly observations. Let's move on!"

"How shall be avoid being thrashed by these creatures?"

"We'll cut them with our blades as we rush through."

This they proceeded to do, slashing and thus harming, the silent carnivores as they ran on, for some minutes or so, until they appeared to dip into another valley, descending rapidly down a slope until they reached the bottom.

"This is it," said Ifunka solemnly. "We've reached the heart of mighty Ffushkar. We cannot be far distant from the home of the Shaffu—the accurséd sons of Asharru."

"Well, then," Shem replied. "Let's hurry until we reach the edge of their domain, so we can observe whether our brother be still alive."

"Even if he be not," said Ifunka, his voice tremulous with anger and anticipation. "I intend to strike a blow at the heart of their tribe and see blood pour like flooded water over the paths and ditches of their untouched land. Let them ever fear for their safety and rue the day that they offended Ifunka Kaffa."

"You sound like one possessed."

"I am possessed—with righteous indignation."

"Careful, brother, remember Tvem's warning."

"My heart boils, though I remember what he said. Fear not, I *can* control my wrath."

Just then, Ifunka stepped into something warm and soft. Shem heard the plopping sound and they both looked down at once to find Ifunka's foot heel-high in a soft, foamy white ball of cream—or what looked like cream.

"Afflish's forkéd tongue!"

"Ha, brother!" Shem laughed. "It looks as though you've stepped in it this time!"

"Stepped in what?"

"A ball of white cream—or perhaps an egg?"

"There are no eggs this size and girth."

Ifunka bent down and poked the ball with his finger. Collecting a small amount on the tip thereof, he brought it to his nose.

"Hardly any smell."

He tasted it.

"Agggg!" he exclaimed. "It is foul beyond words." He gagged.

"Let me see."

Shem knelt down to look at it.

"Remove your foot," he requested.

Ifunka lifted his boot, which reluctantly exited the ball, covered in a layer of white filth which was painted a ruddy shade of red due to the glowing trees all about them.

"It seems soft but not liquid—rather like a secretion of some kind."

"What could possibly be big enough to secrete a ball of this size? Surely it isn't excrement?"

"If it be, it comes from an enormous creature."

The ground rumbled, as if a stomach deprived of sustenance, and seemed to move beneath their very feet.

"Brother!" Ifunka cried. "We'd better move!"

"The worms—it must be the worms!"

"That was worm excrement!"

As these words left their lips, the trees shook and leaves fell off the branches. A mound of earth lifted up in front of them as they rushed forward.

"Back!" Ifunka cried.

Like a spout of water, the soil lifted up to a point and then gave way to an enormous mouth, a pallid, coarse tip—phallic yet grotesque—eyeless, blind, a figure of death and senseless malice. Its body lifted up and, succumbing to gravity, thwapped down sharply on the forest floor like a piece of meat slapped onto a butcher's slab. Its slit-like mouth opened wide to reveal three rows of sharp, knife-like teeth, brilliantly-white, within a pink, fleshy interior. Breathing holes on the side of its head sucked deeply and a hot, pungent breath came belching out of its hideous, deadly orifice. Snake-like in its movements, it came charging after them, its head as big as a man's chest and each tooth a finger's length from base to tip.

"Run!" Ifunka screamed as they darted around it and onward through the valley. The worm, a *ffaika* or 'forest-worm', slithered after them at great speed, only hindered by the jerk-like oscillatory motion of its movements, causing it to crash, ever and anon, into tree boles and rocks. Undeterred by these perpetual mishaps, it continued on, gaining ground on the hapless monks, who had no recourse but to keep running and hope for some deliverance from their fate—a fate, indeed, terrible to imagine. Death by worm is, truly, a horrible thing; to be sheered in half by razor-sharp fangs and slowly devoured through many feet of digestive juices which gradually reduce one's flesh to a pulp-like mush, until suffocation or blood loss causes one's heart to beat no more—such is the fate of the worm-devoured.

The ground beneath them began to tremor and shake violently like the sheets of a troubled sleeper's bed, tossing to a fro. Two mounds of earth sprung up before them and hideous, sickly heads burst forth to reveal their gleaming teeth. Flailing violently and slapping one another, they lifted themselves up and crashed down onto the leaf-bestrewn floor. The two monks involuntarily dispersed, Shem to the left and Ifunka to the right, such that the worms, in violent contortions, raced in both directions, with two on Shem's tail and one on Ifunka's. Yet this was not enough! Three more mounds of soil welled up like bubbles spewing forth lava from the mouth of a volcano, hurling clods of soil to and fro—two to the right of Ifunka and another to Shem's left. The odds were now well-and-truly against them. The last strands of hope seemed to be drifting from their grasp. The worms' mouths snapped together like so many lobster claws slicing victims from head-to-toe. At last, as their legs began to seize up through over-exertion, and they panted what seemed to be their last, Ifunka came upon a path of stones, each one ground flat, of a large circular circumference, the one placed after the other in a straight line heading towards what appeared to be a ditch some *oksha*s away in the distance. Ifunka leapt onto the first stone and then continued running. The worms followed along, to the sides of the path, being unable to go through stone and unwilling to go on top of it—perhaps natural instinct to avoid exposure to enemies.

"Shem!" he called out. "There's a stone path. Come towards me! Go to your right!"

Shem turned towards Ifunka's direction and ran with every last ounce of energy, leaping onto the stone path as the nearest of his pursuers lunged, lifting into the air, over the path and, having missed its mark, smacked its mouth firmly into the ground on the other side.

"Wait!" whispered Ifunka. "They can't see us."

It had dawned on Ifunka that the worms were following the sound of their footsteps. He and Shem both froze and ducked down, holding onto the stones. The worms carried on moving, as if anticipating the continued movement of their prey when, discerning that the sound had stopped, they likewise paused. Raising their bulbous heads, they swung back and forth, hoping to bump into their mark. The monks kept perfectly still, hugging the rock for dear life. The worms proceeded to rub their faces along the surface of the rocks until they came upon the monks' backs. Two large worms rubbed their mouths up and down the monks' bodies and, sensing something there, proceeded to extend their meaty tongues which, like slime-soaked giant slugs, doused their robes in thick, gooey saliva. Ifunka struggled to keep still as the mucousy muscle wiped across his ginger curls, the saliva running down his temple and over his eyelids. The tip of the other worm's tongue touched Shem's nostrils and almost felt its way into his mouth. He grasped his blade firmly and, saying a silent prayer within his innermost being, pulled it from the scabbard and thrust it into the head of the beast, piercing it through the chin and crown of its head. The blade was firmly lodged and the worm flailed up and down, retreating in chaos. The other worms, alarmed, lifted their heads and danced back and forth, like cobras stunning a mouse with their gyrations.

"They can't see us," Ifunka whispered. "We rush them one by one, then immobilize them."

"There's too many."

"Five remain. You slice two; I'll cut the other three."

They stood up and, on the count of three, rushed at the worms, one after another, slicing their leathery bosoms open with knife and sword, spilling purple blood on the damp, ruddy forest floor. The injured worms flailed and retreated while Ifunka and Shem leapt back onto the path and rushed onwards towards the ditch. They slowed down as they reached its edge, leading to a moat—rather than a mere ditch— surrounding an inhabited settlement—the base of the Shaffu. The moat was not full; in fact, it had only a stream at its bottom, so Ifunka and Shem gently descended and approached with caution, hoping to taste the water. However, as they bent down to sip, they noticed that the sun had just descended over the horizon and the sky was beginning to darken. Mist descended upon the moat and obscured their vision. Faint lights appeared and began to encircle them.

"The *shan*!" Ifunka whispered. "They guard this moat. They are all around us!"

"What shall we do?"

"Leap the stream, run through them and climb up that ledge."

"Impossible—they'll catch us."

"What choice do we have?—sit here and wait for them to kill us? Damn the *shan* and damn the fear they put into our hearts. Damn them to Gahimka!"

"Wait! The verse! The *Yonff Poltiffog*! Chant it, brother!"

"Yes, it worked before. Why shouldn't it work now?"

As they began to chant the holy words *'Roimelaffsholem roimemavtilei! Ramtukum gel poltiffavtilei...'* the *shan* melted away, as if anticipating the rest of the verse. The mist, too, subsided, leaving the brothers alone in the midst of the moat.

"Praise be to the Great Spirit!"

"Exalt His name!" Shem cried.

"Careful, let's keep our voices down. There'll be watchmen for sure."

"With worms and *shan* and a thousand *kobotv* of thick forest on every side to keep them safe and secure?"

"Even so, there is no underestimating these vicious cowards."

"Cowards are we?" came a voice.

The monks froze.

"Tseshayn-zen kha ftâkh-ish (we are not cowards)*!"*

"What tongue is that?" Shem whispered.

"The tongue of the Shaffu!" Ifunka replied.

"Shaffu!" the voice rejoined. *"Ffadh-Shaffu ftâkh-ish! Kumkha-Sharru okh-ish, eyn-fach atolsha-zen Khanshaff-eym* (we are the Sons of Shaffu. I am Kumkha-Sharru, watchman of the walls of Khanshaff)."

Ifunka turned to face the warrior whom he divined, through the similarity of Shaffi to Tremni, to be called Kumkha-Sharru. The warrior was clad as Jyoff had described, dressed in a long black robe held tight with a thick leather belt and brass buckle, carrying, in one hand, an axe with a long haft and sharp, iron head and, in the other, a jagged blade designed to rip flesh and bone with every blow, making all attempt at healing vain. The victims of their blows would surely die as blood spilled and flesh, mangled beyond recognition, hung hazardously off the bone.

"I am Ifunka Kaffa, a monk—a simple monk—and this is Shem Effga; we mean no harm. Take us prisoner, great warrior."

"Ftosh kha vamdha-yish, khaffshik (That is not possible, infidel)*!"* came another voice.

To their left, another warrior, similarly-clad and armed, appeared. Both faces were obscured by their hoods.

"Nayakht-Offash okh-ish (I am Nayakht-Offash)*!"* the second watchman continued.

"Why don't they just kill us?" Shem whispered.

He stared at one and then the other, his heart racing. There was no way to overcome such skilled and powerful warriors.

"If they speak Tremni, they should be talking to us in Tremni."

"They're toying with us and, at the same time, I think they're cautious. We're the first to reach so far into their territory and live."

"If we can kill them both, before they sound the alarm, we'll still have the element of surprise."

"Indeed, but how? Tvem only taught us the first two movements of the nine-fold path."

"Ha, ha, ha!" Kumkha-Sharru laughed. "Kill us? We are endowed with excellent hearing and we do speak your foul, *khaffshik* language."

"Khaffshik?" Ifunka did not understand.

"Infidel," he replied. "Ye infidel scum! What impetuous pieces of filth to come this far into our sacred territory and befoul it with your unclean feet. *Khaffshik* filth! Great Spirit-worshipping bastards! We *do* know what to do with you. Your bodies shall burn on the pyre in sacrifice to mighty Asharru, who dwells among us in the flesh. Yea, we shall feast upon your meat and crack your bones to suck away the marrow within. Your blood shall fill our goblets and your skulls shall decorate our Great Hall. The fire shall cleanse the unbelieving filth from off your

29

cursed bodies by the grace of Asharru, who is born of eternal flame, while your god is naught but imagination and idle fancy. I laugh at your Tamitvar and its pretentious verses. I spit on your monastic vows and your meaningless prayers. Now, I shall take you prisoners so that we might sup on your virgin flesh."

"Virgin! Ha, ha, ha!" Nayakht-Offash laughed in scorn. "Bastard virgins! Come and feel the fire!"

"If you are going to kill and eat us, what motivation do we have to give ourselves up?"

The watchmen laughed.

"What choice do ye have, monks? Your puny arms can barely hold a butter-knife, let alone a man's blade!"

"Let's say that's true," Ifunka continued. "It would not be fair, or honourable, surely, under your god or mine, for both of you to fight me at once."

"Single combat, then?" Kumkha-Sharru was intrigued. "I have nothing to fear from thee, *khaffshik*! Come, then, face me and see what the result shall be. I shall only maim thee so thy flesh shall remain sweet!"

"Well, then, come watchman—face this puny monk," Ifunka challenged him. "Let's see who the infidel really is."

He unsheathed his sword, still wet with purple blood. Shem stood away from him, his back resting on the bank. Kumkha-Sharru raised his axe and jagged blade and charged at Ifunka. Ifunka stood, motionless, as if numb to the danger and certain death that rushed towards him with such rapidity. Then, counter-intuitively, he sheathed his sword and pulled a staff which he had fixed to his back. Holding it with both hands, as he had been taught by Tvem, he stood, like a rock, his feet firmly placed and steadfast. The foeman was only one *oksha* in front of him. Ifunka breathed in deeply and exhaled. Then, swiftly and mechanically, he raised his stick in a defensive position, blocking his enemy's first blow from the axe. Before the fiend could strike again, he knocked his enemy on the chin with a swift upward motion of the staff. Then, grasping it on the end, like a sword, he thwacked the watchman across the head, cracking his skull in the process. Thus, with the second movement of the nine-fold path, he had mortally wounded his attacker.

Nayakht-Offash, enraged, rushed to attack his friend's killer. Shem leapt forward and struck the watchman's knees with his staff, cracking his knee-caps. Immobilized, his weapon thrown by the fall, the watchman flailed on the ground in agony.

"Finish him!" Ifunka ordered as he withdrew his blade to dispatch Kumkha-Sharru.

"Finish him? Is that what we've become—murderers?" Shem protested.

"We have killed clay men, have we not?"

"They were beasts—these are men like us."

"They are *not* men like us," Ifunka replied sternly. "These are blood-thirsty infidels who spit upon the Holy Tamitvar. They curse the Great Spirit. Death is quick justice for the unbelievers."

"Is this justice or vengeance, brother? What would Tvem do?"

"Are you blind, Shem? He would send these brutes to their quietus as swiftly as you have smashed that infidel's knee-caps!"

"I fear for our souls if we do this thing."

"Your souls?" the fallen watchmen grunted. "What souls? You *khaffshik*s are flesh only—flesh to be eaten. Within you is only a pale ghost which shall wander, hungry and forever miserable, in the bowls of Tremn. We, the children of Asharru, the living god, shall dwell forever in his eternal realm, Asharraff."

"Lies!" Shem exclaimed. "I want to save your life and you insult us with these putrid lies?"

"If you will not do it, Shem, let the burden rest on me. I shall spill their blood."

"Do it, fools!" Nayakht-Offash challenged them. "I shall live forever. Asharru lives—the Great Spirit lives not!"

"Lying scum!" Shem shouted, enraged.

He raised his staff and brought it down on the watchman's head, splitting his skull open and releasing a torrent of blood upon the ground. Ifunka grabbed Kumkha-Sharru by his forelock and, lifting it to reveal his still-unconscious face, slit the watchman's throat, blood spurting out across the muddy banks of the stream, dying it red. Ifunka's hands and arms were soaked in warm blood, his face splattered with droplets thereof. Wild-eyed and exhilarated, he exclaimed:

"Praise be to the Great Spirit! Thus die all who oppose the truth—all infidels and oppressors."

"There's no going back now, is there?" asked Shem rhetorically. "We'll have to kill them all; every last one of them."

"They're pure evil, Shem. They deserve to die."

"Even so, are we the dispensers of divine justice?"

"We're monks—we are His agents."

"In any case, let's clean up, eh? We need to get into that town and avoid detection."

"We don't have much time before the next lookout comes to replace the first watch. Then the alarm will be raised. We'll have to hide well."

"Come then!"

They washed their hands and faces in the stream and then began to climb the ledge. When they reached the cusp, they peered over but could see only a thick, stone wall topped with battlements consisting of a crenellated parapet with triangular merlons; arrow-slits were visible within the crenels. Whether these were defended or not, they could not easily surmise. Yet, if there were watchmen in the moat, there would have to be more defensive soldiers lining the battlements. Doubtless, within the city itself, there would be yet more watchmen.

"Stay low," urged Ifunka. "There might be eyes on the walls."

"What shall we do?"

"We stay silent—we creep up—kill the guard."

"Then what—the city is swarming with infidels."

"We'll have to find a house, tie up the inhabitants and keep quiet until we can figure out where Brother Ushwan is being held captive. We'll go from there."

"Go from there? The odds against us are impossible."

"But we are in the right. We are followers of the good religion. The Theocracy be damned, we shall do something here which shall reverberate throughout the ages. We shall drown these curséd evil-doers in their own blood, tear them limb from limb; only death can make them pure.'

"Well, then," said Shem. "Let's go. If we are going to do this thing, let's do it."

"Go!"

They scampered to the wall and began to climb, fixing their fingers in the crevices, nooks and crannies and pulled themselves up, stone by stone, until they reached the parapet. Ifunka was first over. He peered across the battlements and, seeing no guard, lifted himself up and over. Shem followed.

"Keep close, brother," Ifunka cautioned.

"Where are they—where are the guard?"

"They could be moving around as we speak—around the circumference of Khanshaff. Quickly!"

"Can't we just go over, without killing the guard?"

"They'll be the first after us, once they discover that the two watchmen are dead. The more we kill, the safer we shall be."

They stealthily moved along the ramparts until they spotted two watchmen—they evidently always move in pairs.

"We rush them, stab them quickly, then descend the inner wall."

They did as planned, stabbing the watchmen through the chest and back before they could retaliate. As the lifeless bodies sank to the cold stone they carefully descended into the city, which was dark enough that they appeared as mere shadows moving across the face of the lofty stones, unremarked and unnoticed by the oblivious Shaffu. The houses of the Shaffu were large, two stories high made of large stone blocks fixed together with cement, buttressed by wide balconies on the upper floor and red-shingled roofs. Windows consisted of numerous coloured glass planes in a circular shape. The walls were bestrewn with *yenksh*-vines—thick, rough, red rope-like plants hanging from the roof. They climbed up the first vine they came across and, with much exertion, reached the balcony.

"Right, we capture—not kill—them."

"Agreed," Ifunka replied.

Swords sheathed, they raised their staffs and circled the balcony until they came to a door leading into the house.

"Dare we enter?"

"In the name of the Great Spirit," Ifunka replied softly.

The door creaked open and they found themselves with a torch-lit room covered in richly-intricate carpets and tapestries, covering the walls, and cushions all around. The room was empty but there were obviously inhabitants around, and perhaps servants also. A sweet smell of incense pervaded the chamber, creating a sense of harmony and tranquillity, which they had not expected to find in the heartland of impiety and disbelief. They felt out-of-place and uneasy about when they would encounter another of the Shaffu and who it might be. Hushed voices, and a door opened, or slid open rather, and two figures, ravishingly beautiful, stepped into the room.

CHAPTER XV.
Ârva

~

Two light-green women, one with long, black tresses reaching down to her elbows and the other with short, chestnut-brown curls, stepped over the threshold and into the room which Ifunka and Shem had just entered hoping to kidnap the inhabitants and set up base within. Like the other Shaffu they had so far encountered, their skin was radiant, verdant and shimmering, like marble, smoothly-polished, catching light. Their eyes were dark-brown, mysterious. Their features, likewise, were statuesque, as if they were hewn out of a solid block of stone, rather than living, breathing Tremna. Their chins, cheeks and brows were prominent, and their eyes somewhat sunken within their sockets, yet they were immensely—almost ethereally—beautiful, like angels descended from Ganka—more splendrous in appearance than any icon or idol, more brilliant than any mural or tapestry, and more luscious in their seductive effulgence than any man could have conceived in his wildest fancies.

Their heads rested upon long, delicate necks and well-proportioned bodies, well-endowed with femininity, with long, elegant hands and feet. The long-haired beauty was dressed in a long, Tyrian-purple nightdress which hung from her body like a veil, hiding her best features. The other woman, more servile in her manner, was fully-dressed in the attire of a maid-servant; white stockings hugged her calves, resting upon mocha-brown slippers. Her dress, descending to the knees and extending to the elbows, was of the same colour, fashioned from *meb*-goat wool. The dress was loose around the legs but tight around her fulsome bosom and reached up to, but not covering, her collar-bone.

Ifunka and Shem were dazzled by their beauty and stunned that such creatures of grace and perfection could exist among a race of demon-worshipping infidels. How could savages produce such specimens of rapturous gorgeousness? How could such foul creatures have conceptions of modesty, to the extent that their women were covered up even within the fastness of their dwellings, when modesty itself is an inculcation of the precepts inscribed within the holy verses of the Tamitvar, spoken by the tongue of Votsku who saw and communicated with Hashemaff himself? So disturbed were they that their conflicted emotions, born of passion and fear, consumed them entirely and they both dropped their staffs and gazed at the women in abstracted wonder. They, for their part, froze and stared wide-eyed at the home-invaders, terrified by their potential intent, the long-haired one grasping her maid's hand firmly with her right, tremulous and disturbed.

"Khuff, khuff ftâ-ga shift-ôn-ish (what, what do you want)*?"* the mistress cried. *"Yeff Predh-bara-yeym okh-ish. Ftam-ôn eleyn okh-ish* (I am the daughter of the High-Priest. I have money)."

"I am Brother Ifunka Kaffa," said Ifunka, unable to fully comprehend the woman. "And this is Brother Shem Effga of the Holy Order of the Brothers of Bishgva. We are followers of the Right Religion of the Sacred Tamitvar. Our brother monk was captured by the people of this city, the Shaffu; we have come to liberate him. Are you one of the Shaffu?"

He extended his hand to the woman in greeting but she jumped back, her maid embracing her.

"Do not fear! Even if you are one of them—we can liberate you as well, not only from this accurséd city, but also from the shackles of unbelief. All your sins, all your impurity shall be washed away when you embrace the Right Religion. You will become a daughter of truth and worthy of admittance into the Gardens of Ganka, the exalted Paradise, where rivers flow in abundance and angels sing their lofty, sweet melodies in realms of eternal and absolute bliss."

"I don't think she understands a word, brother," Shem interrupted him. "Look at her, trembling with fear; she's one of them. She's an infidel—let's tie them up and be done with it."

"No!" he turned to Shem. "We're infidels to them as well, remember? She's like a *gisht* led astray by a wicked *yeshka* in *gisht*-skins! We can save them both from their sins and take them back with us!"

"As what—wives???"

"Is not Brother Ffen married?"

"Against his will! We're still monks! Are you blind with lust and passion?"

"If this be blindness, I embrace it. Look at those, yes, like two *tvung*-deer, so sweet and innocent."

"You're thinking with your *ozetv* and not your mind, brother."

"Vâ ftâ-ga kheyff-ôn-zen-ish? Kha kheyff-krâ! Kheyff-go dheym-ôn okh-ish (why are you two fighting? Don't fight! I hate fighting)*!"*

"She... she wants us to stop fighting."

"How do you know that?" asked Ifunka.

"Look at her facial expression. She's upbraiding us!"

"She's brave to stand up to her potential abductors so. She has fire in her belly."

"Kha kheyff-krâ (Don't fight)*!"* she repeated.

"Listen," said Shem. *"Kha* is *ca*, the Vocatae word for 'not'. *Kheyff* is *kaffain*, the Tremni word for 'fight'. *Krâ* is our imperative suffix, *-kra*. She's saying *nif kaffainkra* ('do not fight')."

"Yes," Ifunka was excited by this discovery. *"Okh*, she keeps saying *okh-ish. Okh* must be *okt* ('I') and *-ish* must be the copular suffix, *-itv* ('to be, exist'), 'I am'. What did she say before, *yeff* something?"

"Yeff (daughter)*!"* she cried. *"Yeff Predh-bara-yeym okh-ish* (I am the daughter of the High-Priest)*!"*

"Yeff—perhaps it means *yep* ('daughter')," said Shem. *"Predh?* Perhaps *pret*, the archaic Tremni word for 'priest'."

"Predh-bara must be *pretkubara* ('priest')... priest what?"

"-yeym... perhaps *–yeng* ('of'), the genitive suffix," said Shem.

"Ah, yes, she's saying *okt yep pretkubarayengitv* ('I am the daughter of the priest')," Ifunka surmised.

"Okay, so their language is not far distant from ours. We can get information from her; perhaps to find Brother Ushwan."

"Ushwan?" asked the mistress. *"Khaffshik kel vish-ôn ftôn-ish* (the infidel whom they found)."

"Khaffshik!" Shem cried. "Do you call our friend—our brother—an infidel? How dare you!"

Shem picked up his staff as if to thrash her.

"Yai!" she screamed in fear. *"Kha vep-krâ khaffshik* (don't touch me, infidel)*!"*

"Now you call me a *khaffshik*?!"

"Shem, calm yourself. We call them *oshokipatve* ('infidels'), so let's not take offence at that. They *oshok* ('cover') the truth and deny the holy word. These two, however, are simply ignorant. If we speak to her—to them—we could save their souls."

"Well, then, brother. If that is what we must do to satisfy your conscience, let us do it. Right, then, let's try to speak to them. *Shem Effga okh-ish* (I am Sheff Effga)."

He placed his hand on his breast to indicate that he spoke about himself.

"Ifunka Kaffa okh-ish (I am Ifunka Kaffa)," said Ifunka. He did the same.

"Ârva Yeff-Khalam-Sharru okh-ish ffi khô, Meyla Yeff-Ashka-Hafta khô-yish (I am Ârva Yeff-Khalam-Sharru and she is Meyla Yeff-Ashka-Hafta)," replied the mistress.

"Excellent, we have introduced ourselves," said Ifunka triumphantly.

"Khuff ftâ-ga shift-ôn-ish (what do you two want)*?"* she asked.

"She wants to know what we want," said Shem. *"Shift* must mean 'want'. I'm assuming *–ôn* is a suffix, rather like the Vocatae *–von*, indicating a present or active participle. She's basically asking what we 'are wanting' or are 'wanters' of. *Ushwan okh ffi okh…"*—he gestured to Ifunka.

"Ftâkh (we)," she corrected him.

"Ushwan ftâkh shift-ôn-ish. We want Ushwan," Shem continued.

"Khû khâka ftâ-ga-n-ish-ô (he is your brother)*?"*

"Yes," Ifunka nodded. *"Khû khâka ftâkh-an-ish.* He is our brother.

We are monks, um… *ftâkh*, no, the predicate should come first, I think, in your language. Um…"

He pointed to Shem and himself and then performed the *wegvash*, keeping his hands shoulder-length, palms facing upwards, and then the *beffesh*, bending over with hands touching knees, imitating prayer.

"Predhel-zen (monks)," said Ârva, helping him.

"Predhel-zen ftâkh-ish," he said. "We are monks."

Ârva, the mistress, looked at Meyla, her maidservant, who was bemused, and then back at the two monks.

"I don't think she's met monks before, eh Ifunka?"

"I think you're right, Shem."

"Ifta-krâ, predhel-zen, shubay-zen okh-an ftâ-ga-yish (come, monks, you are my guests)."

"I think she's saying, 'come, monks, you are my guests,'" Shem interpreted.

"Well, then, yes, we accept," said Ifunka, not knowing how to say the equivalent in Shaffi.

"Heleyd-krâ (sit)," she motioned for them to sit.

The two monks sat on the opposite side of the room and rested their backs on the exquisite yet comfortable cushions. The mistress herself, Ârva Khalam-Sharru's daughter, sat on their right, on the adjacent side of the wall, in a cross-legged posture, her gown covering her feet and knees. She motioned for Meyla, Ashka-Hafta's daughter, to fetch some refreshments. Ifunka quickly became uncomfortable as he noticed that Ârva was staring right at him—deeply—her eyes meeting his, almost seductively, or were his baser passions playing tricks on his higher consciousness? His heart burned within him; he felt it raging like a far-flung blaze, conquering his reason, challenging his self-restraint. What power could two eyes hold over his staunch reserve? Those same feelings which overcame him when he first encountered Maina Shiboff, the farmer's daughter, returned from whence he had banished them during his long-suffering and self-abnegation. How he had fought against his very flesh, its natural disposition, its hormonal urges, as a boy! How he had wished he could take Maina in his arms, disrobe her and lay together with her in carnal satisfaction! Yet that vision, that hope of everlasting Ganka, kept his roaring heart in check, dampened his internal flame and quelled his lower nature. Now, however, the lower was gaining ground on the higher, reaching out from the dungeon where it had been confined and pouring forth, with tinctured hue, into the crystal waters of his abstemious disposition.

The mistress remained silent, intent only on Ifunka, her eyes fixed, her breaths constant; Shem felt as if he had melted away into nothingness, so much had she ignored his very existence. After a few minutes of this 'stare-off', Meyla returned with a silver tray bedecked with plates of nibbles, what looked like a teapot, saucers and tea-cups—they hoped it was tea she was serving and not something forbidden. The maid placed the tray before them, within reach of both Ârva and the monks.

"*Khatvish-krâ* (eat)," Meyla said as she offered the food to them.

There were three plates, one of white biscuits, covered in powdered icing sugar, one of blue, fudge-like cubes, and another of yellow *meb*-cheese balls.

"*Shiz ftâ-ga shift-ôn-ish-ô* (do you two want to drink)?" asked Meyla.

"*Shiz?* Drink? Yes, but drink what?" asked Ifunka. "*Khuff shiz?*"

"*Fôn* (wine)," she replied.

"*Fôn?* Like 'wine'? Sorry, *kha, kha*," he said firmly.

"*Kha* (no)?" Meyla was shocked at his refusal.

The 'teapot' was actually a carafe of wine.

"*Hamta fôn-ish* (wine is good)," Meyla insisted.

"No, *kha hamta fôn-ish* (wine is *not* good)," Ifunka explained. "*Predhel-zen ftâkh-ish* (we are monks)."

"*Fôn kha shiz-ôn predhel-zen-ô* (monks do not drink wine)?" Meyla asked.

"*Rî* (yes)," replied Ârva. "*Fôn kha shiz-ôn ftôn-ish. Shaz her-krâ* (they do not drink wine. Bring juice)!"

Meyla rushed back to the kitchen and fetched a pitcher of red liquid—deep red.

"*Zash-shaz* (*zasht*-juice)," she said as she filled two silver goblets of the stuff.

Ifunka tasted it.

"Ah, juice," he said. "*Zash* must be *zasht*-willow!"

"*Zasht*-willow juice, interesting," said Shem.

"*Hanav-ôn ftâ-ga-yish* (do you two like it)*?*" asked Ârva.

"Ah, *rî... hanav-ôn okh-ish* (yes... I like it)," Ifunka replied.

"What's she asking?"

"*Hanav*, from Vocatae *anaux*. She's asking if we like it."

"Ah, of course. *Rî, rî*," Shem concurred. "Very *hanav*, thank you."

"Very much *hanav*?"

"I'm improvising. Our tongues are similar; she'll get the idea."

"*Okh... fôn shiz-ôn okh khon-ish yôdh predhel kha okh-ish* (I... I will drink wine because I am not a monk)," said Ârva as Meyla poured her a glass of wine. As a servant, she could not herself drink while on duty. Ârva drank with relish, smiling at Ifunka as she did so.

"Look, brother, how do we know she's not married?" said Shem as the thought occurred to him. "Her husband could be on his way home."

"I hardly think she'd be so bold if she knew we'd be discovered at any moment."

"Perhaps that's her plan."

"And then what? The husband will surely kill, or at least thrash, her for having us in her house. No, look at her eyes. She desires me... she wants me. But why; she knows I'm a monk."

"That girl back in Habka village knew you were a monk as well."

"We'll never speak of that incident again." He paused. "And her name was Shiga."

"So you remember her name, then?" asked Shem with a chuckle.

"Hush!" Ifunka whispered angrily.

Meyla poured her mistress a second cup of wine and then refilled the goblets of the two monks with more *zash-shaz* (i.e. *zasht*-willow-berry juice). Ârva winked.

"She winked at me," said Ifunka, almost enthusiastically.

"She probably had something in her eye."

"No, she did, I'm sure of it."

"Meyla," her mistress called. "*Dhey-krâ, ftôn-am dheyk-krâ* (dance, dance for them)."

Meyla moved to the centre of the room and, much to the monks' amazement, began to dance. It was erratic, sensual; she gesticulated wildly, spun round, shook her hips, increasing in speed as she did so, until it reached a high tempo and she threw herself forward and crouched down.

"She dances as if possessed by some ethereal beat we cannot even hear," Ifunka commented.

"*Can't* we hear?" asked Shem. "I can almost hear it, as if her movements bring the music into being."

She rose again and continued dancing. Shem seemed entranced, just as Ifunka was mesmerized by Ârva's eyes. Suddenly, she stopped and Shem clapped and slapped his hands on his knees enthusiastically. Meyla smiled.

"Well done, my darling, well done!" he said.

"Darling?"

"I misspoke."

Shem's cheeks were flush.

"*Khû ftâ shift-ôn-ish-ô* (do you want him)*?*" Ârva asked Meyla.

"*Rî* (yes)," she replied innocently.

"*Nâ khâm-zen gukh-ôn ftôn-ôm aff-îm ftôn khon-ish* (if they remain virgins, they will be killed)."

"*Gin-ôn okh-ish* (I understand)," Meyla replied.

"Brother," said Shem, worried. "What do they want with us?"

"*Khâm?* What is *khâm?*" Ifunka pondered. "I... I can't work it out quickly."

"*Khû aftem-krâ* (take him)*!*" Ârva ordered.

Meyla reached down and grabbed Shem's hand.

"*Ifta-krâ* (come)*!*" she said firmly as she pulled him up.

Entranced by her beauty, he could not protest as he was drawn away and out of the room.

"Shem!" Ifunka cried as he bounced to his feet.

"*Sha, sha, sha, sha!*" Ârva shushed him quickly, rising to dispel his alarm. "*Kha nash-krâ* (don't be afraid)."

"Don't be afraid? What is she going to do with Shem? Where is she taking him?"

"*Okh-ifft taftâ ftâ-yish. Okhsh-zen-shivt taftâ ftâ-yish. Shandh okh-an-shivt goff ftâ-yish* (with me you are safe. In my arms you are safe. In my bosom you are happy)."

Her words were soothing, calming.

"What… what do you mean?"

"*Ifta-krâ* (come)," she said in a gentle tone, invitingly.

"Come? Come where? I'm here."

"*Okh-shivt* (to me)," she replied.

"*Ftâ-shivt?* To you? Why?"

He suspected her intent and it terrified him.

"Look, Ârva, *predhel-okh-ish*. I am a monk! Do you know what that means? I can't be with a woman—ever! *Gin-ôn ftâ-yish-ô?* Do you understand?"

"*Gin-ôn okh-ish* (I understand)," Ârva replied. "*Yûm vâ* (But why)?"

"Why? Because we serve the Great Spirit alone. He is our God; He made everything, don't you understand? The trees, mountains, valleys, you and me, our forefathers, even Afflish himself. Even your Asharru is His creature. All power, all might, all sovereignty belongs to the Great Spirit, Who rules over all things, Who sees all things, Who hears all things, Who knows all things. Even now, in this room, He sees us and hears our words. I can't speak your language, but do you get something—anything—of what I'm saying?"

Her face betrayed confusion.

"*Kha gin-ôn okh-ish* (I do not understand)," she said.

"You don't understand? Alright, let's mime for a bit and learn some words. Make"—he mimed making something with his hands.

"*Khulff*," she translated.

"Spirit"—he mimed a soul leaving a body.

"*Vabakh.*"

"Great"—he spread his arms wide.

"*Khan.*"

"World"—he stretched his arms to make a circle in the air and spun around.

"*Areft.*"

"God," he said as he mimed an all-powerful being zapping the wicked with bolts of lightning. He simulated the sound of each bolt: *"Tsu, tsu, tsu."*

"Tesh."

"One"—he indicated one finger.

"Dhi."

"Excellent, and… serve, like Meyla. Meyla serves"—he mimed Meyla presenting the silver tray.

"Khûmey."

"Yes, so… *Tesh dhi-yish* (God one is)."

"Dhi Tesh-ish (God is one)," she corrected him.

"Sorry, *dhi Tesh-ish. Khan-Vabakh khû-yish. Areft khulff-ôn khû…* (God is one. He is the Great Spirit. He create the word…)"—he did not know the past tense.

"Areft khulff-ôn khû mon-ish (He created the world)," she completed his sentence.

"Excellent, yes. He created the world. *Khû khûmey-ôn okh-ish.* I serve Him."

"Gin-ôn okh-ish (I understand)," she said.

"You understand me? Excellent indeed. Where shall we go from here?"

By speaking in Tremni, as well as Shaffi, Ifunka was hoping to teach her the basic structure and sound of Tremni, so that she could also acquire it.

"Yeff Khalam-Sharru, Predh-bara, okh-ish. Oleym ftâ vish-ôn ftôn-ish, ftarka-ffish ftâ yamakhsh-ôn ftôn khon-ish, yôdh khâm ftâ-yish. Khâm okh-ish fikh yûm khâm-go lish-ôn okh khon-ish, nâ okh khodh-ôn khôff ftâ khon-ish (I am the daughter of Khalam-Sharru the High-Priest. When they find you, they shall sacrifice you on the pyre, for you are a virgin. I am a virgin also, but I will give my maidenhead to you if you will love me forever)."

She spoke with a sense of urgency, her lips trembling with every word, each one of which was flavoured with the spice of passionate longing. Ifunka struggled to keep up with the words but they flowed out of her sweet lips too rapidly for him to retain them in the storehouse of his memory. So deeply had a bond been forged between them, however, that the very gaze of her eyes spoke words of meaning in the depths of his inner fabric. This meaning was one of love, but the outer meaning of her words evaded him. He could only surmise that she spoke using a conditional form, that there was burning involved, and that she loved him forever, or something to that effect. Did she love him? The idea burned brightly in his heart.

"*Ftâ khôff okh khon-ish* (I will love you forever)," he replied. "I will love you forever. But I am a monk and I cannot touch you. *Yûm predhel okh-ish ffi ftâ kha vep-ôn okh...* (because I am a monk and I touch you not)"

"*Vâmt-ish* (can)," she completed his sentence.

She now resorted to miming in order to make herself understood. She extended her hands to represent two beings. Wiggling her fingers on the right hand, she lowered her voice and said "*Shaff!*"

"Man," Ifunka translated.

She did the same on her other hand and raised her voice: "*Ftom!*"

"Woman," said Ifunka.

Then she joined her hands and wiggled them together, imitating sexual intercourse: "*Sheylav.*"

"Relations," said Ifunka.

"*Kha sheylav* (No sexual relations)," she said, simplifying her speech. "*Khâm khû-yish* (he is a virgin)."

"Ah, *khâm* means virgin, yes."

She next imitated a big fire: "*Ftarka!*"

"Pyre," he translated.

She mimed a man or beast being sacrificed and pointed upwards to God: "*Yamakhsh.*"

"Sacrifice."

"*Khâm okh-ish* (I am a virgin)," she explained, pointing to herself.

"Ah, you're a virgin; very noble of you."

"*Khâm ftâ-yish* (you are a virgin)," she pointed at him.

"Yes, I am as well."

"*Ftarka-ffish khâm-zen yamakhsh-ôn ftôn-ish* (they sacrifice virgins on the pyre)."

"They sacrifice virgins… on the pyre!"

The blood drained from Ifunka's cheeks as he realized the

implications of what she was saying. The Shaffu sacrifice virgins on a pyre and eat their burnt flesh. She was offering to sleep with Ifunka if he would love her forever.

'What an innocent request,' he thought. 'From the mind of one who knows not the rules of the Holy Tamitvar. Shem! He was taken away by Meyla!'

They were both in the same predicament, being forced by circumstance either to accept the possibility of death or to sacrifice their morality and risk the punishment of the hereafter.

"You want me to sleep with you?"

He was conflicted.

"*Rî* (yes)," she replied in the affirmative, grasping the intention of his words. "*Ftâ khodh-ôn okh-ish* (I like you)."

"But why, Ârva? We've only just met. Why do you love me? *Vâ okh khodh-ôn ftâ-yish-ô?*"

"*Yashff ffi shîff eynîm-zen-shivt envakh-ôn okh-ish* (I see truth and beauty in your eyes)," she explained.

"Truth, beauty? In my eyes? I see in myself only sin and shame. Even this whole journey, this entire quest to save Brother Ushwan, is a fool's errand. I have no life—no future. The Theocracy is a sham, but you don't even know what the Theocracy is, do you? You don't even speak a word of Tremni! The wider world is out there, Ârva, and it is full of lies and deception! I've really come to throw my life away—cast it into the gates of destiny. I killed those watchmen like dogs, because I am full of pain and frustration. How can I even convince you of the truth? I just want to shed my blood upon the dust and ascend to Ganka! Is that too much to ask… is it, Ârva? What is there to love in me? Why do you see something in my eyes? Where is my truth? Where is my beauty? I'm a freak. Look at my face. Is there anything natural about this beard? Look at me!"

Tears streamed down his face. Pushing the silver tray aside, Ârva crawled over to him and wrapped her arms around him; he wept even more, sobbing into her shoulder. She held him so tight—so tight that all the worries of the world melted away within her comforting embrace; pain and misery, hopelessness and despair, left his heart as an abiding sense of consolation overwhelmed him. What wonders could the feminine embrace evoke? What mysteries lie hidden within the arms and breast of womankind that cast away the evil shadows of self-pity and remorse? Such power does the grasp of woman wield, that every care, like morning's dew, does fade away in light of sun's brilliance. His face he buried deep within her warm and welcoming bosom as she held him yet tighter. She cushioned her head in her hands and lifted it towards her own, such that the two faces gazed one within the other's , like one soul staring within the mirror of itself. At that moment, seized within the grasp of passion, he kissed her—her lips like *bauff*-bee honey, sweet, of soft yet fulsome texture. She kissed him back, her redolent, thick locks of jet-black hair caressing his blushing green cheeks, radiant with boyish youth's summer bloom. Her cheeks, likewise, were red like rose-blossoms, her eyes alive with a primeval passion that has propelled the course of evolution. Ifunka was on a knife's edge, ready either to fall into temptation or, if he recovered his senses, to flee from her ensnaring charms. Could this be more than a mere dalliance? Was she anything more to him than a mere trifle? Yet he had confessed his love for her, not mere love but love forever, and she had done the same.

Two virgins locked in embrace born of passion's spring, which had long been welling up within the aquifers of their hidden longing. She kissed his right cheek, softly, and then down his neck, again and again, caressing his other cheek with her delicate palm. He reached and grabbed her pure-black tresses and held her head gently, kissing her brow. She looked up at him and brought her lips to his again, kissing him fervently, passionately—an experience which far surpassed, in the pleasure it bestowed, what he had fondly imagined when reading the Tale of Yeshga and Yimna, or the poems of longing penned by the illustrious Hashpa of fame renowned. Thus they remained, locked in firm embrace, kissing and petting one another with almost helpless abandon. Yet innocent, child-like, they did not know what to do with themselves. Unlocking herself from his firm grasp, she lay back on the cushions in the corner and stretched out like a newly-blossomed flower. Inviting as her recumbent body lay, her eyes burning into his soul, his reason emerged from the shackles of desire.

"Ârva, I cannot do this," he said. "The Great Spirit knows all, sees all, hears all."

"Ifunka, I love you," she said in the nasally tone of the Shaffu. "Forever."

"You… you speak Tremni?"

"I hear you and I speak."

"You learn."

"I learn."

"I want you but it is forbidden. No can do."

"Kha vâmta (Not can)*?"*

"Yes."

"Love is forbidden?"

"No, not love. I love you truly. I love God—the Great Spirit—with all my heart and soul. He created me, just as He created you."

"He… created the world," she said.

"Yes, that's right. You are a fast learner."

"You learn fast," she replied, and giggled.

"Your laugh is like sweet music to my ears," said Ifunka.

"I don't… understand."

"Ârva, we are in an impossible situation. I have come to rescue Brother Ushwan or to die, and I will kill as many people as it takes to achieve my goal; whoever crosses our path will die. What can I do with you? How can I save you?"

"I don't understand all. But you take me; you take Meyla. Love is all. You my man; I your woman. One man, one woman, forever."

"You want to be my wife? You want me to be your husband?"

"You are my husband. I am your wife."

"I wish it could be so."

"No monk; Shem no monk. You Ârva husband; Shem Meyla husband. Monk no; you are man. You are man."

"I can't just stop being a monk. I'm ordained. I'm sworn to the service of the Great Spirit. I am a member of the Holy Order of the Brothers of Bishgva. They're my brothers—Ushwan is my brother."

"Ushwan is your brother," she reasoned with him. "I am your woman—I am your wife."

"You don't understand. We're not the same religion, and there's a marriage ceremony, a ritual."

"I… Great Spirit… *Khan-Vabakh khedhi-yôn okh-ish* (I believe in the Great Spirit)."

"*Khedhi?* You believe in the Great Spirit? What about Asharru, the false god of your people?"

"*Kha yashffâ Sharru-yish* (Asharru is not true)."

"Asharru is not true?"

"I not believe Asharru. You are true; Great Spirit is true."

"One God?"

"One God," she affirmed.

"Well, then, repeat the *Spiktomog Kedwayeng*, the Testimony of Faith, and then wash yourself completely and change your clothing; then you may enter the Right Religion of the Sacred Tamitvar. Repeat after me:

Tesa lek okt kedi; Tamitvar Kubara okt kedi; okt spiktomo ffel Wabak Kakan Owaman Aretveyengfi Wonff ffakvaz-inyengfi Tremfitv. Okt spiktomo ffel Votsku envaipat-vitvkaimim Hashemaff Ashamad yonffe yashepogyeng edfilant. Ralishwa Affli Tamitvar Kubarayeng okt teko.

("I believe in one God; I believe in the Holy Tamitvar; I testify that the Great Spirit is the Lord of the Worlds and the Master of the heavens and Tremn. I testify that Votsku is the Seer to whom the Archangel Hashemaff revealed the verses of truth. I accept the Right Religion of the Holy Tamitvar.")

He repeated each sentence, line by line, and she copied him, even attempting to mimic his exotic accent. When they had finished, he told her to go and wash herself completely. He mimed washing and said "Bath!" which she translated as *"Vaish,"* and grabbed his hand, taking Ifunka down a corridor and into a large bathroom with a circular bath in the middle and racks of towels and sponges at the peripheries. Ifunka had never seen its like and wondered how such fineries could exist within the depths of savage lands. She called for Meyla, who had otherwise been occupied.

~

As she pulled Shem from the room, his heart raced within him. What did this fawn-like beauty, this rapturous beauty, so sweet he could devour her whole, want with his pious and religious self? So long cut off from meaningful discourse except, that is, with his turbulent companions and the glorious bard who fell to the clay-men (i.e. the wandering minstrel), he felt a loneliness that few could truly comprehend. He was intro-verted, alone, wrapped within the walls of his own self, oblivious to the petty trivialities of small talk, indifferent to pleasantries, obsessed with the concerns and ideas which welled up within the spring of his own profound and innovative imagination. He was a mine rich in inesti-mable gems, a fountainhead of creativity, yet he disliked the boisterous exuberance of others and their ignorant lack of self-reflection. He was reflection personified; he moved within the compass of himself. He did not need the judgement or the regard of others to fuel his own self-image. The contemplative one—this abstracted one—was now drawn away by the current which he himself could not resist, no matter how much the inner-restraint which he had cultivated cried out within the chasm of his enlightened consciousness.

She drew him; her subtle charms, her sultry wiles, her eyes like *tvung*-deer, her lips like sweet *tornish*-cherries in their summer yield. Her chestnut hair bounced and jostled with her every step, light like a feather in vernal breeze. Her hands like yarns of *woffgi*-silk, seductively pulled him through the corridors to her room, up a flight of steps, within the attic. There she lit some *ffentwash*-fat candles and laid out the blankets of *tvung*-skin on her humble bed. It was nothing more than a wide, rectan-gular mattress of *braksh*-straw covered in a *meb*-wool sheet and overlaid with skins to keep her warm. They were directly beneath the sloped roof and there was no window, but it was cozy and peaceful, presenting the perfect atmosphere for intimacy to kindle brightly between two naïve lovers in the fullness of youth and under the heady intoxication of love.

She lay down on the bed and invited Shem to do likewise. He lay beside her, his reluctance washed away by the streams of unbridled desire, his eyes locked on hers with profound intensity. Her face, so dainty and elegant, was embosomed within a ring of buoyant, chestnut locks which danced upon her light-green brow and cheeks. Her eyes—an intense brown—bespoke mysteries of love and longing, which Shem seemed to read like a book appearing within the tapestry of his youthful mind. She caressed his cheek with her hand and he reciprocated—fearful, confused. She was not simply following orders from her mistress by offering herself to him. There was intensity in her expression which bespoke genuine affection and infatuation. She was, like Ârva, innocent of the ways of men, so she seemed almost to be waiting for Shem to take some initiative. He drew closer to her and she did the same, until both were no more than a *ffil*—a thumb's length—away from one another. She wrapped her arms around him and he did the same. They meant to kiss but were afraid, instead gazing one at the other in silent fascination.

At last, Shem moved in to kiss her but ended up planting his lips firmly on her brow. She seized his hair in her fist and kissed him firmly on the lips. He could not free himself from her firm grasp, even if he wanted to, which he did not, and felt her tongue within his mouth—something which he could not decide how he felt about. It was a strange, slightly unnerving, experience. She tasted of *zasht*-berry wine, pungent and, to his unaccustomed taste buds, sickly, yet the warmth of her tongue dancing enthusiastically within his mouth, filled the cup of anticipation.

Suddenly, there was a call—a voice—from below. Meyla released Shem and sat up.

"Meyla, ifta-krâ (Meyla, come)*!"* came the voice of her mistress.

Standing up, she put her dress in order and turned to Shem.

"Saff (sorry)*,"* she apologized. *"Ftâ khodh-ôn kheyâ okh-ish* (I love you forever).*"*

She turned to leave. Shem stood up and followed after her.

"Meyla, don't leave me… ever."

She turned and looked into his eyes.

"What you say?" she asked in imperfect Tremni.

"Heika! You speak Tremni! I say, no go, no go, ever."

"I come," she replied.

"I mean, I want you always; not leave me ever. Together, you and me."

He pointed to her and then himself.

"I come you; we go, you and me; not leave," she said.

"Meyla!" her mistress called.

"Come, come!" said the maid as she took Shem's hand and led him downstairs to the bathroom.

"Khuff shog-ôn ftâ-yish-ô, vonffey (What do you require, mistress)*?"* Meyla asked her mistress.

"Flaffru-fto yîff shift-ôn ftâ-yish-ô (Do you want to marry this stranger)*?"* Ârva asked her.

"Shem, *rî* (Shem, yes)," Meyla replied.

"Fâ Sfikhtom-go Khedhva-yeym ffogsh-ôn ftâ ffaidh-ish ffi lekh vaishiff-ôn-ish (then you must say the Testimony of Faith and be bathed)," Ârva explained. *"Ifta-krâ, ffogsh-krâ* (come, repeat).*"*

Ifunka again said the Testimony of Faith while Meyla repeated after him, line by line. Then Meyla filled the bath with water and bathed her mistress and herself while Ifunka and Shem stood outside the room.

"You came to your senses, then?" asked Shem.

"Yes, did *you?*"

"I don't know. Of all the sins and temptations of the flesh, women are the most enticing. It's like I was not myself. I was possessed by some unnatural force."

"Lust," said Ifunka. "It's all-consuming; difficult to resist. The fires of passion burn brighter than the sun. Did not Tvem warn us? He said that we should become like a hollow reed, sacrificing all ephemeral pleasure for that which is more lasting. He said that all negative energy could be opposed and overcome by positive energy, which is stronger and more effective."

"The eighth teaching."

"Indeed."

"My positive will overcame the lust within me. It's not easy, but then it's not easy to will anything at all and cause that will to result in real actions."

"'Honour is higher than flesh,'" Ifunka quoted Tvem. "'Spirit is higher than matter.'"

The two women emerged from the bathroom wrapped in *meb*-wool towels. They rushed past them and into Ârva's bed chamber where they dressed in white night-gowns, clean and resplendent, glowing in the candle-light. They emerged like white roses, blooming beautifully before the wonder-struck eyes of their lovers.

"Beautiful," said Ifunka.

"Magnificent," said Shem.

"You like?" asked Ârva.

"I like very much," Ifunka replied.

"You like Meyla?" Meyla asked.

"Oh yes, very like; much, much," said Shem.

"You wife me?" asked Ârva.

"Oh, right," said Ifunka, having forgotten the logical conclusion of their religious conversions.

"Ifunka, is this it?" asked Shem. "Are we abandoning our vows?"

"Tvem told us: 'You're *no longer* monks,'" Ifunka replied.

"He didn't mean that literally," Shem protested.

"We have two choices, or three rather: we leave now and abandon these girls," said Ifunka.

"Hardly conscionable."

"Right, we refuse to marry them but engage in sin with them."

"I suppose that would be a grievous error."

"Well, then, the third option is to marry them."

"So soon?"

"Shem, this might be our last night on Tremn. We might be slaughtered tomorrow or burned on the pyre as virgin sacrifices to a pagan god; or we wed these women now and face the prospect of death later. If the Great Spirit will, we will rescue Brother Ushwan and take these girls back to Ffash Valley where Ffen is even now. We'll till the soil, start families, repopulate this forest region, away from the foul corruption of the Theocracy and its moribund institutions. We can build a new life. Our destiny hangs in the balance."

"There isn't time, Ifunka, for us to wed. The night grows short. How shall we search for Brother Ushwan during daylight? What if they sacrifice him tonight, or in the morning? We don't know their customs."

"Tvem said: 'There is always time. We are all given enough time, if we use it well.'"

"Fine," Shem conceded. "Let's do it. Let's get married. I will marry you and Ârva and you will marry me and Meyla."

"We wed?" asked Ârva, her eyes bright with joy.

"Yes," said Ifunka. "We wed now. Shem will marry us. I will marry Meyla and Shem. We are monks so we have the requisite authority to marry others, just as we married our Brother Ffen to his three wives back in Ffash Valley."

They went to the reception room that they had first entered when they sneaked into the house some hours previously. The women and Shem seated themselves while Ifunka spoke.

"Peace and greetings to all who are gathered to witness this holy rite," he said, uttering the traditional formula of greeting used in weddings. "We have come together, in this house, to wed this bird to this root, that is: Meyla, daughter of Ashka-Hafta, who is not present, of the Shaffu, and Shem Effga, son of Shadka Effga, a brother of the Holy Order of the Brothers of Bishgva of the Right Religion of the Sacred Tamitvar, of the Monastery of the Brown Owl. Dost thou agree to wed this fast root?"

Meyla, not comprehending the formula, was silent.

"Say, *harei* ('yea so')," Shem whispered.

"Harei!" she said, enthusiastically.

"Dost thou agree to marry this bird?" Ifunka asked Shem.

Before Shem could answer, they heard a door or gate swing open and then fasten shut behind them.

"Yai!" Ârva screeched before Ifunka put his hand over her mouth.

"Baba okh-an (my father)*!"* she said in a muffled voice.

"This is bad, brother, very bad!" said Shem fearfully. "It's her father!"

"My father," she explained. "Priest of Sharru. I no believe Sharru, he sacrifice me on pyre. I with you; I believe Great Spirit, one God, Right Religion. What we do?"

"Shem? Ideas?" asked Ifunka desperately.

"We kill him; it's the only way."

"Shem!"

"You started the killing, brother; we can't stop now. There is much more blood to shed."

"No kill; no father!" Ârva protested. She was boiling with emotion.

"Ârva!!!" her father called. He had heard voices. *"Sheff ftâ-yish-ô? Khuff velâsh-ish-ô* (Where are you? What's going on)?"

"Baba (Father)!" she called in reply. *"Iftâff okh-ish* (I'm here)*!"*

"We grab him, we tie him up," Ifunka suggested.

Shem gave him a stern look.

"This was your plan originally."

"He's the chief priest!" said Shem angrily.

"Be that as it may, there is no easy solution to any of this. I simply can't murder the father of a woman I love."

"On your head be it!"

"Ârva," Ifunka instructed her. "Stand at the back of the room. Shem and I will grab your father. Meyla will help to tie him up and gag him."

"My father!"

"We won't kill him," Ifunka assured her. "If you want us to live, help us."

She nodded and said *"rî* (yes)."

"Okay, he's coming," Ifunka whispered.

They heard his footsteps as he paced down the corridor and walked into the room. As he stepped over the threshold, Shem extended his staff, tripping him up. He fell forwards with a groan and the two monks jumped onto him, pinning him to the ground.

"Khuff fteff fto-yeym-ish-ô (what's the meaning of this)?" he cried. *"Ârva, vâ loft lâm-ôn ftâ-yish-ô (Ârva, why are you standing there)?"*

Her eyes welled up with tears, her face betraying agony and upset while Meyla followed suit, bursting into a torrent of tears. Ârva shook her head.

"Meyla???" he called out.

Meyla looked down in shame.

"Kha (no)!!!" he screamed and struggled against his captors. *"Khalam-Sharru okh-ish, Predh-bara Khanshaff-eym. Flevâ khaikh-ôn fto akhfeb-ish-ô? Flevâ ftâ-ga-yish-ô! Ârva-yem khuff akhfeb-ôn ftâ-ga mon-ish* (I am

Khalam-Sharru. I am the High-Priest of Khanshaff. Who dares to do this? Who are ye? What have you done to Ârva)?"

"Be quiet!" Ifunka yelled angrily. "You're our prisoner!"

"Ei? Khaffshik-zen! Kha-vamtâ (Ey? Infidels! Not possible)!"

"Yes, you call us *khaffshik*s, but we are the true believers. You are the infidel."

"You call me and my family infidels?" asked the priest in heavily-accented Tremni, his voice burning with rage. "How dare you? You shall die for this! You shall die for this!!!"

"No, just you, priest. Your daughter is one of us now, as is Meyla."

"Khuff (what)*???"* he screamed again.

"Shut him up, Shem," Ifunka ordered.

Shem stuffed a piece of cloth in his mouth.

"No... Ârva... No!"

He could speak no more.

"Ârva, tell him," said Ifunka. "Tell your father."

"Haffli Ralîshva tekh-ôn mon-ish (I have accepted the Right Religion)," she told him. *"Khan-Vabakh khedhi-yôn okh-ish, Tesh dhi khû-yish* (I believe in the Great Spirit, there is one God)."

"Urrrrr," she groaned as he struggled; Ifunka and Meyla tied his wrists together while Shem secured his feet.

"Khodh-paft okh-an Ifunka-yish (Ifunka is my lover)," she continued. *"Khû okh yîff-ôn khon-ish ffi Shem Meyla yîff-ôn khon-ish* (I will marry him and Meyla will marry Shem)."

"Urrrrggg!!!"

He tried to break free. His eyes displayed hopelessness, anger and despair. He had lost what was most precious to him in all the world; he saw only blood and vengeance. They dragged Khalam-Sharru to the edge of the room and Shem guarded him.

"This is making the wedding rather complicated," said Ifunka. "Shall we start from the beginning or shall I just ask you for your consent, Shem?"

"Hmmm," he pondered, keeping one eye on the infidel priest. "Best to start again."

"Peace and greetings to all who are gathered…"

There was a knock on the door—the ground floor entrance.

"…to witness this holy rite."

Knock, knock, knock.

"Brother?" asked Shem.

"They'll go away if there's no answer"

Knock, knock, knock.

"Huh, huh," Khalam-Sharru gave a muffled laugh.

"Why are you laughing?" asked Shem.

Knock, knock, knock.

CHAPTER XVI.

House of Slaughter

~~

"The door, Ârva, get the door," said Ifunka in an authoritative tone.

"*Rî*, my love. Meyla, *ifta-krâ!*"

Ârva kissed Ifunka on the lips and turned, reluctantly, to go downstairs. Meyla grabbed Shem's hands and held them tight.

"I go; I come," she said.

"It's okay," Shem comforted her. "Whatever happens, you are always in my heart."

"I love you," she said.

"And I you," he replied as she joined Ârva and headed for the door.

Ifunka and Shem kept quiet and listened attentively to hear who it might be who had come to the house at so late an hour. Khalam-Sharru struggled with his bonds and tried to shuffle back and forth on the floor.

"Shem, knock him out," ordered Ifunka.

Shem took his staff and, with a solid thwack, immobilized Ârva's father and rendered him unconscious. The girls reached the door.

"*Flevâ-yish-ô* (Who is it)?" she could be heard to call.

"*Eyn-fach-zen* (watchmen)!" came the reply.

"*Khuff shift-ôn ftâ-gei-yish* (what do ye want)?" they asked.

"*Hakvra-krâ! Khalam-Sharru-yem shipktâ-yôn ftâkh-ish* (open up! We must speak to Khalam-Sharru)!" they shouted.

"*Kha, kha iftâff khû-yish* (no, he's not here)."

"*Hakvra-krâ* (open up)!" they repeated.

"*Kha, vâ* (no, why)?" shouted Ârva.

The watchmen banged on the door again.

"*Meyla, yôt kakvra-krâ* (Meyla, open up the door)," Ârva ordered.

"*Yonffey* (mistress)?" asked Meyla.

"*Kha ramai-krâ* (don't worry)," Ârva reassured her.

As Meyla twisted the lock, four armed watchmen burst through the door, knocking Meyla on the floor in the process.

"*Dashvôdh-zen* (bastards)!" Ârva cursed them.

"*Sheff Khalam-Sharru-yish-ô* (where is Khalam-Sharru)?" they demanded.

"*Ftâ-gei yishk-ôn okh mon-ish—kha iftâff khû-yish* (I told you—he's *not* here)!" she insisted.

"*Khû vish-ôn ftâkh khon-ish* (we will find him)," said their leader.

The leader directed two of the watchmen to head upstairs while he searched downstairs.

"*Ftôn eyn-krâ* (watch them)," he ordered the remaining watchman, directing him to watch the two girls.

Ifunka and Shem could hear footsteps on the stairs.

"Right, Ifunka," said Shem. "It sounds like there's two of them."

"This shouldn't be happening. They've come to see Khalam-Sharru and they're not taking no for an answer. Opposite sides of the door!"

The watchmen rigorously searched every room for Khalam-Sharru, until they came to the room where he lay unconscious. The door was open and they could see his unconscious body on the floor.

"*Predh-bara* (High-priest)!" they cried as they rushed into the room to help him.

Ifunka thwacked one of them on the head, knocking him flat unconscious while Shem missed the head of the other but managed to hit him on the back of his neck, cracking the bone. The watchman gurgled bile and foamed at the mouth, choking on his own fluids before falling dead.

"Sorry," said Shem before they started tying up the other one.

"Can't we kill this one?" asked Shem.

"We might need to interrogate him," Ifunka replied.

The head watchman had finished searching the ground floor.

"Baksh-Sharru, Hara-Sheft!" he called the two watchmen's names. "*Sheff ftâ-ga-yish-ô* (Where are you two)?"

No response.

"*Eshai-krâ* (report)!" he ordered.

Again, no response.

He grew anxious. The head watchman called his colleague to follow him and rushed upstairs.

"*Okh-ifft ifta-krâ* (come with me)!" the watchmen ordered the girls to follow him up the stairs.

As they were going up, Ârva grabbed a candle-holder with candle attached and blew it out. Meyla followed her up silently. When they reached the top of the stairs, the chief watchman began frantically to search. The second watchman took the girls into one of the bedrooms. Meyla closed the door behind them, discreetly, while Ârva raised the candle-holder high above the watchman's oblivious head. She, with all her strength, brought it down on his skull, knocking him thoroughly unconscious. His head bled profusely—he was dying. The chief watchman heard a thump.

"Kumkha-Shaffu!" he called. "*Kumkha-Shaffu! Khuff velâsh-ôn mon-ish-ô* (Kumkha-Shaffu! What has happened)?"

There was no response. He was on the threshold of the reception room, where Ifunka and Shem waited to leap upon him in order to deliver his quietus. He turned, unsure of where to go, his back to the room. Seizing the opportunity, Ifunka and Shem thwacked him with their staffs, hitting him on the shoulder and back. He cried in agony and fell to his knees. Shem bonked him on the head and he collapsed. They tied him up and placed him next to Khalam-Sharru and Hara-Sheft, the only surviving captives. The girls dragged Kumkha-Shaffu's body into the room.

"Well done, ladies," said Ifunka triumphantly. "Put his body next to the other dead watchman. Shem, help them."

They laid his still-bleeding half-corpse on top of Baksh-Sharru. Ârva rushed into Ifunka's arms. Her heart beat strongly—fiercely; her cheeks were flush—tears streamed from her eyes.

"I kill *shaff!*" she said, her voice agonized, tremulous.

"What did you say?" asked Ifunka.

"I kill a man!" she repeated, her voice choked.

"That's odd—I'm sure I heard you say you killed someone else," he remarked but his words went in one ear and out the other as she clung to him for comfort, her hands shaking, her body trembling. While he should have been thinking only of comforting a woman in distress, her trembling excited the baser sentiments within his impassioned loins. He released her, or rather, pushed her away.

"Ârva, there's work to do."

She looked at him, confused.

"Shem!"

He was also holding Meyla. The two rocked back and forth in one embrace, like two rocking-chairs locked together in a perpetual exchange of momentum.

"Yes, brother?"

"We need a bucket of water and some salt. We're going to interrogate the infidels."

They sat up the three prisoners and splashed water in their faces. They all awoke with a start. Frantic eyes looked one at another and then at their captors, including Ârva and Meyla, who were now cold in expression—even to her father—looking sternly on.

"*Ârva! Meyla!*" shouted Khalam-Sharru. "*Khuff akhfeb-ôn ftâ-ga-yish-ô* (what are you two doing)?"

"Speak Tremni, father!" she shouted back at him defiantly. "I am not Shaffu."

"Unholy child—ingrate!" he shouted. "I raised you pure, through sixteen years, touching no man, yet here you are: the slut of a *khaffshik* dog???"

"He not touch me; we marry soon—today."

"Over my dead body!!!"

"You die? Die! You are *khaffshik*. I know truth now. One God—one Great Spirit—He make everything. He make sun—He make moons—He save my soul. You teach me Sharru; you teach me lie—death my soul: Gahimka!"

"Gahimka, Ganka! These are lies of the *khaffshiks*! I am your father—you believe me!"

"No—your eyes are not truth! I see eyes with light. I see Ifunka eyes; in them truth and beauty."

"One day! One day and all my world is ruined! One day! One day!"

"That's enough!" said Ifunka. "Your only task in life now—all three of you—is to answer my questions. You give us what we need, you might get to live. At the most, one or two of you might live. At least one or two of you will die; I can guarantee you that. If you lie to me, I will kill you. If you don't answer me, I will kill you. If you try to escape, I will kill you. If I feel like it, I will kill you. Is that understood, Khalam-Sharru?"

"Yes," he replied in an indignant tone.

"Watchmen?"

"Yessss!"

"Why did the watchmen come to this house tonight?"

No one answered.

"Shem?"

Shem took a knife and cut the two watchmen's cheeks. They squirmed with pain. Then, taking salt in hand, he smothered it all over their wounds. They twisted their heads and necks, grimacing yet more, but they did not answer.

"Ârva, Meyla, don't look," Ifunka advised. "Their feet!"

Shem raised one of the watchmen's axes in order to dismember the captives' feet.

"Wait, wait, wait!!!" pleaded the chief watchman.

"Hara-Sheft is my subordinate. I am responsible for his actions. Do not take his feet!"

"Answer us or you will die!" shouted Ifunka.

"Leave Hara-Sheft; he will answer you nothing without my command."

"Very well, then," said Ifunka. "Then we don't need him. Shem!"

Shem raised the axe and brought it down with full force, striking off the watchman's head. The dead man's body shook briefly and gorged the commander and Khalam-Sharru in a sea of blood; Shem's face was covered with it; the wall was splattered.

"Ah, ah, ah, ah!!!" the commander screamed repeatedly and in quick succession. *"Kha, kha, kha, kha* (no, no, no, no)*!!!"*

He burst into tears.

"His soul is now in Gahimka," said Ifunka, who almost seemed to relish the spectacle. "Where seas of fire burn the infidels through all eternity. There Afflish the Accursed reigns, until the time when he shall be chained up and cast into the abyss. Gahimka is the abode of denial—the place where all evil-doers shall receive their reward. Do you want to receive your reward, watchman? Do you want to join your friend?"

"Hey, hey, hey, hey," he said, trying to calm Ifunka. "Calm down! I will tell you everything!"

"You weak dog! You're going to pander to this *khaffshik shiflakh*—this piece of filth?" Khalam-Sharru upbraided him.

"Shem, teach Khalam-Sharru a lesson in politeness," said Ifunka.

"Ârva, keep your eyes closed," warned Shem.

He took his knife and cut the priest on the shoulder, rubbing salt deep within the wound.

"Ahhhhhh!" he screamed.

"Do you like it?" asked Ifunka. "I love salt—it gives just the right flavour to everything, doesn't it?"

"I thought monks were better than this," said Khalam-Sharru as he clenched his teeth in agony. "It's all driving you mad, isn't it? You're no better than us. You're a murderer!"

"I do what I have to do," Ifunka replied angrily. "You demon-worshippers killed my family—my uncle and aunt—the only people who ever loved me. Then you took my friend, Ushwan, from me. You make us travel through this whole forest, through *yeshka*s and bandits, lake worms, forest worms, *shan* and watchmen. Clay men—they took our friend, the wandering minstrel; Ffen—he's left behind in Ffash Valley. I've lost everything!—everything! But I'm going to get Ushwan back. Ushwan will not die at your hands, false priest! That watchman was not murdered; he was one of you—the murderers! You eat people—you sacrifice virgins to a god that doesn't even exist! Is it murder to kill infidels who are themselves murderers? I think not."

"Doesn't exist?" asked Khalam-Sharru. "You will see him in the flesh! And, one way or another, you will both die. If my daughter doesn't repent, she will die also—virgin or no. If she and you are virgins, you shall both burn on the pyre. If not, there is an even worse fate for all of you. One way or another, you are all dead. This is *our* city, mighty Khanshaff—holy Khanshaff. There are six thousand residents within these walls alone, and a dozen small villages and outposts throughout this region, which is Shaffnâ, the realm of real men! Can you overcome us all, fools? For what?—for one monk—this Ushwan you keep talking about? He's nobody and we shall eat him. Even his bones shall be cracked open so that we may suck out the juicy marrow and boil them in our soup—so hearty and delectable! Are you going to kill me, monks?"

"We'll see," said Ifunka, trying to conceal his anger and sadness. "Watchman!" He turned to the remaining watchman. "Why did you come to this house?"

"The moat guard did not return and the wall guard on this flank have also disappeared. We came to alert Khalam-Sharru, the priest. He sits on *Marakh Dairshan-eym*—the Council of Thirteen."

"What is the Council of Thirteen?"

"Twelve elders, one chosen from each of the twelve boroughs of Khanshaff. They're selected by *Marakh Ffû-daikh-naff-eym*–the Council of Fifty-Nine, which consists of the chief priests of every borough, the headman of each village, the commanders of the watchmen, and the *Metshu*—the Sage."

"Who is the Sage?"

"He is a mystic who can speak to animals and trees, see visions, and channel the voice of Sharru."

"So, this is Sharru in the flesh?"

"No, Sharru lives in the *Ffâna*—the Temple, within the Inner Sanctum, with his companions, the Priestess and her four maidservants. Sharru rarely leaves his sanctum but the Priestess emerges from time-to-time to confer with the Sage and officiate at high sacrifices and ceremonies."

"Is the Sage on the Council?"

"Yes, he is the chief of the Council. He's been travelling of late, but is due to return soon."

"It is clear, then," Ifunka concluded. "That Sharru is a fiction—a fantasy kept alive by the concept of the 'Inner Sanctum'. This Priestess is nothing more than a deceiver and a liar."

"Oh, you would not say that if you saw him—and saw her!"

"How; why?"

"He is glorious to behold—a living god!"

"Impossible. Have *you* see him?" asked Shem.

"No," the watchman admitted. "But my grandfather did."

"Nonsense!" shouted Ifunka.

"It's true," averred Khalam-Sharru. "And *I* have seen him."

"You *would* say that!"

"Tell me, virgin," Khalam-Sharru continued. "Will you still love my daughter when you see the Priestess? You will not keep your virginity so easily then!"

"I love Ârva and no other."

"Have you ever loved another?"

"What? I—that's inconsequential."

"Your 'love' is nothing more than the urges of your *khaffshik* loins. It will pass. And then another beauty will captivate you and Ârva will fade like a lost memory, even as your previous beloved has faded from your memory."

"I won't hear this!"

"But you must! I am on the Council of Thirteen and I know more than you. Your plan is hopeless; trust me. As soon as the rest of the Council know what you are doing, this whole city will be up in arms. That watchman—do you know his name?"

"No."

"Ask him then!"

"Very well, who are you, watchman?"

"Sharru-Mashda," he replied. "Member of the Council of Fifty-Nine.

"When the Council of Fifty-Nine notice that their colleague is missing, what do you think will happen then?" Khalam-Sharru taunted him. "Will they give up and go home? Six thousand Shaffu shall descend upon you and you shall most certainly die, in the name of Sharru, the true god!"

"Praise his name!" said Sharru-Mashda. "He is *mashda*!"

"*Mashda?*"

"Magnificent," Khalam-Sharru translated.

"Well, we do not need you any more, Sharru-Mashda. Are you willing to take the Testimony of Faith and leave the accurséd illusions which you are currently suffering from? Will you cast out Asharru from your heart and embrace the Right Religion of the Holy Tamitvar?"

"Never!" he replied.

"Good; that eases my conscience," said Ifunka matter-of-factly. "I forgot to ask Hara-Sheft, though his answer would have been the same. Shem!"

"Wait!" Khalam-Sharru pleaded. "He has answered your questions!"

"The last answer was unsatisfactory. Do it!"

Shem raised the bloodied axe, still dripping wet, and hewed off Sharru-Mashda's head.

"Now; where is Brother Ushwan?" Ifunka asked with a slight smile.

The blood and violence was getting to him, warping his mind.

"You should have asked Sharru-Mashda; I'll tell you nothing."

"You look thirsty. What say we give the councillor a drink?"

"Indeed," agreed Shem as he reached for the wooden bucket full of water.

Grabbing him by his thick black hair, Shem shoved his head into the bucket. He struggled. Ifunka held him down. Ârva got up and left the room in tears. She couldn't handle it; neither could Meyla, for, whatever disaffection she may have had for her father, she could not tolerate seeing him harmed in any way. Khalam-Sharru struggled like a wild boar, trying to break free from his bonds.

"Enough!" said Ifunka, just as the priest began to succumb to oxygen deprivation.

Shem released him from the bucket, his face pale green, wet and panicked. His eyes were wide, alarmed, his hair dishevelled, veins pulsating on his forehead and neck.

"All right; I'll tell you," he said. "If you promise, by your Great Spirit, not to kill me now."

"If you attack us or try to escape, we must kill you."

"Very well, but for no other reason. Agreed?"

"Agreed," said Ifunka.

"Right, then. Your brother, Ushwan, is being held at the heart of the city, in the dungeon of the sacrificial offerings, which is located below the Council Headquarters, adjacent to the Temple of Asharru. It's heavily guarded and Ushwan is due to be sacrificed tomorrow, along with twelve other virgins: six men and six women. We're awaiting the return of the Sage, who is due to arrive from a recent journey in time for the ceremony."

"What happens at this sacrifice?"

"The Sage and the Priestess will officiate, in the presence of the Council of the Thirteen and the Council of the Forty-Nine, as well as a crowd of spectators, in the Square of Sacrifice—the courtyard of the holy Temple. The sacrificial virgins will be stripped naked, smothered in oils and fragrant perfume and their private parts covered with a red loin-cloth of *woffgi*-silk. One each of the male and female offerings will be selected by the Priestess and given a choice: the man will be given the option of giving his virginity to the Priestess while the woman will be offered the choice of giving her maidenhead to the Sage, thus escaping the fire."

"Does anyone refuse?"

"Ha, ha, ha," Khalam-Sharru laughed. "When they have been ravaged, the man and woman are thrown to the sacrificial *ffaika*—the forest worm who lives within a chamber underneath the temple; eaten alive and digested in its fearsome belly."

"Ah, I see," said Ifunka. "So, it doesn't happen often then?"

"It happens all the time," he replied. "Then the number is completed by taking two virgins from the watching crowd."

"How do you know that someone is a virgin?"

"The Sage knows."

"So, to accept the Priestess or Sage is to kill other innocents. Why do they choose that fate?"

"The Priestess is irresistible. You shall see and you shall succumb to her charms. The Sage also; he can melt a woman with his eyes, so powerful is his capacity for seduction."

"I think you underestimate us," Ifunka retorted. "I can make your daughter quiver and sigh with a mere glance."

"Bastard!!!" Khalam-Sharru cried.

"Ifunka!" Ârva called.

She entered the room.

"I be your wife soon. You listen me! No more hurt *baba* heart. He is infidel, but my heart is big. I love him. *Baba*—" she turned to Khalam-Sharru. "Ifunka not kill you. You love me; he love. Help me."

The priest's heart melted within him.

"Ârva, I forgive you," he said. "I've always doted on you and I had high expectations for your future, even that you could become a new maidservant for Asharru himself. I'll make this deal. If you, Ifunka, take my daughter away and forget about Ushwan, I'll let you go and pass this whole thing off as a kidnapping. No one will know who you were and there will be no consequences for your actions. Take care of my daughter and Meyla and keep them happy. That's all I ask."

"No!" Ifunka cried. "I can't leave Ushwan. We've come too far for that. We've shed too much blood for that. I shall love your daughter with all my heart, as Shem loves Meyla, but I will free Ushwan, even if I have to kill the Sage, the Priestess and the whole Council!"

"You're going to get killed, you foolish bastard!" Khalam-Sharru shouted. "And my daughter is going to be sacrificed on the pyre! Even if you take her maidenhead, she's going to be fed to the worm. Do you not understand that?"

"Accept the Great Spirit as the one true God," replied Ifunka. "And Votsku as the Seer who revealed the Holy Tamitvar through the inspiration of the Archangel Hashemaff."

"You deluded fool!" Khalam-Sharru cursed him. "I can never accept your *khaffshik* religion. Save my daughter and save yourself!"

"I believe in one God; I believe in the Holy Tamitvar," said Ifunka, ignoring him. "Shem; lock him in here. It's your wedding night. I'll marry you and Meyla. Then I'll take the first watch, for four hours. You can take the second watch. Then Ârva... no, Meyla. Ârva is too close to him. Rejoice, brother, tonight you shall be married!"

They secured Khalam-Sharru, tied him to the door, gagged him and left him to his own devices while the four companions cleaned up and changed into fresh clothes; they then went to the secondary reception room in order to complete the marriage ceremony. Ifunka repeated the first part of the ceremony and then asked Shem:

"Dost thou agree to marry this bird?"

"Harei!" he answered enthusiastically.

Shem kissed Meyla passionately and they all rejoiced. Ârva brought some food from the larder: a round, salted loaf of bread called a *ftelish* (or *tvelish* in Tremni) and a type of yoghurt made from *meb*-milk called *mebshâsh*. They enthusiastically ate up. Ifunka then begged his leave and returned to watch Khalam-Sharru in the blood-soaked, corpse-strewn reception room.

Meyla and Shem repaired to their bedroom where she hurriedly divested herself of her garments to reveal the fullness of her soft, silky-smooth and fulsome figure, her curls bouncing over her supple neck and sweet bodily features; beautifully light-green skin shaped into wide curves of ideal proportions. She seemed to him a symphony of beauty, a luscious repast dying to be kissed, touched, caressed and fondled. He threw off his own vestments and joined her on the bed as they playfully touched and explored each other's bodies in the innocence and full-flower of youth's blossoming maturity. Their love was intense, new, a combination of pain and pleasure satisfied by the safe knowledge that they were now united in wedlock, joined in a life-long union sanctioned by the Great Spirit, which made their pleasures legitimate and yet more potent.

As the newly-weds consummated their wedded bliss, Ifunka watched the priest intently and was, in turn, watched, hawk-like, by him. Ârva had been sent to bed, like a dutiful child—she was only sixteen after all. Meyla was yet younger—fifteen—but in the full flower of her womanhood. Hour after hour, Khalam-Sharru watched his foe with hate-filled eyes until, eventually, Ifunka could sustain his gaze no more and burst out:

"What is it, demon-worshipper? Do you hope to kill me with your eyes?"

"You have taken my life from me!" he replied.

"Oh, I have taken your life from *you*?" Ifunka replied. "You infidels killed my uncle and aunt. I had been abandoned by my parents—they were my only true family, and now I have nothing left but my brother Shem and your daughter, whom I love. I have saved her soul from eternal damnation. You tell me who has taken what from whom?"

"She is all *I* have. Her mother, Lîfa, died in childbirth; and Meyla— she is like a daughter to me as well. Do you think us incapable of love?"

"I do not."

"Yet you kill us indiscriminately?"

"You slaughter innocent men, women, and children like sheep— nay, dogs! You burn virgins alive to placate a false god!"

"Asharru lives—we, as the Council, are privileged to see him. Some love him; we, as priests, are *supposed to* love him, but every one fears him. He does not die but lives eternally in the flesh. If he lived in your city and you knew no other god, would you not worship him? We are following only what our forefathers followed."

"God does not want innocents to be sacrificed on a pyre. He wants us to do good and worship him. Listen, the Holy Tamitvar says, **'oshoki-patve ffogash: etv gel ffonashmozin parlaktant aftokti parlaktilei; hash reffeleim sapi tvakim Wabak Kakan lishantilei. Vocarum: Ramut elenarum, om venda—lei!—phel uom cub sapiem hithio cub paterioceiCum cultaphunmonathalei'** ('the infidels say, we worship only what our forefathers worshipped; yet the Great Spirit has given each man a choice. Say: choose God, O people—yea!—even He who created you, male and female, from clay and water')."

"Our god demands fear and vengeance."

"If you can see him, flesh and blood, he is not a god, but a man. God is a Spirit who speaks through His Archangel, Hashemaff."

"You have great faith, monk. Now, I do not hate you. I do not believe in your invisible god, but I bless your marriage to my daughter."

"You've placed me in an awkward position; I have you captive."

"I understand. In any case, your watch is over. Get your friend, my erstwhile torturer, to come."

"It's his wedding night."

"Nevertheless—fair is fair. You're tired. I can't sleep with you here; no man loves his son-in-law. Go on!"

Ifunka walked to the corridor.

"Shem!" he called out.

Shem leapt out of bed, still completely nude, and threw on his robes.

"Husband!" Meyla woke up in alarm.

"Don't worry; I'm taking the watch. Get back to sleep."

"*Rî* (yes)," she said and covered herself in the warm blankets.

Shem rushed downstairs and took up his position. Khalam-Sharru fell sound asleep as soon as Ifunka left the room. He'd been speaking the truth. Ifunka decided to check on Ârva. Peering into her room, he found her fast asleep, breathing softly like an angel, her chest lifting the silken blankets with every exhalation. He had not been given a room so he spent some time exploring the house, room after room, until he found one which satisfied his tastes. The Shaffu were unusual amongst inhabitants of the planet Tremn in that they were accustomed to using soft beds. He found, however, one mattress which was sufficiently hard, being stuffed full of *braksh*-wheat; a bed perhaps intended for a lesser servant.

"Decadently soft," he said before laying on its rough sheets. "What would the Abbott say? Yet lying with my face in Ârva's bosom; that would I do!"

Washing his hands and face in the washbasin, he performed the *kashafftishatvin* prayer and went to sleep. Ârva woke him at around dawn. He awoke gently as she kissed his brow. Opening his eyes, he saw her delicate neck above his face.

"Am I in Ganka?" were his first words.

She giggled and smiled.

"You say Ganka; tell me more about Ganka."

Her smile was like a vast river, dazzling white in the noon-day sun.

"Ganka is Paradise; an endless expanse of redolent gardens, luscious and beautiful beyond imagination; rivers with endless mossy banks, fresh springs of never-depleting wine, pure water, and milk; mansions of solid ruby, diamond, and emerald; temples of marble, gold and precious stones; never-ending banquets of succulent food to delight every taste; glorious music, heavenly carols sung by a limitless host of white-winged angels, harps, *mimgeffs*, and other heavenly instruments in hand, their voices instilling an ecstasy most complete; wide-eyed companions, virgins of every hue, from pure white to darkest black, with silken hair and luscious beauty, sufficient to delight every righteous man."

"Will you forget me in this Paradise?"

"No, no companion of heaven will ever surpass you."

She kissed him again, this time on the lips.

"Let's not get carried away," he said. "It's time to pray."

"Pray?" she asked.

"Yes, you know, to the Great Spirit."

"What is prayer?"

"It is communion with the Great Spirit."

"We talk him?"

"He hears all, remember? We can talk to Him and He speaks to us."

"He speak to us?"

"Yes, but not in words—more in feeling. It's like when I look in your eyes and you in mine. You feel what I want to say without me saying it."

"Yes," she said.

"There, you see? Now, let me show you."

He got up and performed his ablutions, directing her to do the same. Then they performed the *kashroim*—the dawn prayer—together, with her copying each of his movements. He said each line of the prescribed verses slowly so that she could copy. When they had finished, he asked her:

"What do you think, then, of prayer?"

"Good, good. When we do it again?"

"There are five prayers: the *kashroim*, said at dawn, the *kashatvin*, said at midday, the *kashashom*, said in the afternoon between midday and sunset, the *kashammanaffob*, said in the evening, and the *kashafftishatvin*, said at midnight. These five times are times of remembrance. The prayers differ slightly at each time, the *kashashom* being the longest, but you will learn with time. You or Shem can teach Meyla the proper method."

"Yes, Ifunka, my love. I make you food."

"Ah, very well, thank you. You are too kind."

He wasn't sure if she meant she had already made it or was going to make it, but he thanked her nonetheless.

"Husband, all is for you."

"As I am all yours."

Ârva accompanied Ifunka to the secondary reception room where he joined Shem for breakfast. Meyla was busy watching Khalam-Sharru.

"What's the plan?" asked Shem as he finished his meal, which consisted of sweet bread, called *shîmva* (*shimwa* in Tremni), warm milk (as the monks were forbidden wine), honey and *zasht*-berries.

"We have to free Brother Ushwan before the sacrifice later today. How far are we from the dungeon and temple?"

"Meyla tells me one *kobotv* and about ten *oksha*s. We're at the edge of the city and we must make our way to its centre."

"In that case, we must dress in the garb of the Shaffu until we reach the dungeon, take out the guards, free Ushwan, return to this section of the wall, scale it and flee back into the woods with Meyla and Ârva."

"That's going to be challenging. We don't look or act like Shaffu and we barely speak any Shaffi. How are we going to manage it?"

An idea occurred to Ifunka.

"We use Khalam-Sharru."

"Are you mad? He's our enemy. We tortured him last night!"

"I spoke to him. I believe he can be convinced if it means his daughter's life."

"I think you are right," agreed Ârva in her best Tremni, which she had been practicing for several hours since waking up.

"Your Tremni improves by the minute, Ârva—or should I say Arwa?"

"Arwa?" she struggled to pronounce the name, especially the 'w' sound.

"Yes, the Tremni equivalent of your name."

"If you want," she replied, ever agreeable, extraordinarily so for a sixteen-year-old.

"Come, let us confer with your father, Arwa, and see if he accepts our plan."

They headed to the reception room where Khalam-Sharru and Meyla were both awake.

"Good morning, Khalam-Sharru," said Ifunka. "I trust that you slept well."

"For one in bondage, yes," he replied.

"Have you eaten?"

"Yes... but enough frivolity. Your brother dies today. Have you made up your mind? Do you wish to leave peacefully with Ârva and Meyla, abandoning Ushwan, or do you intend to proceed with your rescue plan?"

"What do *you* think?" asked Ifunka.

"Very well, then you must release me or kill me, or leave me to be found, days later, starved and dehydrated."

"I have another plan," suggested Ifunka. "Look, if you don't accept my plan and play your part, not only will you die but your daughter will be captured and killed."

Khalam-Sharru's eyes were wide with shock.

"Listen, all of you," said Ifunka earnestly. "This is how it is. Shem and I will don Shaffu attire and Ârva will accompany us, as she is a trusted member of this community and city, speaking on our behalf. If we are captured, she will be captured and implicated."

"Never!" cried Khalam-Sharru. "You twisted and dishonourable *khaffshiks*!"

"Calm down," said Ifunka in a placating tone.

"Alternatively, the girls remain here—innocent—whatever happens, and you accompany us to the dungeon, help us to gain access and we leave with Ushwan unharmed. As an accomplice, you will be killed if you don't come with us back to our civilization. Those are your options. Choose wisely."

Khalam-Sharru considered for a moment and then nodded his head, his eyes betraying shame and remorse.

"Good," said Ifunka. "Untie him, Shem. He can help us to dispose of the bodies."

They unloosed his bonds and began to remove every trace of the watchmen. Their clothes they burned in the hearth-fire and the naked corpses were chopped up, wrapped in cloths and thrown into the rubbish bin—a large wooden container which was daily emptied and collected by the city cleaners. They also disposed of the blood-stained carpets, burned their bloodied clothes, and washed and donned Shaffu attire. All of this took the space of two hours.

"Excellent," said Ifunka when they had finished. "There is but one more thing to attend to before our plan gets into motion. Ârva, Meyla, Shem, Khalam-Sharru, today is either our day of victory or the day we die, all of us, either to the worm or the pyre, or the watchman's axe. Shem and Meyla, you are both married and I congratulate you on this consummation. It behoves every man, before he dies, to wed, so that he may taste the delights of womanhood while yet alive in the flesh, while to do so unlawfully, that is, without the bounds of wedlock, and the bonds thereof, is to incite the wrath and terrible indignation of the Great Spirit. Therefore, I wish to wed my dear Arwa, formerly known as Ârva, ere we depart to our destiny."

"I would be honoured to marry you both," said Shem. "You are, besides Ffen, my oldest friend, so I welcome it. I only ask you, Khalam-Sharru, to give your consent."

"I do," he replied reluctantly.

"Very well; begin," said Ifunka.

Shem proceeded with the ceremony and the couple recited the marriage verse, after which Meyla and Khalam-Sharru clapped. They ate yet more sweet bread and milk to celebrate and then made ready to leave.

"Are we going yet?" asked Shem. "You haven't consummated your marriage."

"Oh, is that so?" asked Ifunka.

Ârva laughed.

"I'd almost forgotten."

"A monk to the last," laughed Shem, teasing him. "Full of more reserve and shyness than a school-boy in oversized robes."

"I was such a school-boy once, pure and innocent," said Ifunka. "I never thought I'd touch a woman, let alone 'in that way'. I also never thought I'd kill a man—yet here we are. I should probably stop calling myself a monk. I'm more a vigilante than a monk, or a lone soldier."

"More like Ishmael in battle, hewing the necks of the infidel Biknogs in glorious war," said Shem.

"It's kind of you to say that."

"Get to it, then, Ifunka, consummate your marriage."

He took Ârva's hand in this. She kissed farewell to her father, whose eyes welled up with tears, though as a man he was loath to show them, and they headed to her bedchamber.

"Here we are," said Ârva, her face wreathed in smiles.

The sixteen-year-old girl was in the full blossom of her youth, her eyes full of hope and expectation, her body fresh and ready for whatever the world had to offer. For her, this was the beginning of her life, not the end of something past. Suddenly, a bell rang, resonating throughout the city.

"What is that?" asked Shem.

"I can't be—time is moving faster than I anticipated," said Khalam-Sharru.

"Time moves at the same speed everywhere," replied Shem.

"I mean," said Khalam-Sharru. "That we have been taking our time. It's the third hour before midday."

"And what is to happen at midday?"

"The Council of Thirteen is meeting."

"So?"

"So! I am on the Council. By then it will be apparent that three sets of watchmen have vanished, a member of the Council of the Forty-Nine has vanished and all hell shall break loose. Watchmen will flood the city, searching all houses, strangers will be arrested and interrogated, and the sacrifice may be expedited."

"Then we have no time to lose!"

"Yes, while your monastic brother is engaged with deflowering my precious daughter!"

"I'll get him," said Shem.

He climbed the stairs and called through the door.

"Ifunka, brother! We have little time."

"Shem—do you rather want us to burn on the pyre?"

"To be honest, brother, the worm doesn't seem like a much better option."

"Brother, I'd advise that you put the worm aside for now that we may attend to the matter at hand."

"Ten minutes, my friend, and the matter at hand will be attended to."

"Very well," Shem conceded.

He returned to Khalam-Sharru and Meyla.

"He's thinking with his *ozetv* again, I'm afraid," he explained. "Ten minutes, he said."

"Right, Meyla and Ârva will stay hear armed with swords in case the house is invaded. You and Ifunka are dressed in the garb of scribes."

Shem was dressed in a long, black overcoat, velvet-black doublet and breeches and white stockings. He also wore a black, brimless cap and black, leather shoes. Khalam-Sharru was dressed in the black robes of a councilman with Tyrian-purple overcoat and a high, *meb*-skin hat—the same colour-with a long, black tassel. His waist was girdled by a Tyrian-purple sash and his feet were adorned with sandals. He carried an ebony-black sceptre of authority in one hand and, at his side, was armed with an ornate silver-handled curved dagger in a silver bejewelled sheath.

"You will have to use these two knives as your defence," Khalam-Sharru advised, handing Shem two daggers to put in his black leather, silver-buckled belt. "I will give Ifunka the same, once he is ready."

"Before we leave, let us pray," said Shem.

"Do as you will," said Khalam-Sharru.

"Great Spirit!" he sat on his knees. "Protect Meyla, Ârva, Khalam-Sharru, Ifunka and this servant, from evil and mischief. We seek only thy will. We desire only thy glorification and praise. We kill, not out of hatred, but in accordance with thine all-conquering justice and equity. Lead us to victory over the infidels and forgive us our sins and the sins of our forefathers. In thy holy and exalted name; *Raffal!*"

"*Raffal,*" repeated Meyla, meaning 'even so'.

Rising from prayer, which Khalam-Sharru had judiciously abstained from—he being a priest of Asharru—they descended the stairs and waited for Ifunka near the entrance of the building. A few minutes later, Ifunka could be heard to descend the stairs and was dressed and ready-to-go. Khalam-Sharru handed him the dagger.

"Where is Ârva?" her father asked.

"She is ill-disposed at present."

"Understandable. Now then, neither of you speak on the way. I will do the talking but you will kill the guards when we reach the dungeon. I will then escort you, along with Ushwan, back to this house. Is that clear?"

"Crystal," said Ifunka.

"Excellent. Then let's go."

They opened the door and stepped out onto the streets of Khanshaff.

CHAPTER XVII.

Khanshaff

~⸲

The sky was overcast, rain-laden clouds moving gently over the deep-red forest and lofty walls and houses which composed the secret city of Khanshaff, nestled, like a polished ruby, resplendent within the heart of Ffushkar. The houses were all rather similar: two, three or four stories high with balconies and round windows, laden with vines and hanging flowers. The streets were full of Shaffu who appeared perfectly Tremna except in their apparel and a preponderance of dark hair contrasted with bright green skin. Ifunka did his best to conceal his red hair and keep a low profile. He noticed that it was mostly men who moved about the street with few but older women around. It was apparent that most Shaffu women lived relatively sedentary lives within their capacious dwellings; this saddened Ifunka somewhat. Shem was awed by the symmetry and beauty of the city—a city which harboured such evil and unrighteousness. They moved through alleyways and around bends, swiftly and discreetly, avoiding main thoroughfares and plazas. They passed through the edge of the market, where fruit and vegetables, sandwich-vendors and pots-and-pan shops were frequented by old ladies and black, green and brown robed shoppers and businessmen. So busy were they that barely anyone glanced at the three swift-moving figures who paced through the tangled streets with a purpose. Within no time, they had reached the centre of Khanshaff.

The Council Headquarters—a round, *tvagshaff*-like structure of hewn granite surrounded by dozens of watchmen vigilantly staring in all directions. The Temple—*Ffâna* as the Shaffu call it—was opposite the Headquarters.

They paused behind a corner, looking out at the plaza. Ifunka and Shem were full of trepidation, as this was a make-or-break situation.

"How are we going to get past those watchmen?" asked Ifunka.

"I said not to speak. If anyone hears us speaking Tremni, we're all dead," said Khalam-Sharru. "We walk coolly and calmly towards the building. I will speak to the guards—you keep quiet. If all goes well, we enter and then go down to the dungeon. Understood?"

The monks nodded. He signalled and they walked out onto the plaza, in full exposure to the guards and passersby, who eyed them intently. The moments that they passed through the crowd and up to the gate were excruciating—they seemed to move slowly—painfully slowly. When they reached the entrance, the watchmen greeted him:

"Marakh-fach, ftâ hufft-ôn ftâkh-ish (councilman, we greet thee)!"

"Ftâ-gei hufft-ôn okh-ish (I greet you)," he replied. *"Iftâff ifta-yôn okh mon-ish khaffshik shâkh-fach envakh* (I've come here to see the infidel prisoner)."*

"Dift-krâ, khaff Sharru-yeym-shivt (come, in the name of Asharru)!"

The companions entered the Council Headquarters, which were bright and spacious, lit with myriad candles, as well as natural light passing through its manifold windows. The floor was adorned with a mosaic of variegated geometric designs while the entrance-hall was ringed with fearsome statues of robed watchmen with no faces, axes and swords ready to attack. They reached a stairwell at the far end of the hall and descended three flights, until they found themselves in a corridor leading to a single wooden door guarded by two special guards dressed in bronze armour with cuirasses, spiked helmets, greaves, gauntlets and leather belts. Their armour dazzled resplendently in the subtle, flickering glow of the wall torches. They approached the guards slowly, cautiously, aware of their disadvantage in arms and armour.

"Ftâ-gei hufft-ôn ftâkh-ish (I greet you)," Khalam-Sharru greeted them.

"Sharru khan-ish (Asharru is great)!" they replied.

Ifunka felt like saying 'The Great Spirit is Greater' but held his tongue.

"*Khaffshik shâkh-fach shift-ôn envakh ftâkh-ish* (we want to see the infidel prisoner)," said Khalam-Sharru.

"*Eikhu khaffshik-ô* (which infidel)?" they asked.

"*Predhel* (the monk)."

"*Ftûkh* (forbidden)!" they replied.

"*Ftûkh* (forbidden)???" he exclaimed. "*Flevâ okh-ish khôr-ôn ftâ-gei-yish-ô? Marakh-fach okh-ish* (do you know who I am? I am a councilman)!"

"*Khôr-ôn ftâkh-ish* (we know)," they replied without emotion. "*Yûm shîkh Metshu-yô khavâ-yish* (but the Sage has commanded this)!"

"*Khuff ffogsh-ôn Metshu mon-ish-ô* (what did the Sage say)?"

"*Predhel vâmt-ôn envakh eft khû-yish* (no one can see the monk but he)."

"*Hamta* (very well)," said Khalam-Sharru.

Pulling out a dagger, he swiftly plunged it under the cuirass, piercing the guard's bowels and kidneys. Before the other guard could cut him down, Shem and Ifunka drew swords, swung at the guard, one blow hitting his calf, which was only protected by leather leggings, while the other bounced off the cuirass, serving only to imbalance him. The guards both fell to their knees, dropping their pikes. Khalam-Sharru picked up one and plunged it into one guard's neck, bathing the corridor in a sea of blood, while Ifunka added to the expanding pool of sticky stuff as he slashed the other guard's shoulder, cutting part of his neck, including his jugular vein in the process.

"The first time I've shed the blood of my own kind; I'll not forgive you for that, monks."

He grabbed the keys off one of the fallen guards' belts.

"We are all one species and one kind," said Ifunka. "The children of Inta."

"*We* are the children of Asharru," Khalam-Sharru retorted.

"So you say," replied Ifunka. "Though I don't believe it."

"Let's be careful; there may be other guards within."

Khalam-Sharru opened the creaky, old wooden door and entered the dark dungeon. It was a small cavern, of natural formation, containing thirteen cells, lit by torches along the wall between each cell, which had round entrances barred diagonally with copper bars. The prisoner, hopeless and dejected, lay on the cold, hard beds of solid rock and stared at the ceiling of their cells. Ifunka and Shem searched each one until they found Ushwan—a lean, despondent version of himself, withered like a dead leaf, his eyes fixed on a dripping stalactite which formed a yellowish cone with rippled skin, rather like a spiky gourd.

"Ushwan," said Ifunka in a gentle tone. "It's us."

He neither acknowledged their presence, nor did he respond. He simply remained motionless—as if paralysed.

"Ushwan! Ushwan!" said Shem. "It's useless; he's numb in his senses. What have you done?"

He turned to Khalam-Sharru.

"I haven't done anything—I'm not their keeper."

"Nevertheless, you're Shaffu. Your people do this routinely. Have you tortured him?"

"Almost certainly—as you have *me*."

"We did it for a righteous cause. What do you do it for?"

"Is torture righteous? You believe in doing good—we believe in doing what Asharru wills—good or evil."

"You admit that you are evil?" asked Shem.

"By your standards, perhaps. In any case, however he's been treated, we have to extract him—immediately."

"Ushwan—look, you've got to snap out of it. We have to go," said Ifunka in an urgent tone.

Ushwan turned and looked at them. His face was stone-cold, as if he had been drained of all sensibility and feeling.

"You're just ghosts—phantasms conjured by my sick mind, mateys. Jolly good effort for trying to rescue me but I'm afraid you don't exist. I'd rather you all disappeared, actually; I can't bear to remember pleas-anter days."

"We're real, Ushwan; we're here to save you!"

"Open the cell, Khalam-Sharru, so we can prove it to him."

"I'm looking for the keys," replied Khalam-Sharru. "Give me a moment!"

He found the key and opened the cell. Ushwan sat up, alarmed.

"Phantasms don't usually open cells?" he said, confused.

"Because we're real, Ushwan, real as you."

"By God!" he exclaimed. "Is it true? How have you crossed such a distance and overcome such odds?"

"Faith, brother," said Ifunka. "And the Will of the Great Spirit."

"We had help from some friends along the way," explained Shem. "Even a wandering bard who showed us the way, and an elderly sage called Tvem, who taught us the basics of the nine-fold path."

"A wandering minstrel?" exclaimed Khalam-Sharru. "That's peculiar…"

The monks rushed into the cell and embraced their friend—the goal of their long journey. Tears streamed down their faces—they could not believe how fortunate they were; how many tests and trials they had overcome, how many lives had been sacrificed, how many dangers they had faced, how many sufferings they had endured. And Ushwan—how he had suffered, how *he* had endured days and weeks of distress in the dismal dungeon, fearing for his life, not knowing when the inevitable would come. He had lived through nights which seemed to stretch for all eternity and days filled with bleak misery, deprivation of every pleasure and kindness, meagre, tasteless food, lack of every comfort or satisfaction.

"The other cells; we must open them also," said Shem as he wiped away his tears.

"Are you mad, monk?" asked Khalam-Sharru. "We're already too large in numbers. How do you expect us to save them all? That wasn't the deal!"

"We have a duty to these people," said Shem.

"The only duty I have is to myself and my daughter."

"Shem, I'm afraid he's right. We can't save them."

"Ifunka!"

"What do you want us to do?" asked Ifunka. "Bring thirteen prisoners on the streets, scale the wall with all of them, avoid the watchmen, worms and *shan* and still make it back to civilization alive?"

"We've overcome so many odds!" Shem protested.

"This is one too many!"

"At least let us open their cells. They're going to die anyway."

"Perhaps you're right."

"Mad—the both of you! I won't do it."

"You don't have to, Khalam-Sharru. Just give me the keys!"

"No."

"Well, I'll get them from the guard."

"Alright, take them!"

Khalam-Sharru gave Ifunka the keys. He opened each cell, reviving the disturbed prisoners who all reacted, at first with disbelief and then jubilation. Six men and six women, from every corner of the Old Central Kingdom which borders on the Great Forest of Ffushkar, viz. from the provinces of Okayeshvi, Ritvator and Ffantbav. Merchants, apprentices, nuns and novices—they were all virgins—young and old—snatched away by their insidious captors.

"Listen, all of you," said Ifunka. "I've freed you; but that's all I can do. You have a chance now, to escape, which will mean overcoming the watchmen outside this building. Brother Ushwan, Shem and I, along with Khalam-Sharru, must go alone. Stay here ten minutes before you come after us. I can't help you further."

"You can't just leave us," said an elderly nun. "I'm a sister from Ffantplain; my name is Mela Shiffwoff. Can a brother abandon a sister?"

"A sister? How unusual. I've not met any sisters before! Nevertheless, the answer is 'yes'. We must leave you, I'm afraid, because there's no other option."

"We don't stand a chance!" protested a lanky merchant. "Look at me—I'm skin and bones. I've never been a strong man—a fighting man."

"Trust in the Great Spirit, my friend," said Ifunka.

"Look, Ifunka, this isn't right!" said Shem.

"What is right, then, Shem—that we all die"

"No, that we all should live!"

"Help us," said the merchant. "My name is Wenta Shainbev and I am a cloths merchant. I have an elderly mother who needs me. Oh, please won't you help us?"

He burst into tears.

"I want to get married, have a family," said a young lady, about seventeen years' old. "I'm Ffila Tvedraff; I'm an only child. Without me, my poor parents will have no grandchildren!"

"I've never been kissed," said another woman, about twenty. "Love, passion, sweet love-making, have all eluded me till now. Oh, death is a horrible thing! Please help me! My name is Shatva Shilbam."

"Enough!" shouted Ushwan. "We all want to live, but what are you all going to do about it?"

The prisoners looked one at another.

"Who doesn't want to live? I'd gladly die for all of you, but you've heard them. They've come to rescue me, and they have only one chance. Help and you might have a chance too."

Ifunka whispered in his ear: "They can't help us."

"Of course they can!" Ushwan replied fervently. "You're here to save me, chaps, so lend me your ears. Two of them will dress in the armour of the guards."

"That takes care of two of them. What about the other ten?" asked Ifunka.

"They are transporting the prisoners, old boy," said Ushwan.

"Impossible," said Khalam-Sharru decisively. "The watchmen will not believe that all the prisoners are being moved at once. It's incredible—utterly incredible. They'll alert other councilmen who will forthwith dispatch us all to the realm of death and destruction."

"A conundrum—a bloody puzzling one to be sure," said Ushwan. "Kasharoo—that's your name isn't it?" He turned to Khalam-Sharru.

"No, Khalam—…"

"Yes, yes, all right—something foreign. Anyway, do you know any discreet or hidden routes out of this confounded piss-post?"

"Language!" Ifunka protested.

"The tongue moves as the spirit lists," Ushwan replied. "Anyhow—what and whatever—do you have a solution or not, Kasheroo?"

"Khalam-Sharru!" he shouted. "And yes, I do."

"Why didn't you tell us about this earlier?" Shem asked.

"Never mind that!" said Ushwan. "Go on, Kashrut, tell us the what—and—wherefore."

"You mean the what-and-whereto?" corrected Shem.

"Whatever! Let Kashby tell us."

"Khalam-Sharru!"

"Go on, man!"

"I *will* have my name pronounced correctly!"

"I was just ribbing you. Take the feather and jump."

"What?"

"Kalam-Sharru."

"Good enough. As I was saying—there is a way out through the emergency escape tunnel, which the councilmen had constructed for purposes of egress in case of siege or invasion."

"Excellent!" Ushwan rejoiced. "We're saved—all of us!"

"Perhaps," said Khalam-Sharru. "But we have to enter it from the Council Chamber itself"

"So?"

"So, we must climb the stairs to the main lobby, get past the watchmen at the door to the chamber, enter the chamber, kill any witnesses within—if there are any—and then enter the tunnel. If we succeed in that, well, if the twelve succeed in that—for we must go back to my house to find Ârva and Meyla—then you will have to avoid the *shan* and forest worms, walk through countless *kobotv*s of deep forest without provisions or a tent and reach civilization. Even then, you're dead."

"Dead? Why?"

"Tell us what you were up to *before* you got captured," Khalam-Sharru asked Ushwan.

"Reading, I suppose."

"Reading? About what?"

"About bandits—about the demon-worshippers."

"And then?"

"I was walking to the privy to relieve my bladder when I was suddenly surrounded by four men in black who gagged and restrained me, blindfolded me and carried me away in a cloth bag."

"How did they know you had read about us; how did they know your habits of relieving yourself and the location of your cell?"

"I haven't the foggiest idea!"

"Ha, *khaffshik* cattle!" Khalam-Sharru laughed. The companions frowned.

"Hold your tongue, infidel!" Ifunka warned him.

"Who are the ignorant—who are the infidels? How about your bishops—your priests?" Khalam-Sharru asked. "You do not know the half of it! We have lived here, at peace, for millennia, because your theocracy sustains us."

"You work for the Theocracy?" asked Shem.

"You amuse me, monks!" he replied. "The Theocracy works for us!"

"Lies!" cried the nun.

"Misinformation!" cried another.

"Let him speak," urged Ifunka.

"We protect the Theocracy—remove its enemies, cull its excess population, for a fee of protection; a hundred thousand *patsimad*s per year, a thousand *meb*-goats, three thousand *zig*-chickens, five hundred ells of *woffgi*-silk, and a hundred *ffentbaff*s. See you not how splendorously-arrayed is our great city? This is the wealth of Kubbawa, the taxes of your people sustaining ours—the top predators—the children of Asharru!"

"Say you are speaking the truth; what would happen if the Theocracy stopped paying and supporting you?"

"We would march on your cities, towns and villages, raping, pillaging and burning them to the ground. We would slaughter and eat your men, women and children. Asharru, with one flick of his finger, would reduce your walls to ashes and melt your swords and spears. We would not stop until all of Tremnad were cleansed of the *khaffshik*s, so that Shaffu might reign from the Seas of Matvakakan and Offlising unto the Seas of Yatvegab and Sogyishifa!"

"I see," said Ifunka. His heart sank; the nun fainted in disbelief."

"You don't even want to believe it," said Khalam-Sharru.

"It doesn't matter, does it?" Ifunka replied. "The Theocracy is a lie!

If we survive this thing, we'll have to teach the truth and undermine its foundations. Truth lies in the heart, not in priests and clergy."

"Asharru will not tolerate it!"

"Asharru be damned! He can't stop the truth."

"Would you kill a god?"

"I would kill a man," said Ifunka with firm determination. "Nevertheless, let's do this. We must try to save the prisoners if we can."

"Very well," said Khalam-Sharru reluctantly. "Follow me."

Two of the sturdiest prisoners donned the armour of the guards, and they all ascended to the entrance hall. Khalam-Sharru and the two pretended guards stood at front. They slowly made their way to the council chamber door. The two guards on either flank of the door eyed them suspiciously.

"Khuff shift-ôn ftâ-gei-yish-ô(what do you all want)?" they demanded.

Khalam-Sharrus spoke: *"Marakh-ôn okh-ish; kha okh fteyn-krâ* (I am a councilman; do not question me)!"

"Saff, saff (sorry, sorry)," they apologized.

Khalam-Sharru entered the chamber, followed by the others. There were three councilmen at the council-table, staring in wild disbelief at the mass of prisoners.

"Khuff fteff fto-yeym-ish-ô, â Khalam-Sharru (what is the meaning of this, O Khalam-Sharru)?" asked one of them.

"Lock the door! Bar it!" Khalam-Sharru ordered.

The pretended guards barred the door with a sword.

"Kherffê! Yoibê (rebellion! Intrigue)!" one of the councilmen cried.

"Zeft-Sharru," Khalam-Sharru addressed him. "No one can hear you when this door is shut. The room is sound-proof; one of the glorious and ingenious features contrived by our great minds in order to preserve the dignity of our great Council!"

"Temni? Shfikh-ôn ftâkh-em Temni-shivt ftâ-yish-ô (Tremni? You are speaking to us in Tremni)?"

"Yes, Tremni, my new adopted tongue," he replied. "Why are you so surprised? Everyone must die some time."

"But why, Khalam-Sharru?" asked another councilman. "We are your friends! Why have you released the *khaffshiks*?"

"I protect my own," he replied. "I'm sure you can understand that, Shâl-Dey. And you too, Ftel-Daff. You have a daughter. Mine would have died had I not come here. This *khaffshik*—" he pointed to Ifunka. "Will take her to safety."

"You're dead for this," warned Zeft-Sharru. "Sharru shall kill you all—and your precious daughter!"

"I think not," he replied. "Kill them!"

The pretended guards hesitated.

"We'll do it with you," offered Ifunka.

The two monks charged the councilmen. Unarmed, they were quickly cut down and dismembered, their blood in pools soaking the mosaic floor with its sticky warmth, like paint spilled from an artisan's paint pots. Their screams split the air but did not penetrate the council-chamber door or walls.

"Come this way," called Khalam-Sharru.

He led them to the back of the chamber, where a circular mosaic of blue, azure, white and black adorned the wall. Pressing a seemingly random selection of stones, the mosaic swung counter-clockwise and sprung open, revealing a stone tunnel structurally supported with metal ribs.

"This descends half a *kobotv* and then two *kobotv*s out of the city, beyond the reach of the forest worms. A path lined with stones leads one hundred *kobotv*s north to the outskirts of the village of Weffbar. From there, one can make one's way onwards to any other location."

"Weffbar?" Ifunka asked. "The name sounds familiar."

"It shouldn't," replied Khalam-Sharru. "It's a small and insignif-icant village."

"Go on then, friends, we must take another route. Remember, the Theocracy is a lie," Ifunka instructed them. "Tell others so that the message may spread."

"We will," said Wenta Shainbev.

The twelve prisoners all made their way into the tunnel before Khalam-Sharru sealed it behind them.

"Right," he said. "Now we must make our exit. We must return to my house post haste. We'll gather supplies and scale the walls."

"Can't we use this passageway?" asked Shem.

"No, we must give them time to escape and it's too suspicious. The murdered councilmen shall soon be discovered—even before we return. We must leave straightaway!"

They exited the chamber, closing the door firmly behind them and proceeded to leave the Council Headquarters. They moved swiftly through the town until they reached Khalam-Sharru's house. Overjoyed, they rushed to the door and entered. There, Ârva and Meyla had been waiting in anticipation. They embraced their lovers, and Khalam-Sharru, with joy. Ifunka introduced Brother Ushwan, who was delighted, as always, to meet beautiful young ladies.

"How do you chaps know such charming ladies?" asked Ushwan.

"That's a long story," replied Ifunka.

"Well, I should like to hear it, old boy."

"We haven't much time," said Khalam-Sharru.

"Nevertheless, fill me in on the main facts."

Ifunka described, in brief, how they met and then married the girls.

"Fantastic! Absolutely bonkers but fantastic nonetheless. I say, I never took you chaps for ladies' men; I suppose I've underestimated you. Well done, boys; absolutely smashing!"

"Yes, well, we have much more to tell you of our journey, but we're pressed for time."

"I'm no stranger to the ways of women myself."

"Well, surely the Sage ascertained your virginity."

"No, old boy—we've seen no Sage. Anyway, whether I am a virgin or not is none of your business."

"Ah yes, he's supposed to be on his way from a journey," Shem remarked.

"Yes, the Sage should be arriving today," Khalam-Sharru agreed.

"How can you know that with any accuracy?"

"The Sage is not an ordinary man; he can see things which are invisible to other men—he can speak to trees and to animals and hear what they say; he can even move small objects with the force of mental will alone. He knows things no one else knows—how, we do not understand."

"But what is the source of his power?"

"It is inherited, generation after generation. It's said that he comes from the purest lineage."

"Blood alone cannot give men power," said Shem.

"Some say the *mîmra*—a field which embraces all of reality."

"The *mimra*? Yes, we've heard of it," said Ifunka.

"Well, *I* haven't," said Ushwan. "But I'm sure you'll tell me all about it."

"The *mimra* can only be used by the righteous," said Shem. "Tvem told us so."

"Perhaps," said Khalam-Sharru. "I don't fully understand the nature of his powers. Anyway, pack up your provisions. We need to scale the wall and get out of here. It's only a matter of minutes before someone discovers what's amiss."

"I pack everything," said Ârva. "With Meyla help."

"Excellent, let's be off," Khalam-Sharru suggested.

Each companion, including Ushwan, had a rucksack full of food and other necessaries, as well as water-skins. Ushwan was given full Shaffu attire in order to blend in during the journey. Khalam-Sharru also carried a skin full of wine. In addition, they were supplied with a dagger, ropes and other equipment. Khalam-Sharru left first, examining the surrounding area and observing the wall. He called the others out, one-by-one.

"The wall is too dangerous," he said. "We can't go that way."

"Why ever not?"

"Look, the wall is heavily guarded. They must have discovered that the watchmen stationed there have been murdered."

"Well then, what can we do?" asked Ifunka. "We're doomed."

"No—if we scale the wall we'll look duplicitous. If we exit the main gate we can invoke my authority."

"Well then, let's go to the gate," said Ifunka.

"Alright, let's hurry!" said Khalam-Sharru.

They went through the backstreets and alleys, avoiding attention, until they made it to the vicinity of the main gate which was secured by six guards, three on each flank, similarly clad as the guards in the prison.

"Follow my lead—do not speak a word!" he warned.

They approached the gate, Khalam-Sharru in front, followed by Ifunka, Shem and Ushwan, each with hoods raised and faces obscured. The guards stood at attention and greeted the companions:

"*Sharru khan-ish* (Asharru is great)!" they proclaimed.

"*Sharru khan-ish* (Asharru is great)!" Khalam-Sharru returned the greeting. "*Ftâ-gei hufft-ôn ftâkh-ish* (I greet you)!"

"*Vâ khâd-ôn ftâ-gei-yish-ô* (why are you leaving)?" the chief guard asked.

"*Ffamlîsh Veft-eym-em dift-ôn ftâkh-ish* (we are going to the village of Veft)," Khalam-Sharru replied.

"*Vâ? Kulft-fto yamakhsh-go khaffshik-zen-eym-ish* (why? Today is the sacrifice of the infidels)."

"*Shîb khôr-ôn ftâkh-ish, yûm baba okh-an enval ftâkh khon-ish* (I know it, but we are going to visit my father)," he explained.

"*Hamta* (very well)," the guards accepted.

They opened the gate and allowed the companions to go through unhindered. The other side of the gate was guarded also; the guards merely stared on as the companions took the main road leading into the dense forest of *zasht*-willows, bifurcating at a point where it led either to the villages to the south or the territory of the forest worms to the north. The direction they took was curved away from the way that Ifunka and Shem had taken to reach Khanshaff.

"What did the guards ask you?" asked Ifunka when they were a safe distance away.

"They said the sacrifice is tonight and asked why we were leaving."

"What did you reply?"

"I said we were going to visit my father in the village of Veft."

"Well, are we?"

"Yes and no; it will be safer that way. We'll stay in the village tonight and go to the deep forest tomorrow. They will think we've gone directly to the forest."

"But you've told them we're going to Veft."

"Initially—but we're actually going to Sharmakh, two *kobotv*s to the west of Veft. I'm not visiting my father at all."

"Well, then—at least we're safe now, whatever route we take," said Shem.

"I wouldn't be sure of that," said Ushwan.

"We are free from the city—that's what counts," argued Khalam-Sharru. "Tomorrow we'll enter the forest from a point they do not suspect. Then we'll move swiftly back along the route you took previously."

"To Lake Ffush and then Ffash Valley where Ffen is awaiting us. There we will fortify the Valley and build a new life," said Ifunka.

"Very well, my old life is finished," Khalam-Sharru continued. "The people of Sharmakh will keep us safe. They are my vassals. My family has ruled Sharmakh for three hundred years, since they inherited it from the Sage of that era."

"Inherited? Why did they inherit from the Sage?"

"That's not important," Khalam-Sharru replied abruptly, shrugging off the matter.

They continued along the path for two *kobotv*s, until they saw a cart approaching from the distance.

"Let me do the talking," advised Khalam-Sharru.

When the cart was only a few *oksha*s distant, they saw that it was a hay-cart pulled by a single *ffentbaff*. At the head of the cart was a farmer with a *geltv*-hat and a thick brown robe and sandals. The cart halted as the driver tugged on the reigns. The *ffentbaff* grunted and stopped.

"*Ftâ-gei hufft-ôn okh-ish* (I greet you)," greeted the farmer.

"*Ffi ftâ hufft-ôn ftâkh-ish* (and we greet thee)," Khalam-Sharru replied.

"*Sheff dift-ôn ftâ-gei-yish-ô* (where are you lot going)?" asked the farmer.

"*Veft-em dift-ôn ftâkh-ish* (I'm going to Veft)," he replied.

"*Veft? Ffâm-em dift-ôn okh-ish* (Veft? I'm going to the city)," said the farmer, indicating that he was going to the city. "*Yamakhsh-go envakh okh-ish* (to see the sacrifice)."

"*Hamta. Hamta ish-krâ* (well, farewell)," said Khalam-Sharru.

"*Hamta ish-krâ* (farewell)," he said in kind.

"*Shakhrô-krâ* (wait)!" came a voice.

"*Khuff* (what)?" asked the farmer. "*Vâ* (why)?"

A cloaked figure emerged from the back of the hay-cart. His face was obscured by his hood. He walked slowly up to Khalam-Sharru, Ifunka and Shem, looked at each one carefully and then told the cart driver to go without him:

"*Dift-krâ, â okhlensh. Okhlensh-zen khozen-ish* (go, friend. These are my friends)."

The cart-driver nodded and continued on his way, leaving the stranger with his new acquaintances.

"*Okhlensh-zen-ô* (friends)?" asked Khalam-Sharru.

"Friends, yes," replied the stranger in Tremni.

Startled by this revelation, the companions pulled out their daggers and swords.

"Who are you, devil?" Khalam-Sharru demanded. "Why do you speak Tremni?"

"I don't know you, stranger," he replied. "But Brother Ifunka and Brother Shem are my friends and former companions. I've been looking for them for ages. Is this Brother Ushwan?"

"Damn it, man, who are you?" Khalam-Sharru repeated.

"Can it be?" asked Shem.

"Yes, it is," said the man. "It is I—your friend—the bard."

"Praise be to the Great Spirit!" Ifunka cried.

He rushed to embrace his friend.

"Indeed. *Heika! Heika!*" cried Shem.

"Old friends!" exclaimed the bard joyously.

He held them both tightly.

"Show me your face, man. Shall we not also greet you?" asked Ushwan.

"Hold on a moment!" replied the bard. "I have not seen my friends in many days. Give us a moment!"

The bard held Ifunka and Shem's hands in his grasp.

"Tell me," demanded Khalam-Sharru, suspicious. "What is your name? And how came you to speak Shaffi?"

"Shaff."

"*Shaff?* That is our word for 'man'!"

"No, it is Tremni for mellifluous—like honey flowing."

"Very well," replied Khalam-Sharru, unconvinced. "What is your surname?"

"Tolwa—and I'm from Weffbar, if you must know."

"Weffbar? That's on the edge of our territory! Show yourself!"

"Khalam-Sharru, do not disrespect our friend," said Ifunka. "He helped us to reach this place before he was lost to the clay-men."

"Yes, well, how did he survive? Have you considered that?"

"I'm sure he'll tell us in good time!" Ifunka defended him.

"Leave him alone, infidel!" Shem exclaimed. "What do you know of true friendship and sincerity? He saved us! He almost gave his life for us!"

"Yes, trust me, Shaffu villain!" Shaff cried. "I am who I say I am."

"Then show your face!" Khalam-Sharru boomed. "Or shall I run you through with my blade?"

"*Hamta,*" said Shaff in Shaffi. "Or 'very well' as the Tremna *khaff-shik*s say."

"Shaff?" Shem was confused.

The bard raised his hood.

"*Metshu* (Sage)*!!!*" Khalam-Sharru cried.

"Indeed, I am the Sage and you are my servant—and cousin—Khalam-Sharru. Asharru be praised! He has delivered you all into my hands."

Ifunka and Shem tried to grab him, only to realize that their wrists were bound with a firm rope. Ushwan and Khalam-Sharru raised their daggers. Shaff, with a flick of his wrist in the air, knocked the blades out of their hands telekinetically.

"Impossible!" Ushwan exclaimed.

Raising his own staff, he hit Khalam-Sharru and Ushwan on their heads, deftly and with one swing, knocking them unconscious in the process. He grabbed the girls and tied their hands.

"Shaff!" Shem screamed. "*Who* are you?"

"I am the chosen servant of Asharru. I have indeed led you here, as sacrifices to the great god of all. I am no bard—I am the Sage, filled with terrible power and malice. I am no friend to either of you."

"We loved you—we believed in you!" cried Ifunka.

"Your faith, then, was in vain, fools!" Shaff scorned them. "I am the servant of the great and powerful one—the living god—who has gifted me this power. I am called Ffûtish-Sharru by birth—the razor-sharp sword of Asharru, and I am the Lord of the Shaffu; I am Shaff-Nayakht-go by reputation, the Man of Darkness, and I am *Metshu*—the Sage!"

With another blow of his staff, he knocked Ifunka and Shem fully unconscious.

CHAPTER XVIII.

The Sage

~

A voice spoke softly, beautifully, reciting a poem in a melodious tone:

"Vukt–ramtiffog kakshu shipon ishkikim itvkra / ffant kakshureffur ffoltavt kakshuffash / Kanshaff kakshufi, kakanfi, kraifi yaokra! / amantv Ffushkaryengzivt lamavt tvatorffash / Asharru nashiffah, Asharru gera itvkra / vairo kamame affrayeng shiyizovt zatvffash / offtishilem patrik shumavt yaokra! / rumiog Asharruyengim talkra ffash!"

("The sun—its brilliant glow be told / Shines brightly o'er the city bright / Khanshaff—lo!—brilliant, great, and old / stands eternally in Ffushkar's might / Asharru fearsome, Asharru be bold! / shall swiftly drink the blood of virgins cold! / Lo! The fire burning in the night / Fire send them thus to Asharru's hold!")

Ifunka awoke slowly; his eyes were heavy and he felt a powerful pain move through his whole body like water flowing from a spilled beaker. The poem rang in his ears, consumed his thoughts as he struggled to assert control over his bruised and aching body. He found that he was suspended, his arms in iron manacles hanging from the wall and his feet likewise cuffed. He struggled, tried to tear himself free, but it was useless. He was imprisoned, shackled to a cold stone wall, his clothes ripped from his body to reveal a muscular physique perfected through much travel, fighting and travail along the journey. His hair was dishevelled, his head bruised and cut, and his arms and legs lacerated. His bare feet were bruised, barely able to sustain the weight of his languid body. He was naked, save for a loincloth, and the room in which he found himself was cold, such that he shivered intensely. He looked around frantically to see if he could find his companions.

"Oh, believe me, they are safe," said a voice. "At least as safe as you are."

"What is that supposed to mean?" he cried.

"I only mean to say that we have not beat them more than you have been beaten—nor any less."

"Damn you! Damn you!" he cried.

"Oh, my dear monk, is that any kind of language for a pious man such as yourself to use? Is not every moment a fitting occasion for devotion and praise of your Great Spirit? What do you hope to achieve through curses and hatred?"

"I mean to know where I am and where my friends are."

"Quite safe. Did you enjoy the poem? It's a translation from the Shaffi—not as beautiful in *khaffshik* tongue, mind, but still I managed to render it in good enough form, don't you think?"

"Shaff, is that you?"

"Shaff? That is a mere pseudonym. You may call me Shaff-Nayakht-go, Ffûtish-Sharru or, quite simply, the Sage. I shall call you *khaffshik*."

"Look, Shaff. Show yourself. I can't bear this trickery. For old times' sake, at least give me the courtesy of seeing you."

"Do you hope to convince me to release you by virtue of our previous friendship? That was all a charade, *khaffshik*, an ingenious charade which revealed your true purpose and allowed me to anticipate your arrival here, in my glorious city."

"What do you gain by all this, Shaff? Isn't it clear to you that we mean only to save our friend and get out of here? We're not virgins any more anyway. What would you gain by killing any of us?"

"Oh, it's not as simple as that," he replied matter-of-factly. "Not at all. You mean to tell the world about this place—to inform them of the conspiracy which lies at the heart of the Holy Theocracy of Tremn. I can't allow that—no I can't. If I allowed that, it would mean the end of our way of life. You see, you had to be stopped, one way or another. Whatever pretence of friendship I may have evinced towards you, my real intention has always been to scope out the land, find suitable victims for sacrifice and identify any potential threats to Shaffnâ."

"I see," Ifunka replied. "But tell me where my friends are, at least. I need to know."

"Why should I care what you need or want?" asked the Sage.

"Because I believe there is good inside you."

"Then you believe wrongly. I do not believe in good or evil—only in what is best for Shaffnâ, in obedience to mighty Asharru."

"He doesn't exist!" Ifunka cried.

"Doesn't he? You shall see soon enough, when you are face-to-face with him."

"Are you going to kill us?"

"That is for Asharru to decide; he is all-wise."

"Damn it, Shaff! Let me go!!!!"

Again and again, Ifunka tried to break free but it was no use. The iron shackles could not be escaped. The Sage laughed and walked away; his footsteps could be heard receding. Ifunka was left alone with despondent thoughts and battered body. He had obviously been beaten or dragged to the prison or dungeon where he was currently being held.

"O Great Spirit! Help me!" he cried as he pulled at his shackles.

Sinking into despair, he fell to his knees and wept.

Hours seemed to pass—or perhaps only minutes; he couldn't tell. It seemed as if all were lost: their plan, their escape, their reunion with Ushwan—all was in vain. His beloved wife, Arwa, whom he cherished as dearly as his own heart and soul—would he ever see her again? The Sage would doubtless have no care for any of them; they would all certainly be sacrificed to the false god that the Shaffu worshipped. Blood alone seemed to satiate his voracious appetite for terror. With all hope drained from within him, Ifunka thought of only one thing: to kill Asharru should he come face-to-face with him and avenge his wife and friends. If they were already dead, he would take down as many of the Shaffu as he could before spilling his own blood in the dust. Death was a consolation if all other reason for living were taken away from him.

These black thoughts were interrupted by a loud, scratching sound, as if something metallic were being dragged along the stone floor. Within moments, a figure emerged around the corner of the chamber which he tenanted. He was large, bald and fearsome, his skin bright green, his eyes yellow, his mien and build terrifying and malicious. He wore only thick leather trousers, his torso adorned with rippling muscles and a brutal-seeming physique. Altogether, he appeared to be an embodiment of cruelty and was massive in size, with a grin indicative of sinister intent. In his right hand he carried a large wooden club and in his left a leather lash. As Ifunka looked on, terrified, the man whipped his lash and laughed heartily.

"*Shakh-Sharru okh-ish* (I am Shakh-Sharru)*!*" the man cried as he whipped the lash again. "I am your torturer!!!"

"What do you seek to achieve by torturing me?"

"For the pleasure of Asharru!" the man replied with a grin.

He raised the lash and whipped him, again and again, tearing at the monk's flesh. Blood trickled down his breast and abdomen, forming pools near his feet. Ifunka cringed with each blow, his teeth clenched, his body taut, every punishing crack of the whip leaving piercing wounds on his chest. Then, setting aside his whip, he raised the club and approached him. He held it gleefully, patting it in his other hand, as Ifunka's lashed and terrified body quivered against the frigid stone. Raising it high, he swung down to deliver punishing blows to Ifunka's legs, arms and torso. Ifunka coughed and spat gobs of blood as his muscles and flesh were successively pulverized by Shakh-Sharru's sadistic enthusiasm. After some minutes, which seemed to drag on for eternity, the torturer delivered a final blow to Ifunka's stomach, causing him to violently vomit blood and bile before collapsing into a torpid state of half-consciousness. Shakh-Sharru chuckled, cast aside his blood-stained implements and left the battered, half-dead monk to breathe his last—or so he thought.

Shem awoke to find himself tied with his arms behind his back and his feet shackled. He was much bruised and scraped but otherwise in good condition. He looked around to see where Ifunka was but could not find him. He saw only the two girls—Meyla, Arwa—and Khalam-Sharru and Ushwan, similarly enchained, standing to his left and right respectively. They were on a wooden platform constructed in the middle of a square and surrounded by thousands of onlookers who eyed him (and the others) intently. It was still not yet sunset, but the sacrifice was being prepared. The Sage, Shem's erstwhile friend, could be seen pacing back and forth on the platform, ensuring that each of the prisoners was well-secured and that all arrangements had been made satisfactorily.

"Excellent!" he said. "All is ready. The sacrifice shall commence in two hours."

"Two hours?" asked Shem. "Shaff—my friend—don't do this."

"Shem, Shem, Shem!" the Sage replied. "Food for the worm! The mighty *ffaika* shall rise from its dungeon lair and consume you and your friends. May the last thought you have be of betrayal and despair. Then shall you realize that the Great Spirit does not exist and Asharru is your true god!"

"What of the poem you read to us all those days ago?" asked Shem. "You said: 'All wisdom, truth and knowledge beneath the words concealed—The key is not in monastery or temple, but in the lover's heart'. Where is your love; where is your heart, Shaff?"

"These words are mere trinkets which I collect within the treasury of my mind," he replied. "I am the collector of truth and wisdom. I am the judge of right and wrong, knowledge and ignorance. I am the Sage, the knower of things as yet unknown to mortals such as yourself. Asharru speaks through me; I am his mouthpiece and pawn. What do you speak to me of mystic sentiments for? Will they save you? Will they engender within me some petty sentiment or sympathy? Will they bring up some nostalgia for our brief friendship—itself a subtle lie? I think not. Accept your fate, which is to be eaten by the worm."

"Fate?" asked Khalam-Sharru. "I am a high-priest of Asharru, yet even I know that there is no fate. You can still release us, Sage; we only wish to go on our way and live in peace. We have no desire to spread your secrets."

"Oh, but you've done worse than that already," the Sage asserted.

"Have you not released twelve captured virgins who are, even now, on their way to the rest of Tremnad? What do you say to that? You have already revealed our secrets! Yet we shall find them, slaughter them and all the villages where they dwell. Whole settlements shall be wiped off the face of Tremn!"

"You can't do that!" cried Shem. "Is this what your god wants?"

"Indeed," replied the Sage. "He delights in blood and burnt flesh. He desires that all *khaffshik*s shall die and meet their eternal punishment—a punishment they are born to endure."

"Let Meyla and Arwa go at least," Shem pleaded. "They have nothing to do with this."

"They are guilty by association," the Sage replied. "Are you happy with yourself? You have doomed them to this fate. Furthermore, your 'rescue' of the thirteen virgins has doomed thirteen other souls from our own people who shall now be sacrificed—virgins—innocent young men and women who shall die in place of those you saved. You have condemned them to death by your actions; think on that!"

"Where's Ifunka?" asked Ushwan. "You've got to tell us that at least, old chum!"

"Oh, we have special plans for him!" said the Sage.

"Fiddlesticks!" Ushwan shouted. "Utter tosh! Tell us where he is! What's *his* fate?"

"Who is the mastermind of all this—who is the most responsible?" the Sage asked rhetorically. "He will be punished specially—for his special part in these crimes. Now I must leave you all for a while but, worry not, I will return to watch your gruesome deaths."

The Sage left them to stew in their misery.

Ifunka was beaten—defeated. His body was bruised and broken, his spirits crushed, his flesh disfigured. With his last ounce of strength, he recited the *kashffitod*—the prayer in difficulties—the words slipping painfully off his wearied lips: *"Ay Wabak Kakan! Kam Tai, hari nif aftokti tvanfa, ffitodefi akshefi shotomefiyo aftokti Tai tatvkrafa, Kalf Nahonlasht, Yikwafftaka, Owaman ffakvazinfi aretve lotvshivfiyeng!"*

"Dreadful, isn't it?" said the Sage, who had returned to gloat.

"Great Spirit…" muttered Ifunka.

"I'll give you one final gift," said the Sage. "An audience with the great god himself, Asharru."

"What….?"

"You will see that he is not only real but glorious, his splendour blinding your eyes with the rays of his magnificence."

"Great Spirit… is one."

"Ha! Will you say that in the face of the real god?"

"Yes…"

The Sage raised his wooden staff and whacked the monk squarely in the face. Ifunka grimaced and spat a gob of blood which dribbled down his chin and onto his already-bloodied chest.

"Pain and suffering is the eternal reward of the *khaffshik*s!"

"There is… one God!" he said with great effort.

"One hour remains until the sacrifice. Prepare yourself, for you shall not die until after you have witnessed the death of all your friends and thirteen innocents who will replace the *khaffshik*s that you freed. They are of our own people, young and innocent, whose lives you have now robbed. Then, and only then, when every last hope and happiness is removed from before your eyes, Asharru himself shall take your life and dispatch you to your eternal punishment. Is that not sublime, false monk?"

Ifunka did not answer.

"Asharru shall visit you when he pleases. Otherwise, I bid you *adieu* until the sacrifice. Fare thee badly, *khaffshik*!"

Ifunka was left alone for a while. His thoughts raged, tossing and turning like furious waves in a sea storm. He thought of the mysterious owl, the 'Watcher' who had spoken to him before. Where was that supernatural being now? Had it forgotten him? And what of the Great Spirit? The Great Spirit should surely protect him, but it seemed as if had been completely forsaken. In his heart of hearts, he called out to Votsku, to Hashemaff, to the angels above, to his departed uncle and aunt—to anyone; but no answer came.

After a while, he heard footsteps—light footsteps like those of a woman. Then, suddenly, a dazzling beauty appeared before him; a woman of ravishing beauty stepped into the cell and appeared before him like sunlight at the break of dawn. Her features were all perfectly-formed and balanced, his hair black and silky smooth, reaching to her waist; her dark-green eyes were hawk-like, piercing; her skin was forest-green and smooth. She was dressed in a flowing, red skirt which reached the tip of her ankles, revealing well-manicured toes and delicate feet raised up by high-heeled shoes, her thin waist bare and her bosom concealed within a red, silken top which hung from her body like a serviette covering a cherry tart. She wore a ruby-encrusted gold necklace, diamond-covered bangles and earrings. Her skin was redolent with a sweet, musky odour, and every move and her gait was elegant and refined. She walked towards him—slowly, cautiously—and then cupped her hands beneath his chin in order to hold his face.

"What ails you, lover?" she asked.

"Who…. you?" every word pained him like a thorn in his side.

"What are words when passion speaks?" she said. "For the sweet-nectared flower, there is no question of the bee's identity."

"What… in Gahimka???" he swore.

"Now, now—finer language than this is fitting," she advised him. "For I am a lady of the divine effulgence. I am the highest maidservant of Asharru himself—even the High-Priestess. My thighs have robbed a thousand virgins of their dignity and held within their tight embrace the manhood of the living deity himself."

"Blasphemy…" said Ifunka.

She looked deeply in his bruised eyes.

"Do you desire me?"

"No…"

"Your mouth says one thing but your eyes say another. Man is an animal—ravenous, hungry, desirous, full of passion and rage. You are all of those things, corruptible and weak. Woman is the weakness of all men."

"Not… I…"

"So you say, but what do your thighs say? What does your breath say? What do your eyes say? They say you want me. They say you need me more than a *yeshka* desires flesh or a dying man one drop of water."

"My wife…"

"She shall soon be dead and so shall you, but I shall live—I shall continue as the days roll on and the mountains sink to dust. When the seas boil up and mighty Vukt consumes its planets—even then shall I stand alongside my lord—Asharru ascendant—who shall consume stars and star systems in his engulfing wrath! Think then that once you were within me—once you filled my cup with your essence. I am the sea which consumes the essence of countless men. Within me, you shall always be remembered. What think you, *khaffshik*?"

"No!!!" he cried.

"I could take you if I wished, but I prefer to conquer men willingly. Even now, your resistance is weakening, and your bloodied thighs bend beneath the force of my radiant beauty."

Ifunka shook his head defiantly.

"This is the ruby of attraction," she continued. "One of the treasures hidden within the caves that lie nested beneath this city. Khanshaff was built on this very site because of the powers which are hidden within the ground. The ruby gives me immortality of the flesh and power of attraction over others. No one can resist me."

She pressed the ruby against Ifunka's forehead. His mind exploded with passion, his thoughts benumbed, his mind and conscience diminished.

"Feel my power! Feel my charm!"

Ifunka could not resist the ruby's influence. He neither spoke nor resisted as she kissed his forehead and lips.

"You taste of *khaffshik* blood and sweat," she said. "Guard—unshackle this one and wash him. Cover him in *tvung*-deer musk and *gebnav*-rose water and send him to my chamber."

The guard appeared but looked confused. Irritated by his lack of comprehension, the High Priestess repeated her request in Shaffi and left: *"Poftekh–fto garchodalff-krâ ffi khû vaishiff-krâ. Vûl-ftung-ifft ffi shogi-gevnâv-ifft khû shôkh-krâ ffi offlîzefft-em okh-an khû tâl-krâ."*

The guard did as requested, unshackling the weak protagonist, washed him down with a bucket of water and replaced his clothes with a long, silken robe. He took Ifunka to the chamber and placed him on the bed, covered him in musk and rose-water. Then, tying the wounded man's hands and feet, he left the chamber and locked the door. The water had revived Ifunka somewhat, stimulating his senses and stimulating his power of reason. He sat up and tried to free himself from the ropes which bound his hands and feet. He struggled, biting the ropes, pulling at them and trying to rub them against the corner of the bed. His exertions, however, were unsuccessful, leading him to roll off the bed and onto the hard, marble floor, which sent jolts of agony through his already-bruised and battered body. Lifting himself up, he managed to get to his feet, hopping all the way to the door. Finding it locked, he then hopped to the window, looking to see if there was some way he could escape through that portal. Suddenly, the door opened, and the High-Priestess came in, dressed in a white, silk robe, similar to his own, revealing the contours of her sultry body. Ifunka looked at her with disgust, his eyes enflamed with rage born of hatred for the Shaffu and their manifold injustices.

"Have you forgotten the ruby?" she asked. "Do you think yourself powerful enough to overcome its influence?"

"If the Great Spirit wills," he replied. "But whence does this ruby gain its potency?"

"You're mining for information, I see. Well, let's just say it comes from the heart of the system of caves which lie beneath the Ffâna. The Sage also, derives his power from a jewel—the emerald of insight, which he wears around his neck beneath his clothes. None of this knowledge, however, will avert your fate, my rabbit. I will feast on your life-essence just as the worm shall feast on your flesh and bones."

"If I am to enjoy your body," Ifunka replied. "How I can do so with my feet and hands tied?"

"Do you hate to be dominated, my lover?" she asked. "It is no shame to be overpowered by one as ravishing as myself."

"But you deprive me of the delights of feeling your body with my hands, of grabbing your thighs and breasts."

"Well, then, I shall release you," she said. "So that your pleasure shall be complete, and I may struggle with you in mutual embrace."

She untied him slowly, while kissing his hands and feet, the brilliant ruby dangling from her neck. As she stood up before him, he felt the ruby's influence radiating against his breast—but she was short, at least a foot shorter than he, so the ruby did not face his temple as it had before. The influence, therefore, was not complete. As she pressed her body against his, and began to disrobe him, he quickly grabbed the ruby in his hand and tugged hard, pulling her neck in the process. The chain did not break, however, and she pulled backwards, trying to free herself from his grasp. They struggled against one another, each pulling hard to escape the other. She punched and bit him while he jerked the chain again and again, sometimes choking her and sometimes digging it into her neck until, at last, he managed to pull it over her hair, scraping the skin on her forehead and nose in the process and ripping out some of her silky-smooth locks. She screamed and slapped him in the face, punching his shoulder and head-butting him in the chest. Ifunka was knocked backwards, dropping the ruby in the process. She jumped on top of him, pinning him down, and grabbed his neck in her hands, trying to choke him to death. With his right hand, he managed to punch her in the chin, knocking her off of him, such that she tumbled sideways, colliding with the bed. Ifunka picked up the ruby and made for the door.

"No!" she screamed. "You shall not escape me thus, *khaffshik*! That door is locked!!!"

She leapt to her feet, grabbed a metal lamp and threw it at Ifunka's head, bashing him on the temple. Ifunka fell to his feet and held his face and forehead in agony. She rushed up to him, grabbed the lamp again and hit him over the back of the head, causing him to bleed profusely. Ifunka fell backwards, half-conscious.

"You just can't make it easy, eh, rabbit?" she said, her voice bubbling with anger and passion, his lips drooling. "Shall I punch you again or shall you relent?"

"Infidel," he muttered.

She slapped his face and grabbed his hair in her fist.

"Take it like a man," she said, pinning him again, attempting to pull off his robe.

Ifunka reached with his left hand for the ruby. He managed to grab hold of the edge of the chain and pull it towards himself. Grasping it in his hand, he felt the carved edges of the ruby and held it tightly. Lifting the ruby, he placed it on her forehead. Her eyes opened wildly as she realized what had happened.

"No, you cannot control me!" she cried.

"It's too late, I'm afraid," Ifunka replied.

"No, I am the High-Priestess… I have the power… I rule over my victims."

"Now, you are my victim," said Ifunka angrily. "Get off me!"

She stood up and wrapped her robe tightly.

"Help me up."

She lifted Ifunka up.

"Now, you are going to take me to the Ffâna!"

"Why???"

"Take me to the caves… show me where the ruby and emerald came from."

"No, even I do not know where they came from. These were discovered before I was born."

"Do not delay! Take me there or I shall kill you."

"Kill me? Kill your lover?"

"You are *not* my lover! Arwa is my lover!"

"Listen, rabbit, I shall do as you ask, if you spare my life."

"Perhaps. Take me there, help me to find other jewels such as this and I will use them to destroy your false god and free my friends."

"There is no time for that!" she warned him. "Less than an hour remains until the time of sacrifice. Your friends shall be killed before you reach the place you seek."

"Even if I go to my friend directly, I will be killed before I can release them. There isn't any other option! Take me to the caverns now! There's no time to lose!"

"Very well, but the guards shall be suspicious."

"Give me a weapon—a sword."

She reached under the bed and grabbed a *ffutish*-blade.

"That's been there all this time! You could have killed me with it."

"Where's the fun in that?" she laughed, throwing him the sword.

"Stay ahead of me; pretend to hold me in your power."

"That's not difficult," she replied.

He concealed the sword beneath his robe and followed behind her, hand-in-hand. She took him down the corridor and into a stairwell. They descended seven flights of stairs until they reached the bottom-most floor, which was lighted only by a singular torch. Grabbing the torch, she lighted another and handed it to Ifunka.

"You can let go of my hand now," he said.

"I know—but I rather like it. Can't I?"

"I'd rather not—I am a monk, after all."

"Very well."

"So, we're already inside the Ffâna?"

"Indeed, on the bottom-most floor thereof, where it meets the cave-system. These are ancient—little-touched by the Shaffu. We built our whole city above these caves at the command of Asharru, countless thousands of years ago."

"Don't you see?" said Ifunka. "Your power derives from a ruby—the Sage's power from an emerald. Do you really think Asharru is a god? His power must also derive from a precious stone. If I can find another stone, perhaps I can defeat him."

"Have you come to destroy our faith, monk?"

"No, I have come to reveal the truth."

They moved through the dark cavern, turning round bends and long shafts or corridors, ducking when the ceiling descended and avoiding stalactites and stalagmites reaching down and up from the ceiling and floor. It was damp, wet, and cold—they seemed to descend for ages, deep into the bowels of the earth. Their torches but dimly pierced the pitch blackness which engulfed them like an impenetrable veil. Their journey continued—on and on—until they reached a ledge; thankfully they saw it in time. Feeling around, they found steps carved into the ledge, descending back and forth in a zigzag pattern down to some unknown bottom beneath. These stairs they followed, carefully adhering to the wall to avoid an untimely drop until, finally, they reached the bottom of the cave-system. There they lost all sense of direction as there appeared to be an open, immense space all around them, in all directions, wrapped in absolute blackness and eternal darkness.

"Methinks we're in Gahimka itself!" Ifunka exclaimed.

"No, we're in the depths of Khanshaff—maybe even bordering on the realm of Asharru himself, Asharraff."

"Do you think he emerged from the darkness, then, like a worm from the clay?"

"This is his place of origin, yes, or the gateway to his place of origin."

"Which way shall we go?"

"Ask the ruby—it shall lead you."

Raising the ruby, which was fastened round his neck, he said: "Show us the way to the place of treasure, from whence this ruby was found."

At that moment, he felt moved to proceed directly forwards, as if driven by a hidden power. They proceeded until they reached another roofed cavern, taking them yet further down into the depths of the earth, descending gradually as the roof dipped, until they had to climb on their hands and knees through the small space that remained. This passageway they followed for a while until they reached yet another open chamber within the rock. The large, open space was larger than they could discern, their light barely illuminating twenty or thirty *oksha*s in any direction. What they could see, however, was that the space was not entirely natural, the floor being purely smooth, as if flattened and smoothed out by ancient people eons ago in the distant past. They continued onwards, their footsteps echoing loudly, until they reached a ring of stone posts which extended more than forty *oksha*s across and around a vast hole in the middle of the chamber. When they entered its circumference, spherical lamps illuminated themselves on each post, casting the entire the chamber in an ethereal glow. It was electronic lighting, powered by some hidden source below, a technology which the Tremna of this era were entirely unaware of and incapable of understanding.

"What is this?" asked Ifunka. "Where is the light coming from?"

"There are powers within here which hark back to the dawn of time," replied the Priestess. "This was all built by Asharru when he entered our world, more than two hundred thousand years ago."

"If that is true, where did he come from?"

"From the one you call Afflish, the Lord of Fire, whom the priests call Haff-Lîsh, which in our tongue means 'Flame-Sire'."

"I suppose you think Afflish the Accursed is a god?"

"Yes, though we do not worship him and his existence is not explained to the masses. We only teach the people of Asharru, because he is their god. We, the possessors of knowledge, know of the existence of Haff-Lîsh, who lives in another world; Asharru is his servant."

"So your power—the Sage's power—they all derive from Haff-Lîsh?"

"No, there is an ancient power contained within each stone, which was scattered across the universe at the beginning of all things, when the planets took shape and the men first walked the worlds. Then the stones were cast across the great expanse of the stars to every world."

"We must find whatever power still lies hidden within this circle and I must use it to save my friends."

"If that is what shall salve your conscience, my rabbit."

As they approached the hole, it became apparent that there was a sudden drop into some kind of fathomless abyss beyond which, at a distance of three *oksha*s, was a seeming island, upon which stood a platform with a single cylindrical, coin-shaped object in the centre thereof. It was luminescent green, glowing the darkness—at the centre of everything. Several other objects could be seen on lower platforms circling the island.

"Those are the objects of power!" Ifunka exclaimed. "I must have that coin at the centre!"

"You do not know what it is capable of."

"Whatever power it possesses, I shall use that power for good—to fight evil and destroy Asharru."

"What if the power is too much for you—a mere mortal. What if it controls you?"

"Does the ruby control you?"

"Am I good or evil?"

"Well…" he had no answer to that question.

"In any case, the distance is too far. There is a gap of at least three *oksha*s, and a chasm over which you must leap, descending into absolute darkness. It could be as deep as Tremn itself! The distance is impossible."

"He wouldn't have left these things undefended. The chasm is its defence."

"You don't know that that is its only defence."

"Be that as it may, we need to find some wood and construct a bridge."

"So we're going back up to the surface?"

"It looks like it. We'll have to save my friends first and then return here."

~~

"Where is the Priestess?" the Sage asked. "She was supposed to escort Asharru to visit the prisoner! Where has she gone?"

He looked around her room frantically, peering under the bed, opening the cupboards.

"The prisoner is missing. The Priestess is missing."

He summoned his deacons and ordered them to accompany a detachment of watchmen to search the Temple and the Council Headquarters. No stone should be left unturned, no suspicious person unquestioned, for the sacrifice must go on, and the prisoner must be found. He hated the thought of killing the Priestess. After all, she had served Shaffnâ well throughout the centuries. The ruby of attraction had kept her young and beautiful, seductive and charming—a power of attraction which had even made the Sage a slave to her charms, yet he was not permitted to enjoy them; he—the Sage of all Shaffnâ—could not unwrap her beauty and enjoy the pleasures of her flesh—while paltry virgin prisoners were allowed to do so in order for her to absorb their youthful energy before they were fed to the worm. Where could she possibly be? There is no way that she could have aided the monk to escape. How could that be possible? Yet she had clearly disobeyed orders and would need to be executed—with Asharru's permission of course.

"In any case, the sacrifice must go on!" he said to himself resolutely.

He proceeded to the stage where the four prisoners were tied up, along with thirteen virgins selected from the populace, who had miserable countenances, preferring to be spectators themselves watching *khaffshik*s die rather than victims to their own monstrous god! Normally the ceremony would begin with the selection of the virgins whom the Priestess would enjoy but, since she was temporarily absent, they would proceed with the rituals of sacrifice *in absentia*. The Sage stood in the midst of the crowd, dressed in his flowery Tyrian-purple robes, and unrolled the Scroll of Sacrifice, detailing the rituals, chants and incantations to be used in the ceremony. He knew them all by heart, of course, but the scroll must be used as a matter of form. He unrolled the ancient parchment, looked at the ancient handwriting, and was about to open his mouth to intone the holy words when, of a sudden, an arrow whirred through the air and struck the Sage in the arm, piercing his flesh and spurting blood over his robes, sullying the parchment.

"What in Asharraf!!!" he cried.

"Let my friends go!" cried a voice.

CHAPTER XIX.

Plant Man

~o

A cloaked figure emerged from the crowd, his face obscured by pendant hood. Bow in hand, arrow poised, he leapt onto the platform. The Sage, benumbed by the sudden attack, had fallen to his knees in agony. The arrow had pierced his flesh right through, severing veins and muscles, scraping his humerus—or the Tremna equivalent thereof—releasing spurts of blood which distributed themselves in profusion over his garments and the parchment which he had dropped on the wooden planks. The watchmen, whose duty it was to guard the Sage, rushed forward at the mystery figure, axes and swords raised, to slice and rend the offender. The figure moved swiftly, releasing one arrow into the guardsman to his left, ducking another's blow and stabbing the assailant in the back. Three other guards set upon him. Pulling an arrow from his quiver, he manually thrust it into the breast of one of them. Another swung his axe and sword in a pincer move. The cloaked figure ducked, narrowly avoiding decapitation. Butting his attacker in the abdomen with his head, he knocked the guardsman onto his back. Pulling another dagger from his belt, he lodged it firmly in the remaining attacker's belly. He pulled the daggers free from their dying bodies, leapt onto the surviving guardsman's body and plunged both blades deep into his chest. Retrieving the same weapons, he then cut Shem, Meyla, Arwa, Ushwan and Khalam-Sharru free from their bonds. The Sage—enraged—leapt to his feet, seized the arrow which was embedded in his flesh and snapped it.

"*Sheff khashla eyn-fach-zen okh-an-ô* (where are my other watchmen)*?*" he screamed. "*Shaff-ftosh bakh-krâ ffi lekhta khû khishyâkh-krâ! Khû shûm-krâ! Fteyka-khim khû shuffk-krâ* (seize that man and flay him alive! Burn him! Cast him to the *ffaika*)!!!"

"I think not, Shaff!" replied the cloaked figure. "Today your false god shall go hungry. Where is Ifunka?"

"What do you know of Ifunka? *Who* are you?"

"I thought you were a Sage. Where is your famed wisdom?"

He handed a dagger to Shem while Khalam-Sharru seized a sword and axe.

"Seize weapons: Ushwan, Meyla, Arma. Arm yourselves!" Khalam-Sharru cried. "We're getting out of here or we'll die trying!"

"*Eyn-fach-zen* (watchmen)*!*" the Sage cried, summoning his watchmen. "*Sheff ftâ-ga-yish-ô* (where are you)?"

Watchmen could be observed approaching from the opposite side of the plaza.

"My own people stand like ignorant sheep and do nothing—nothing to save their holy Sage!"

Seizing the sword of a fallen guardsman, he leapt to his feet and rushed at the cloaked figure.

"Die, *khaffshik!*" he cried.

"Who is the infidel?" asked the cloaked figure as he released another arrow—this time into the Sage's other arm—his right—causing him to drop the blade, stumble and fall flat on his face.

"Did you foresee that?" asked the figure. "Let's go!"

The companions, now armed and ready to defend themselves, huddled close together and followed the figure off the stage and towards the temple.

"Where are we going?" Khalam-Sharru asked as he eyed the swarming guards who seemed to approach them from every angle. "This is suicide!"

"We have to find Ifunka!" said the figure.

"*Who* are you?"

"I've been training—preparing for this mission for some time. I followed Ifunka and Shem's tracks, met some individuals they had encountered along the way and found directions to this place. All that remains is to rescue Ifunka and get back to the valley.

"We won't even get to the Temple!" Khalam-Sharru protested.

"O ye of little faith!" said the cloaked figure. "I have a surprise up my sleeve—a few surprises."

As they neared the Temple, a swarm of watchmen surrounded them. For a moment all was silent and still as the watchmen stood poised to rend each one of them into myriad pieces of bone and flesh. They appeared to await the Sage's command, who was some distance behind, being carried towards them on a leather stretcher.

"Each one take the hand of their fellow," said the figure. "And, when the signal rises, follow me."

He reached into his cloak and pulled out three glass spheres and rolled them down his trousers. They emerged at the tip of his boots and rolled an *oksha* or two distant before cracking explosively. A vision-impeding gas arose, blinding the watchmen while the figure pulled the companions past the confused guards and into the Temple. Barring the door with a pole behind them, they rushed for the stairwell which leads to the underground caverns—the same that Ifunka had fled to earlier, accompanied by the Priestess. The guards of the Inner Sanctum remained to assault the companions, whom they overcame with their sheer force of numbers, stabbing and bludgeoning them to death. As they were about to descend the stairs, they could hear the doors of the Inner Sanctum swing open and someone step out. They felt a presence, even without looking—one evil, overbearing and full of imperishable rage. They knew, without setting eyes upon their enemy—that it was he, the false god, the embodiment of negation and darkness—Asharru—the servant of Afflish the Accursed—he whose name the true adherents of the Tamitvar seek refuge from day and night in their devotions.

"In the name of the Lord of Darkness, look at me!" said a voice, deep, seductive, evil.

"You don't exist, false god!" cried the cloaked figure.

"There is only one God—only one!"

"But I am here, standing before you. Worship me, infidel!"

"Let's keep going—what doesn't exist cannot harm us," said the figure.

"But he *is* real," Khalam-Sharru protested. "I have *seen* him!"

"You've seen a man pretending to be a god," the figure retorted. "God is one."

"You sound like a monk, stranger!" replied Khalam-Sharru.

"I was—now I am a free man but still a slave of the one true God—the Great Spirit."

"Ffen—is that you?" asked Shem.

"It took you this long to figure it out?" he replied, pulling back his hood. "Indeed, it is I!"

"But how?"

"Never mind that."

"Ha, ha, ha, ha!" laughed Asharru. "You can't simply wish me out of existence, monk. I am a child of the stars while ye are all bits of tarnished clay! Worship me or, indeed, ye shall all be killed by me—personally!"

"What shall we do?" asked Shem.

"Nothing—we continue," replied Ffen. "If we ignore him, he is only an idea. If we see him, we acknowledge that idea's substantiality. Until we gaze upon him, he is an abstraction, existing only through the faith of his believers, such as this man"—he pointed to Khalam-Sharru.

"Khalam-Sharru," the object of his pointing introduced himself.

"Yes, well, your belief has brought this upon us. The *mimra* embraces both the real and the potential which emerge from the world of similitudes into this world. Asharru's power, being darkness—a negation of all that is good—has no real substance. His power only exists in abstraction, as an idea which becomes real, materializing as you believe in it. Have you not wondered why he hasn't attacked us while we ignore him?"

"He's biding his time, savouring our demise," argued Khalam-hsarru.

"Your fear fuels him; that is his power which realizes itself through the medium of the *mimra*."

"Die, mortals!!!" Asharru boomed.

Khalam-Sharru turned and looked at the embodied deity.

"No!" Ffen cried. "Now he exists! Until we see him, he has no form—only potential. Turn away!"

"I cannot—I am his priest."

"Yes, you are my *khalam*; you were named for me," acknowledged Asharru. "My servants give me being but Afflish gives me purpose. He is the lord of lords, the great dark one who shall conquer the light, who shall extinguish the stars in his everlasting fury!"

"You wish, devil!" Ffen replied.

"Khû bakh-krâ (seize him)!" Asharru demanded, ordering his servants to seize Ffen.

Khalam-Sharru, now under the dark being's spell, grabbed hold of Ffen, who dropped his weapons in surprise.

"Stop it, Khalam-Sharru!" Shem shouted.

Ushwan and Shem both tried to pull him off. In so doing, they caught sight of Asharru. Khalam-Sharru turned him such that Ffen ended up gazing into the creature's face. They beheld a humanoid figure, seven-foot tall with dark red, hairless skin, ripped with veins, a large muscular head with protruding brow, wide eyes—black with yellow irises, white teeth like knives, and long earlobes with silver earrings. He wore armour up to his neck, a glistening cuirass, bevor, pauldrons, greaves, vambraces, gauntlets and other adornments, all of silver appearance but really composed of a metal beyond the ken of Tremna comprehension. In his right hand he carried a six-foot-long pike of the same material and, at his waist, he had a sheathed broad sword, a dagger and some kind of energy weapon—a blaster—on the left-hand side. At his back there flowed a crimson cape which descended to his ankles. He smiled, his vicious pincers of teeth (somewhat obscured by the bevor) shining brilliantly.

"I am Asharru," he said in perfect Tremni. "I speak your tongue as I speak Shaffi, and Vocatae, and myriad other tongues of men—from this world and other worlds. This is *my* planet now—I have ruled it through the Shaffu and the Theocracy for thousands of years. Even the emperors feared me—yea, even Kubba Gven trembled at my mention. The High-Kings of old—they knew of me; they kept their silence. Who does not know me? Who does not fear my master—Afflish the Great, Lord of Darkness? I am real, as you see me before you. Believe what you see, not what is invisible. Where is the Great Spirit? Has any man seen Him? But you have seen me, and I have seen Afflish. We are real— matter and energy. The Great Spirit is composed of what—Himself?

Ha, ha, ha, ha, ha! You follow the Tamitvar, written by a man—Votsku, son of Kemi. He was a man misled by his own fancies. Does all your faith rest on the sayings of one man from the Age of Kings? Wake up and then bow to the god you see before you and denounce Votsku and his book of delusion, and cast the Great Spirit behind you, to the realm of vain imaginings!"

"We're champions of the Right Religion, demon… ruddy, demon face!" challenged Ushwan.

"Your eloquence fails you, monk!"

"Look, evil one," continued Ushwan. "Is there no peaceful way out of this? My friends simply came here to rescue me and wish to leave in peace; no further bloodshed. You must understand that my life was rather imperilled by that sacrifice intended for you. Come, old boy, play the game! Let us go free!"

Asharru laughed heartily.

"How can someone who doesn't even exist be amused?" Ffen pondered.

"I *do* exist, infidel!" the creature cried. "Now, feel my wrath!"

He raised his pike which lit up with an ethereal glow. It burned red and then, directed towards the companions, blasted them with an explosion of energy. They were all knocked off their feet and rendered unconscious. Turning to the main entrance, he motioned with the pike and it opened, allowing the watchmen to pour in.

"Ftôn garsh-krâ (bind them)!" he roared.

The watchmen, amazed to behold their deity, fell to their knees in adoration.

"Lâmi-krâ (rise)!" he commanded. *"Ffi ftôn garsh-krâ. Heshnîsh dhîl-im ftôn adhem-krâ ffi gaff-ôn ish-krâ ffeyka-yem ftôn lîshum-ehê! Yîlâ yamakhsh-go kheyâ shîb khon-ish. Metshu okh-im erim-krâ! Khû ffaidh dhîd-ehê okh-ish* (and bind them. Take them back to the platform and make ready to feed them to the worm. It shall be a special sacrifice indeed. Bring me the Sage! I must heal him)!"

The watchmen, eager to please, complied, binding the unfortunate companions with fast ropes and bringing the Sage to Asharru. Spreading his hands over the Sage's recumbent body, he was enveloped in a ruddy glow. Healed and refreshed, the Sage leapt off the stretcher and prostrated himself before the dark being.

"My lord, what is thy command?"

"Find the Priestess, bring her to me for judgement, and find the other monk. He is too close to great power. Kill him before he endangers the holy temple. If you fail to kill him, you shall die and I will deal with him myself. Is that understood?"

"Yes, lord," said the Sage submissively.

"Very good. I shall be waiting in the Inner Sanctum where I shall be pleasuring my handmaidens. Ha, ha, ha, ha, ha!"

He continued chuckling maniacally as he retreated into his chamber. The Sage called five watchmen to accompany him as he headed down the staircase which leads to the underground caverns beneath the temple.

Ifunka and his erstwhile captor, the Priestess, were near the base of the staircase when they heard the pitter-patter of footsteps far above them. Someone or some people were descending rapidly near the entrance.

"They're coming," whispered Ifunka. "We won't be able to get any wooden planks to form a bridge."

"Quickly—we must return to the treasures below."

"But how shall we reach them?" asked Ifunka.

"You fear too much, my sweetness. There is always a way but we must reach it before they come for us. My life is void if you do not succeed just as my heart is void if devoid of your love."

"My heart belongs to another," said Ifunka firmly. "Arwa is my true love."

"Khalam-Sharru's daughter is a mere child. I can teach you the fullness of true passion and bliss."

"I think not, Priestess."

"Let's go; perchance we can find a place to stow away and enjoy one another."

"Focus!" he urged her. "Take us back to the treasure and help me to find a way of reaching it."

"As you wish, my rabbit."

They rushed back from whence they had come, racing to return to the fathomless abyss which protected the ancient treasures of power before they could be espied by the pursuing watchmen. Before they reached the final chamber, Ifunka noticed a subtle light which hovered to the far right of them. He paused.

"What is it? Come on!" the Priestess shouted.

"Wait a moment," he commanded as he continued to ponder the glow which seemed to increase in radiance, flash and then decrease until it became only a faint light.

"I can see it," she said. "But what is it?"

"I thought you might know," said Ifunka, disappointed. "We'd better investigate."

"Investigate? You're going to get us killed. Who knows how many evil creatures live in this pitch blackness?"

"Maybe so," he admitted. "But we were heading for a dead end and certain confrontation with the Sage and his watchmen, who are no doubt making for us as we speak. Soon they will see us and then we will have no choice but to fight or die, or fight and then die, as the Great Spirit wills."

"And if this betokens an even worse fate?"

"As the Great Spirit wills."

"Very well, then," she agreed. "Let's find this light of yours, my rabbit, whether it lead us to doom or fortune."

"Come then!"

They rushed into the darkness, not knowing what lay ahead of them—whether a hidden ledge and precipice or a sheer wall; they could not discern. They continued for some time, never reaching the light which remained ever equidistant with its previous manifestation, as if it either moved constantly in reverse or appeared the same distance at all times by decreasing in size or radiance as they approached or, perhaps, like some distant star, it was so huge and so distant that the distance they traversed was insignificant in comparison with the remaining span of traversion.

"This is taking forever," the Priestess moaned.

"For an old woman, you're considerably lacking in patience."

"Old woman!" she scoffed. "An old woman who could eat you alive, you silly boy!"

Suddenly the light flashed and formed the glowing outline of a door and then disappeared. They rushed towards it and felt the cold, stony door. The light was gone but they could feel the cracks of its edges.

"How does it open?" Ifunka asked.

"Use the ruby," suggested the Priestess.

Ifunka felt for a keyhole and then, taking the ruby, he fit it into the lock, twisted it and the door slowly opened. He then retrieved the ruby and they entered. The chamber was bathed in light, the walls in shimmering gold and the floors resplendent granite. As they entered, the door sealed behind them and they were lost, confused, benumbed by the blinding light and vibrating energy which engulfed them.

"Great Spirit! Where are we?"

"Denor oplisiv (in another place)," said a voice in Vocatae. It was a familiar voice. *"Taila oplisiv* (in a safe place)."

"Who are you?"

"Vocataetae adiemmon leso? Cubenratae adiemmon leso (have you forgotten Vocatae? And have you forgotten me)?"

"What is that voice—it speaks the ancient tongue—the Foxish tongue?" asked the Priestess.

"It's the being—the watcher I saw in my dream."

"You had a vision?"

"I was in a vast plain of everlasting immensity and wondrous light. I saw a great owl which spoke to me in words of mystery. It said it was a watcher but not a god."

"That's impossible. You saw another like Asharru."

"Enra ca anaux Asarrum le (I am not like Asharru)," said the voice. *"Cum hrhauiphut quodcarae le avienutom iliphon amutae le. Enra aerd denor aredae–pheum cub ared levoneic cacansa amenic phel celphic amonirelaph-adrevur enin* (he is an embodiment of evil whereas I am a champion of good. I am the king of another realm—a realm of beings of great power who watch over the galaxy)."

"The gods! The gods of light who oppose the gods of darkness!" exclaimed the Priestess. "Haff-Lîsh and Asharru are in eternal war with the gods of light."

"Nonsense!" said Ifunka. "There is only one God—the Great Spirit!"

"Amaneciu venda noiucmon le–aviumciu amane ca le, pheum cub sing tathe-lonai. Enra Solis le avium Ammon Raetomaehrhon venda noiuc, sonni cabca ieditom vamint le phal xela arretaphaisiv (men have called us gods—but we are not gods, only protectors, defenders of the light. I am called Solis, but your people call me Amon-Ra, by which name I am known also on some other planets)."

"Amon-Ra!" the Priestess exclaimed as she bowed prostrate on the ground.

"Enra Asarrum ca le (I am not Asharru)," said Amon-Ra. *"Ca parla-gutonaitom soji. Sing Ramut phel Cacansa Vabaideicei vam parlagutarum. Cum Amantuad pheum cub veil iosutae. Enra alam Ramutae le, anaux oucau saphai oucau arretaisiv celphic cadolin siphie. Asarrum thehoicra, Preduom, cubtaehrhon caucreaquun quelicuteam vathiacra* (I need no worshippers. Worship only God, Whom ye know as the Great Spirit. He is Almighty and worthy of praise. I am a slave of God, as are all men on all worlds in this limitless universe. Forsake Asharru, Priestess, and atone for thine innumerable sins)."

"Cumen thehoi (I forsake him)," she replied in Vocatae. *"Enra aciaha quelicon le. Caemye di Aman le* (I am a terrible sinner. There is only one God)."

"Amut wav (very well)," replied Amon-Ra.

"Ves ciuamtae coji, om Aerd (what do you want from us, O King)?" asked Ifunka.

"Asarrumtae cuint cone, Iphunca Capha, phada Candaspuic (thou must defeat Asharru, Ifunka Kaffa, son of Kandaspu)."

"Ium vani (but how)?"

The light diminished somewhat, and Amon-Ra appeared before them in an owl-form hovering in the air before them.

"Caemye maitu cacansa amenae phetisie tumragahimae. Tem Mirad Maitu cabca amen uontouog cub gudouogae oucau miraleca leconae into. Tumra maiavadi sarusiv, vanon amantu eldgou ucre zela. Laphatiph, osmoson amena levonap celphic maitu phultiphint lecon (there is a coin of great power on the

island in the midst of the abyss. It is the Verdant Coin which contains a power of control and manipulation of all vegetable life. In the midst of a barren desert, the possessor can grow a mighty forest. Moreover, the bearer of this coin shall himself be transformed into a powerful being)."

"Vani maituciu gesiamconso (how shall we reach the coin)?"

"Celphic revurona (with this bridge)."

Amon-Ra pointed to a thin metal board.

"Raliscra; tem gehrha le (have faith; it is strong)."

Ifunka lifted it and made ready to leave.

"Xohrhocra (wait)!" said the owl. *"Maitu sohrhab varninae le. Hrhuin wonphicra arn egiptusa levontaesip emiphcon* (the coin is full of danger. Master yourself or it shall make thee a vengeful being)."

"Quebaconen, om Aerd (I shall, O King)," said Ifunka. *"Leci deacra, Phada Candaspuic. Maitu ademcra cub Asarrum conecra. Celp oucau le* (then go, Son of Kandaspu. Take the coin and defeat Asharru. That is all)."

They backed away respectfully and then exited the luminescent chamber which vanished behind them. Carrying the metal board carefully, they quickly paced back to the entrance of the final chamber. They were too late, however, as the Sage appeared, fully healed, with a cohort of five watchmen armed to the teeth. They hid in the shadows as the watchmen passed by, hoping to avoid detection. As they approached the abyss, the Sage called for them to halt.

"They're here somewhere. *Hushrev-krâ, shaff-zen!*" he ordered, commanding his men to move out

The guardsmen spread out and searched all sides of the room, every corner, nook and cranny, but returned unsuccessful.

"What shall we do?" whispered the Priestess.

"Amon-Ra must mean for us to succeed somehow. He *is* 'watching' after all."

"I can feel them," said the Sage as he closed his eyes in concentration. "Emerald of insight, reveal the truth!"

As he continued to meditate on the problem, Ifunka felt as if a hidden eye were upon him when, suddenly, the Sage opened his eyes and smiled.

"Loft, shivatish raffli-yog," he said, meaning 'there, near the entrance'.

The watchmen rushed back to the mouth of the cavern, weapons raised. Alarmed, Ifunka and the Priestess ran but were quickly overtaken by the watchmen, who seized them roughly.

"*Ffataff yêsh-zen! Predh-bara-yei okh-ish* (mad dogs! I am the Priestess)!" she screamed in disgust. "*Okh khudhalff-krâ* (unhand me)!"

"Unhand you?" asked the Sage. "How many men have 'handled' you? You're little more than a prostitute."

"I am a Priestess!" she exclaimed.

"Of Asharru? Then where is your loyalty—helping a *khaffshik* to reach the sacred jewels?"

"I was forced," she replied.

"So you claim, but I can see he has already corrupted your mind. Why else did you run instead of waiting for us to rescue you?"

"I was afraid."

"Do you still believe that Asharru is our true lord?"

"I... no," she replied.

"Your own tongue condemns you! I wish I could kill you right here and now but his lordship desires to judge you himself. *Khô teyadhim-krâ* (take her away)!"

"Leave her alone!" Ifunka shouted.

"Oh, I see you are soft for her, Ifunka," observed the Sage. "Have you enjoyed the delights of her thighs? Does she have a place in your heart?"

"My heart belongs to Arwa."

"Don't worry; she'll be eaten by the worm soon."

"Damn you!" Ifunka cried.

"Not so religious now, are we, monk?"

"I shall kill you, Shaff," said Ifunka coldly. "You shall die and this whole city shall burn."

"What power do you have, monk? You're impotent—utterly powerless. Shall I show you something? This will delight you, I'm sure."

He motioned to the watchman.

"*Leib khô-yan gîshem-krâ* (tear off her clothes)!" he ordered. "I want to enjoy her before she is killed by Asharru."

"No, you bastard!"

Bursting free from a watchman's grasp, he grabbed hold of his captor's axe and swung it into the watchman's ribs, splitting his chest. Pulling it free, he lobbed it at the watchman who was about to disrobe the Priestess, burying deep into the watchman's belly, spilling his entrails.

"Kill him!" the Sage cried.

Ifunka picked up his fallen enemy's sword and, holding it two-handed, swung it wildly at the three watchmen who now assailed him. With one blow he slashed a watchman's arm, who tripped and fell in front of the middle watchman's legs, causing him to stumble and fall forward. Ifunka stabbed the fallen watchman in the back of his neck and pierced the other's back, sticking through his lungs. The last approached him from behind. Enraged, Ifunka swung round, blade in hand, simultaneously slashing through the poor devil's belly. Grasping his outflowing intestines and vital organs, the foeman gurgled at the mouth and, vomiting bile, collapsed dead as a doornail. Breathing heavily and exhausted, Ifunka was drenched in blood. His eyes were wild like an angered beast raging in the night.

"Who else will taste death at my hands?" he challenged. "You, Shaff? Come then, bard; spill your blood!"

"You love this woman, don't you, Ifunka?"

The Sage held the Priestess in his grasp, a knife held to her throat.

"I love her as a brother does his sister," Ifunka replied evasively.

"Come now, we're old friends. There's no need for lies among friends. You love Arwa; I understand that. But why do you value this woman so much if you do not love her. Do you not covet her as a lover?"

"Your words offend me, bard!"

"The truth cuts like a blade!" the Sage replied.

"I love you, my rabbit," said the Priestess in bated breath.

"Then bleed for your love!" exclaimed the Sage as he swiftly sliced her neck, which spurted blood in abundance.

Her eyes stared in final shock and her body went limp.

"Nooooo!" Ifunka screamed as he grabbed an axe and, doubly armed, charged at the Sage swinging wildly like an enraged berserker.

He swung his axe and sword in furied motion, striking the Sage's sword with one blow and hacking his knife-wielding arm with the other, causing the Sage to drop both his weapons and seize his mangled limb in agony.

"My arm!" he screamed as his shoulder haemorrhaged torrents of blood.

"I shall rise again in Asharraff!" he cried.

"Don't count on it!" Ifunka quipped as he dismembered the Sage's remaining limbs.

"Death for you shall be slow indeed," said Ifunka. "Savour your wounds as you prepare for entrance to Gahimka and the flames of hell-fire. Fire everlasting shall burn your every limb and flesh while demons shall prod and torment you in never-ending torture. Such is the fate of the infidels!"

"Mercy, brother," pleaded the Sage. "Finish me off!"

"My heart has no more room for mercy," said Ifunka stoically. "Now I feel only hate and rage. I shall tear Asharru limb from limb and raze this city, and all its people—man, woman and child—to the ground."

"Then I shall see you in Gahimka, then?"

"As the Great Spirit wishes," he replied as he set off for the treasury, picking up the metal board and leaving the Sage to bleed to death in utter loneliness, humiliation and degradation.

Returning to the final chamber, Ifunka laid the metal board over the chasm and slowly—cautiously—crossed over onto the central island. Gold and jewels abounded with open treasure chests pregnant with coins, pearls, diamonds, rubies, emeralds and sapphires. Bars of precious platinum were stacked near the middle. At the very centre was a raised platform, like an altar but circular, upon which sat a singular coin which flashed and gleamed in the light of Ifunka's torch. It shimmered green as he approached it. Characters in *ffokatai* script were hewn in a ring around it which read: *MIRAD MAITU SOLISAE–PHEUM CUB DI RUBA MAITUSINAE; AMEN LECONAE CUB UONTOUOG MIRALEC ARRETREVUR* ('The Verdant Coin of Solis, one of many coins; the power of life and control over the vegetable world'). As he read the words out loud, uttering them in solemn tone, he seized the coin in hand. It was cold, smooth and wide; indeed, so smooth and polished was it that he could see his image reflected perfectly.

"What the Great Spirit wills!" he cried as he held it in both hands. "Give me the power, Amon-Ra!"

The coin began to glow resplendently with a verdant brilliance which encompassed his entire body. The glow intensified as it began to hum with some primordial rhythm which dated back to the beginning of the universe. Its power, derived from the primal force of the *mimra* itself, began to flow within him with incredible force and speed, filling his veins and sinews, transforming his inner and outer being. His green skin intensified, his hair began to vanish (including his iconic beard); his irises became a brilliant white. His flesh became firmer, more muscular, and coarse, like the skin of a vine. His head grew a new form of hair, vines hanging down like dreadlocks until he appeared to be a living humanoid plant, devoid of clothes but with modesty hidden by a hairy vine-like exterior which obscured his genitals. He was taller, fitter, more menacing in appearance, yet also noble, like some knight of old watching over the denizens of the land. He examined his body admiringly and then searched for the coin which had, he discovered, disintegrated within him and become incorporated into his body. Whether or not it could be reassembled and retrieved, he could not surmise.

"The power..." he said with a new voice—deeper, more authoritative, stronger. "I am full of power. Methinks I am more than a man and yet something different. I am Plant Man!"

"*Raem Sapie* (Plant Man)," said a voice.

He turned to see the owl hovering behind him.

"*Celp avana iediad le* (that is a fitting title)."

"*Ves celphic leso? Vesenra leso* (what is this? What am I)?"

"*Phultaminttae le–pheum cub amen cub zuldanca maethraint. Egiptus thehoicra, vilma cub hepmi ademiacra cub Asarrum conecra. Taehrhon doun cacansa le, anauxtaehrhon phonasmut cacansa le aviumtaenra ca isic quirb* (thou art changed—invested with power and responsibility. Forsake vengeance, embrace justice and mercy and defeat Asharru. Thy destiny is great as thine ancestry is great but I cannot tell thee all now)."

"*Hepmi? Hepmitomhrhon guodcarone dabrouso* (mercy? Do my enemies deserve mercy)?"

"*Tem quei Cacansa Vabaic le* (it is an attribute of the Great Spirit)."

"*Ithai egiptus le* (so is vengeance)."

"*Egiptus Ramutam le* (vengeance belongs to God alone)."

"*Vesenrahrhon doun leso–vesenrahrhon phonasmut le* (what is my destiny—what is my ancestry)?"

"*Enra ca ucre voca–quirb deacra cub Asarrum conecra* (I cannot say—go now and defeat Asharru)."

Amon-Ra vanished. Ifunka began to walk to the chasm and cross the metal plank when his body sprouted myriad vines which bridged the gap, forming a new vine-rope bridge.

"Marvelous!" he exclaimed. "I can cross any gap! Can I make vines at will?"

He crossed over and then extended his arm, which sprouted vines flying off into the pitch blackness like projectiles until they struck a wall and clung onto its edge, more than fifty *oksha*s distant. Pulling backwards on the vines until they were taut, he sprung forward and out of the chamber until he landed near the corpse of the Priestess. The vines retreated and reconstituted themselves within his herbaceous flesh. He knelt down and lifted the woman's head, holding her on his knee.

"I didn't even know your name," he said as his eyes welled with tears. "My heart has room for your love; you shall be avenged with Asharru's life-blood."

He lifted her limp body onto his shoulders and then looked for the Sage's corpse—it was gone! Looking round, he found a trail of blood, as if he had been drawn away at great speed. Firing more vines, Ifunka continued in leaps and bounds until he reached the base of the staircase. The blood trail led upwards to the Temple—the *Ffâna*—itself. Ifunka's vines shot upwards, clinging to the temple ceiling and, bowing down on one knee, he sprung upwards, flying round the staircase until he reached the main chamber of the temple. There he found himself surrounded by an army of watchmen, poised to kill, while the Sage lay on a stretcher, half-dead, with two attendants cleaning and sewing up his wounds—how he had got there so quickly, he could not surmise. Placing her dead body on the temple floor, Ifunka raised his hands to address the warriors who surrounded him.

"Heal her! Clean her wounds!" he pleaded.

"*Hafkha-yîm khô-yish,*" said one of the physicians. "She is dead."

"She's not dead!" he screamed.

Seizing the physician with vines around his neck, he pulled him to the Priestess's body.

"Heal her!" he ordered.

"Yes, sir," the healer replied and set about washing her neck and sewing up her slit throat.

"Why don't you attack me?" Ifunka challenged the watchmen. "Am I not a worthy foe?"

"Who... is... this...?" asked the Sage, each word uttered painstakingly.

"Do you not recognize your slayer, Shaff?" returned Ifunka. "But I see why you do not, for I am changed. I am something more than I was; I am made new; I am Plant Man!!!"

"Plant... ha... you've taken a coin of Amon-Ra; but Asharru is great."

"Sharru khan-ish (Asharru is great)!" the watchmen chanted in unison.

"You're a dead man, Sage; so where is your false god to challenge me?"

The doors to the Inner Sanctum sprung open and all the assembled watchmen bowed down on one knee. As they all waited expectant—Ifunka included—a booming voice projected throughout the hall:

"I am Asharru—the darkness which follows light! I am the death which shall consume thee while my servants live eternal! I am the giver of life and the remover thereof! Feel my wrath, mortal!!!!"

∼૭

CHAPTER XX.

The Purge

Even as all the assembled watchmen bowed to their deity, Ifunka—now refashioned as the insuperable and empowered Plant Man—stood expectant, but no deity appeared. Rather, all the warriors remained frozen in their pose of subservience and servility while Plant Man stood defiant and erect like a bear rearing its head in the midmost heart of the wilderness. He looked upon the bowing watchmen as his fallen foes, bowing to their triumphant conqueror. Thus did he look upon them as he strutted forth and walked among the motionless enemy and peered into the Inner Sanctum, which was peopled only by several maidservants who eyed him suspiciously.

"Where is the speaker of that voice?" he challenged. "Are you thus non-existent, Asharru?"

"Do you believe in me?" returned the voice.

"I believe in the Great Spirit and the Holy Tamitvar," Plant Man responded.

"Ha, ha, ha, ha, ha!" the demon laughed. "I am also spirit though you cannot see my flesh."

"Where is your flesh?"

"Do you believe I am flesh and blood?"

"If it is true."

"Then here I am."

With a flash, Asharru appeared before him, pike in hand.

"Your belief has given me flesh!"

"As I shall give you death," Plant Man quipped.

Firing vines towards one of the watchmen, Plant Man seized his weapons and sprung at the demon, hacking and slashing at his armour to no avail. The foe responded by thrusting his pike, skewering Plant Man in the process. The pike had pierced him right through the chest but, unharmed, he used vines to propel himself backwards and off the weapon.

"Impossible!" growled the beast. "I have slain you."

"I am unslayable, demon!" he replied defiantly. "There is not even a wound on my body."

His chest was completely resealed. Evidently, his entire frame was now a malleable, vegetable-generating system capable of self-re-generation, projection and controllable appendages and accessories, including vines, leaves and thorns.

"If I can't hurt your armoured exterior, I can kill you through other means," he continued, sprouting numerous thorny vines which wrapped around Asharru's mouth and neck, squeezing tightly with one forcing itself down the demon's throat. He fell to his knees, gargling his own blood, and struggled against the choking vines.

"Yes, die slowly, Asharru. Bleed slowly!"

The watchmen arose to defend their lord, slashing at the vines furiously. As each was severed, Plant Man sent out yet more to replace them. The struggling beast extended his left arm and a beam of energy enveloped the Sage's half-dead body. Miraculously, his limbs extended in white, glob-like masses and then took shape as arms, hands, feet and legs. His wounds healed, and he stood up, reanimated—restored. Picking up two swords, he charged Plant Man head on. Distracted, Plant Man was taken aback by the sudden assault. The Sage easily hacked off Plant Man's arms, causing him to relinquish his vines and fall prostrate. Stepping on his erstwhile killer's back, the Sage raised his swords, poised to deliver a death-blow by severing his enemy's head.

"Revenge is mine!" he cried.

The stricken demon had recovered and stood tall, beaming.

"Finish this pretended plant god!" he ordered.

"I think not!" shouted Plant Man as vines sprung from his back and seized the Sage's throat in an iron grip. His face went from green to blue as he suffocated. Plant Man's arms, meanwhile, had regrown to their original shape and size.

"Release him!" Asharru commanded.

"Heal the Priestess and I shall!"

"She is dead!" replied Asharru.

"Then so is your precious Sage!"

"Very well!"

Asharru extended his arm towards the Priestess. The stitches in her throat fell off and the skin revealed itself. Her flesh lost its tawny pallor and became taut, fresh; organs were reconstituted, her heart began pumping and she inhaled suddenly. Springing to her feet, she looked around wildly, like an animal, moaning and shrieking.

"Now release the Sage!"

"What is this? What have you done to her?"

"Her brain is ruined due to lack of oxygen. You are a fool."

"As are you," he replied as he squeezed the Sage's neck tighter until, gurgling bile, his neck snapped loudly.

He flung the Sage's limp body at the watchmen, who backed off cautiously. Extending his arm yet again, Asharru healed the Sage, who rose once more, vigorous as ever.

"You'll pay for that!" the Sage cried.

"Indeed, you have achieved nothing," said Asharru. "Finish the Priestess!"

Grabbing an axe, the Sage flung it at the brainless woman, hitting her in the chest. She collapsed, dead once more.

"No!" Plant Man cried.

"Futility!" said the demon. "Utter futility! Now submit to me or I shall kill you."

"You cannot kill me," said Plant Man. "I am immortal—pure vegetable life and the power of limitless growth. I cannot be destroyed."

"We have reached an impasse, Plant Man. What do you propose to do?"

"You are sustained by belief, are you not, Asharru?"

"Ha! Your belief sustains me, as do all my servants."

"Yet I believe you shall die!"

Extending his arms wide, dozens of vines shot out in all directions, each one seizing the neck of a watchman and, squeezing hard, each one was strangled to death. Asharru raised his pike to attack but this too was seized by a thick vine which stole it from his grasp. The Sage flung out the vines with his two swords but was seized at the waist and, dropping his weapons, was wrapped around like a python's prey, the vine slowly constricting until his ribs began to buckle.

"You are a projection from the *mimra*," said Plant Man. "I understand now. Once I have killed all your believers, you will not be able to return to corporeal existence but, rather, must fleet away to your master, Afflish the Accursed, and never return. Man, woman and child—all the host of your devotees, shall be wiped off the face of Tremn. Each and every one I shall slaughter, mercilessly, until none remain. This day, all infidels shall perish! This day, truth shall reign supreme!"

Succumbing to their demise, the watchmen collapsed and were relinquished while the Sage, well-nigh suffocated, collapsed. Aiming his hand at the Sage, Plant Man released projectile thorns which embedded themselves in the Sage's skull and neck. He bled out and was motionless. The demon, weakened, fell to his knees.

"I don't believe in you, demon. You have no name. You have no power. You do not exist."

Asharru's body faded like a mirage at the edge of a dune, which evaporates when approached.

"I exist... worship... me."

His words became weak and then, as the image vanished, so too did the sound of his voice. All that remained was silence. Plant Man stood at the epicentre of slaughter, surrounded by a mass of lifeless bodies—asphyxiated, with protruding tongues and frog-like eyes, with contorted faces and spread-out limbs, some on top of others while many clutched their throats, even in death. The bloody corpse of the Sage was the most mutilated yet, even now, Plant Man feared that he might once more spring to life—regenerated—and attack him with merciless fury.

Gazing upon the carnage, he was well-pleased and, having taken it all in, moved to enter the Inner Sanctum. There, he found five women, wondrously beautiful, arrayed in light, *woffgi*-silk garments concealing their bosoms and waists. There was a large wooden bed, covered in gold leaf, a throne of *ffentwash*-bison ivory, meticulously carved, and an assortment of pillows and cushions lined against the wall in Oriental fashion.

"Where did this demon come from?" he wondered.

Searching the throne attentively, he found a small golden disk under the seat. Removing it, he observed that there were small indentations, as if formed through finger-tips pressed into the metal, on the face of the artefact. He felt these with his fingers and then turned it over to find a cursive script on the back. This, being undecipherable to him, he created a pocket at his waist and deposited the object.

The maidservants of Asharru eyed him curiously as he continued to scan the chamber. They were almost characterless—undefined. Disturbed by this, he grabbed hold of one of them with a vine and pulled her to him. She was unstartled, as if nothing could alarm her. Examining her body, he could hear no heart-beat. Picking up a dagger from beside the throne, he made an incision in her chest and, cutting her wide open, found nothing inside, as if she were a mere shell. He clove her head-to-bellybutton and she merely fell into a pile of cloth, like a suit unfastened and discarded. Unsettled by this, he grabbed a torch from the wall and flung it at the cushions and bed, hoping to burn the lifeless automatons to death. He closed the door behind him and sealed the maidservants inside so that they could all be well-and-truly incinerated. Leaving the temple, he espied a throng of watchmen, hundreds upon hundreds, massing in front of him. Seizing the opportunity, he addressed the attendant crowd.

"O people of Khanshaff!" he called them. "Behold, watchmen! I was called Ifunka Kaffa, son of Kandaspu, a monk of the Holy Order of the Brothers of Bishgva, but now I am something more—I am Plant Man, the lord of the vegetable kingdom, and I shall be king over all Tremnad and over all Tremn, and shall put to an end the tyrannical Theocracy and all its corruption and licentiousness. Everyone who opposes me shall be put to the sword and slaughtered. If any of you believe in Asharru and call him lord, I shall slay you here and now and shall burn your accursed city to the ground; even its ashes shall I feed to the *ffaika* and bones shall be playthings for the *ffentbaffs*. Not one of you shall remain alive unless you renounce Asharru completely, accept the Great Spirit as your true God and me as your sovereign liege. I have slain your Sage, burned your Inner Sanctum and defeated Asharru, banishing him to the void of nothingness and non-existence. So tell me, watchmen and people of Shaffnâ, do ye take the cup of submission or that of death?"

"Temni gin-ôn kha okh-ish (I do not understand Tremni)!" shouted one, while another shouted: *"Khuff khaffshik ffogsh-ôn mon-ish-ô* (what did the *khaffshik* say)?"

"Can someone please translate for those two?" Plant Man requested, at which point a cry of *"Sharru khan-ish* (Asharru is great)!" rose up, drowning out further inquiries on his part.

"That's unfortunate," he sighed. "I shall have to massacre them all before supper."

They charged at him, weapons raised. Plant Man merely extended his hands and a wall of trees sprung up from the soil, stymieing their charge. The trees circled round until the watchman forces were completely kettled—walled in by an impenetrable vegetable barrier of thick *kaptitv* trees. The watchmen fell to their knees in disbelief. Burying himself in the ground, Plant Man re-emerged in the centre of the circle, at the heart of the warriors who now had no means of regress or retreat. They turned to attack him, but he dodged their blows, toying with them until, transforming his arms into two great vines with hands-length razor-sharp thorns, he extended them across the diameter of the circle and spun them round at lightning speed, like the blades of a blender, reducing the watchmen to a mass of dismembered bodies and mutilated flesh and bone. He looked upon the carnage and smiled.

"Such is always the fate of the evil-doers," he quipped as he caused the trees to open up and allow him to pass.

He marched through the square until he came upon the now-abandoned platform where his friends were gagged and bound. A formerly-sealed hole had opened in the ground—the opening to the lair of the *ffaika*.

"The sacrifice!" he cried, remembering that his friends' lives were soon to be lost.

Springing forward, he leapt onto the platform and, one by one, released his friends.

"Who are you?" asked Ushwan. "Are you a man?"

"More than that," he replied. "I am changed—I am now a king among men."

"But *who* are you?" asked Shem.

"Do any of you recognise me?"

He looked at Arwa, who stared at him with a mixture of wonder and fear.

"Do you fear me?" he asked.

"I do not know you," replied Arwa.

"That saddens me," said Plant Man.

"Don't tell me it is you?" said Ffen. "You're *different*."

"It is I," he announced.

"Ifunka?" gasped Arwa. "My love?"

"It is I—I was Ifunka Kaffa but now I am called Plant Man."

"But how?" asked Ffen. "You're entirely different."

"I was changed through the agency of the Verdant Coin."

"Verdant Coin?"

"I met a being—a powerful creature which took the form of an owl."

"Owl?" asked Ffen.

"Yes, the mystic owl, my boy," said Ushwan.

"What?"

"While in Kubbawa, I found an old book of legends," explained Ushwan. "The legends from before the revelation of Votsku. The early Tremna used to worship Inta—our great ancestor—and Amon-Ra, the king of the pre-Tamitvaric pantheon. He would take various forms when he appeared among mortals; sometimes as a solar disk or a mighty eye lined with kohl. At other times, he appeared as a man with light-brown skin, or an owl."

"Interesting," said Ffen. "Was it indeed Amon-Ra whom you saw?"

"Indeed it was. He appeared to me in the cavern beneath the Ffâna.

There, in the midst of an island surrounded by an abysmal drop, is a treasury of gold, jewels and diamonds. In the very centre of this treasury lay the Verdant Coin—*Mirad Maitu*—which Amon-Ra urged me to take in order to defeat Asharru. I have done as he requested, slain the Sage— our erstwhile companion—and defeated the false god."

"Marvellous!" exclaimed Ushwan. "Then we can go!"

"Not quite," said Plant Man.

Arwa still eyed him like a stranger.

"Am I so foreign to you—even my darling wife?"

"No, I am always yours," said Arwa as she moved to embrace him tightly.

"Why can't we go now, old boy?" urged Ushwan. "It's time to get out of here."

"Where's Khalam-Sharru?" asked Plant Man, ignoring the question.

"He… he betrayed us to Asharru."

"What!" Plant Man exclaimed. "Then he must *die*!"

"No!" Arwa protested. "He is my father."

"You don't get it, do you?" Plant man sternly answered. "Asharru is sustained by belief. If he has believers, he may return. There is only one solution."

"You don't mean…?" Ffen gulped.

"Yes—I do mean it," he continued. "We must eliminate Shaffnâ and burn this city to the ground—unless the people renounce Asharru."

"Eliminate!" Shem cried. "Genocide?!"

"It's the only way."

"Did Amon-Ra command this?" asked Ushwan. "Is this the will of the Legion?"

"I am the only one who needs to be consulted in this matter. I shall annihilate all the Shaffu, if I must. And I shall destroy the Theocracy and be king of all Tremn!"

Plant Man's eyes were bright—with an inner fire—not one of faith but of ambition and terrible vengeance.

"You've gone mad!" Ffen gasped. "Have you forsaken morality?"

"We cannot follow you in this," said Shem firmly.

"I'm afraid I have to agree, old boy," said Ushwan. "Whatever's happened to you, I pray to the Great Spirit it can be undone. You've gone bonkers—absolutely loony."

"Arwa," Ifunka turned to his wife. "What say you?"

"You want to kill all my kith and kin," she replied. "Which I abhor; but I am your wife and I shall love you for all time. I shall never leave you, for you are my heart."

"And you are mine," he concurred as he swept his beloved into his rough, plant-like arms.

At that moment, the ground shook and the companions turned to see an immense worm rearing its eyeless, hideous mouth and torso from the soil. It moved, slowly but steadily, towards the platform, used as it was to consuming sacrificial victims.

"Run!" Ffen cried.

"Stay behind me, Arwa!" Plant Man commanded.

The others leapt off the platform while Plant Man remained firm.

"Ifunka!" Ffen called. "Save yourself!"

"I am Plant Man!" he roared as a thousand vines burst from the ground and wrapped themselves around the leathery torso of the worm, which squirmed and flailed as it found itself wrapped within a cocoon of sentiently-manipulated vegetable matter. Ffen drew his bow and fired volley after volley of arrows into the worm's neck while Plant Man endeavoured, with some success and against unbelievable resistance, to hold the worm down through force of will. Bursting from its constraints and unaffected by the arrows embedded in its tough hide, it fell upon Plant Man, mouth wide open, devouring both Plant Man himself and a large section of the platform. Arwa, who was some paces behind, screamed and leapt off the platform, falling into Meyla's arms. Plant Man was gone—eaten!

The companions ran—as fast as they could—in order to escape the ravenous behemoth which had obliterated the sacrificial platform and consumed their recently-empowered friend. They fled in the direction of Khalam-Sharru's house, hoping that the worm would not follow. For a while, it flailed to and fro, divesting itself of excess debris and detritus which had embedded itself in the folds of its leathery hide. Then it lumberingly turned and, building momemtum, charged over streets and through the crowd, which rapidly dispersed in alarm and terror as the worm roamed free on a path of carnage. Sundry civilians and other pedestrians were swept up and devoured incidentally—as collateral damage in its determined path of murderous intent. It was targeting its victims—it heard their footsteps, it smelt their flesh—or the pheromones thereof. It desired one thing and one alone: to devour its intended prey. All others were secondary victims to its onsweeping wrath and terrible destructiveness.

As they neared the district of Khalam-Sharru's house, the worm caught up with them and reared its bulky head—like Damocles' sword, dangling over them ready for the oncoming death-blow. At that moment, as they stared up in terror, the worm stalled and began to quiver and tremble. Its motions became yet more tremulous and spasmodic, as if it battled within itself, gripped in agony. Its death-throws grew more and more terrible, until its tough skin gave way to hundreds of bulges which burst open to reveal a myriad thorned vines shooting out like grappling hooks and impacting on the surrounding houses and other buildings, hooking thereonto. The worm was thus pincered and suspended, as if ensconced and embosomed within a living web which grew from within itself like a parasitic fungus, eating it from the very core. It haemorrhaged oozy vital fluids which poured out onto the streets below in a slow-moving deluge.

The worm struggled, in a few more drastic spasms, as its vital energy was depleted and then, sagging, it hung like a leaf caught in a dewdrop-laden spider's web, forged ere dawn's first light. Plant Man soared out of its gaping orifice, gliding past its horrendous fangs, borne by countless vines which lifted and propelled him like so many legs on a swift-moving arthropod. Triumphant—victorious—suspended above the ground, Plant Man appeared as a supernatural being—a demi-god like unto the Greek heroes of old—a being not of Tremn, or any world—exalted above the mere mortals who gazed at their saviour with wonder-filled eyes and awe-struck miens. Such was their amazement that they stood motionless and silent—a silence like the silence before a plunge or before an axe is struck upon the neck of sorry sinner; such, indeed, did they behold him as he descended gracefully to the street-level.

"Here me," he called out, making a second attempt to address the people of the city. "O people Khanshaff and Shaffnâ beyond"—he pause. "Who shall translate on my behalf?"

A watchman who yet remained stepped forward.

"I shall, milord."

"Then repeat what I have said."

He did so: *"Ey Ffendh Khanshaff-eym ffi shîb-yaff Shaffnâ!"*

"I am Plant Man—whom the world has known as Ifunka Kaffa, son of Kandaspu, aforetime."

"Reym-Shaff okh-ish–kheym Ifunka Kaffa ffadh Kandaspu-yiftey khôr-ôn areft akhanffon hant-ish."

"I am your king and sovereign lord."

"Yish ftâ-ga-n ffi ardheyn avma ftâ-gei-yan okh-ish."

"I have slain the Sage and banished the false god, Asharru."

"Metshu aff-ôn ffi darlîsh-tesh Sharru deyanat-ôn okh hant-ish."

"Ye shall worship him no more."

"Khû parlâg-ôn ftâ-gei kha khon-ish."

"Rather, renounce Asharru, worship the Great Spirit and swear loyalty to me and ye shall be spared—nay, ye shall become my army."

"Haftangey, Sharru khat-krâ, Khan Vabakh parlâg-krâ ffi okh-em zeydh parlîff-krâ ffi harî-m ftâ-ga khon-ish–kha, makhô okh-an galî-yôn ftâ-gei khon-ish."

"Fail to do so and ye shall be slaughtered pitilessly."

"Fto flôff-ôn ftâ-gei nom-ish, lekh avshaft-îm khakhêm ftâ-gei khon-ish."

"Heed my command or die!"

"Môn-og okh-an yidash-krâ off hafkha-krâ!"

A large number of civilians bowed and kneeled and began to shout out cries of loyalty.

"Sharru khat-ôn ftâkh-ish (we renounce Asharru)!" some cried. *"Khan Vabakh parlâg-ôn ftâkh-ish* (we worship the Great Spirit)!" cried others, while yet others shouted *"Reym-Shaff lekht-ôn shffu min-ish* (long live Plant Man!" and *"Yish lekht-ôn shffu min-ish* (long live the king)!"

A number of assembled people wavered.

"Slay them!" Plant Man ordered. "And go from house to house and village to village, slaying all who refuse!"

"Ftôn aff-krâ! Ffi ffakhvek-yô ffakhvek-em ffi ffamlîsh-yô ffamlîsh-em dift-krâ, ffi akhav-kheym dhab-ôn-ish aff-krâ!"

Grabbing whatever implements were at their disposal, his newly-minted subjects set upon their fellows and, chasing them down, hacked and rent them to pieces.

"Ifunka!" Ffen cried. "Stop this carnage!"

He raised his arms, pleading to his friend.

"For the love of God, old boy!" cried Ushwan.

They could do nothing as the carnage ensued, blood trickling down the cracks and crevices of the cobble-stone street. The ranks of Plant Man's army swelled, with two hundred becoming five hundred, and five becoming eight, as they swept through the city purging the dissidents—all worshippers of Asharru, and whoever failed to bow the knee to the self-proclaimed king of Tremn.

"Listen to us, brother," urged Shem as Ifunka watched the spreading chaos and bloodshed.

"This is not the way of the Right Religion—this is not what Amon-Ra wants."

"He can stop me if he wishes," replied Plant Man. "But, behold, have I not begun a great cleansing? Am I not ensuring that Asharru shall never return? The Holy Theocracy is a curse and a plague on this world. I shall rid the world of all false priests and bishops. All shall submit to one rule and one king."

"You're mad with power!" Shem protested.

"Would you have said the same to Ishmael the Great when he subdued the accursed Biknogs of Kraina? What about Kubba Gven, the heir of Tsilel, who united all Tremnad under one empire after the demise of Gven Dakit, who had no son? Were these mad with power—or were they heroes of renown? The subtle conspiracy which has hitherto kept the Theocracy under the thumb of Asharru and his minions is over!"

"The coin has changed you, brother," said Ffen. "Will you expect loyalty from us?"

"You are my friends," said Plant Man. "Fear not! I shall not harm you. Now, await me in Khalam-Sharru's house until the city is cleansed.

After we are finished, we head for Ffantplain and then Kubbawa, where the cleansing shall be consummated."

With no way to resist, Ushwan, Ffen and Shem led Arwa and Meyla to the house. Plant Man called the interpreter to his side.

"What is your name?" he asked him.

"Sharru-Khan, milord," he replied.

He was a watchman of medium-build with light-brown eyes and a narrow jaw. His nose was long and arched and his eyes rather too close together, giving a slightly-ridiculous aspect to the man; but, being a freak in himself, Plant Man appreciated these abnormalities rather than being put off by them.

"That name is blasphemous," said Plant Man. "Henceforth you shall be called Tesh-Khan, meaning 'God is Great'. You know these people; therefore, you shall organize our army. I appoint you General. Now go and appoint your commanders and lieutenants. After Shaffnâ is subdued, we gather the army here in Khanshaff in two days' time. I shall appoint a Viceroy to govern Shaffnâ in my absence and then we march on Ffantplain. All boys and men, aged fourteen and over, of healthy body and mind, shall be recruited into our army. All recruits shall take the following oath: 'I renounce Asharru and all his minions and take refuge from Afflish the Accursed. I believe in the Great Spirit and His Seer, Votsku. I swear allegiance and fealty to Ifunka Kaffa, Son of Kandaspu, the King of all Tremn.' Understood?"

Tesh-Khan nodded.

"Very good. Change all blasphemous names and ensure all recruits are armed from the armoury. Gather all *ffentbaffs* and other beasts of burden so that a cavalry can be organized. Dismissed!"

Tesh-Khan bowed and began carrying out his new master's orders. Pleased with his progress thus far, Plant Man surveyed the city, cruising across its streets, filled with blood and severed limbs. Along the edges of the streets and plazas, new trees sprung up at his command and raised their lofty boles to shade the thoroughfares and great open squares which characterized the city of Khanshaff. A thousand thoughts coursed through his evolving mind—how he would revolutionise society, open the frontiers of learning and banish ignorance and corruption. A new Ishmael, a new Kubba Gven, he would revive the glory of Tremn, explore beyond the coasts of the mighty continent of Tremnad and colonise the remaining uninhabited and uncivilized regions of the world, spreading the light of the Tamitvar and banishing unbelief through hilt and blade. A new era would soon dawn, he believed, and a new dynasty be born, through the agency of Arwa's maiden womb.

As he approached the central plaza, he espied a figure amidst the blood and mangled cadavers. It was a lone priest who stood armed and poised for battle.

"You've ruined everything!" he cried. "By Asharru, you have ruined everything! I shall not allow it, Ifunka Kaffa!"

"I am Plant Man!!!" he cried. "Bow the knee or die in your wrath, Khalam-Sharru!"

CHAPTER XXI.

Banners Raised!

~

The two men—if men they both be called, circled one another like two entangled predators locked in combat. Not touching—at least an *oksha* apart, they regarded one another, visages locked in steady gaze, contemplating their next moves. Plant Man, the newly-minted supernatural being, knew he could, with but a flick of verdant finger, quell his enemy and shatter his bones into a thousand sundry fragments. He could strangle Khalam-Sharru with a dozen thick vines, thorns protruding viciously like straws to pierce flesh and drink deep from his bloody veins. The pagan's eyes, deep-gazing, full of rage and abundant determination, were those of a man who saw that his world was ending, like the last ray of sunlight upon the hill-top, reflected on the petals of a solitary flower ere dusk wiped away all trace of illumination; mighty Khanshaff, once the true power behind the Theocracy—the master puppeteer in a performance of falsehood and deception which held all men upon the face of Tremnad within a perpetual delusion! Like the captive in Plato's cavern, the inhabitants of the Theocracy had for centuries lain trapped within a chamber of illusions, ruled over by power-hungry High-Priests and bishops. The benumbed and subdued populace were under the thumb of these theocrats, with Khanshaff serving as a mighty gameskeeper, culling the breeders of discontent.

Khalam-Sharru, a priest of Asharru, a cog within this mechanism of oppression, had lived happily aforetime; yet now his felicity was marred by a small band of *khaffshik* monks who sought to overthrow all things. Why did not Plant Man strike this inveterate infidel down? Why did he tolerate the existence of this traitor? Arwa, his true beloved—her pleading voice rang within his mind, reverberating with words of mercy and compassion.

"*Khaffshik!*" Khalam-Sharru spat his words. "Will you slay me as you have slain my brothers? Will you tear me flesh-from-bone as you have killed the watchmen?"

"What fate they received was born of their infidelity to the Great Spirit."

"What of your lust for power? What of your cruelty to fellow man? Torturer! Murderer! Usurper!!!"

"Hold your tongue, foolhardy mortal!" Plant Man retorted. "I am not that simple monk you encountered as your erstwhile captor! A force of immense power runs through my every vein and sinew—a power of regeneration and vegetative generation."

"Kill me where I stand, filthy dog, or fight me as a man, blade-in-hand!" he challenged him.

Intrigued by this proposal, Plant Man had found a way to eliminate the traitor without bearing responsibility for the act, because the challenge was initiated by Khalam-Sharru himself.

"Equally matched," he said in soliloquy. "Equally matched, the balance hangs level; Arwa cannot blame me for his death. So shall it be then!"

"Do you think, monk, that Arwa can ever forget her father?"

"I am the father of her spirit, as I have freed her from the shackles of Asharru, while it was you who forged those same shackles, link-by-link, and weighted her down with the burden of impiety!"

"Take blade, then, *khaffshik!*" called Khalam-Sharru.

He threw him his sword, which Plant Man caught with evident dexterity.

"I shall bear this axe down upon you and hew this corrupted tree!" Khalam-Sharru cried.

Screaming full-furiously, axe raised aloft, he assaulted the monk with all his might and main. Plant Man dodged and parried, then struck back with deft blows. Khalam-Sharru deflected these with the head of his axe and ducked the third blow. Again they attacked one another, and again, each time avoiding the swinging blades and remaining unscathed. A crowd of onlookers swarmed about them, fascinated and amused by the contest which, in its outcome, betokened the final fate of their once-ascendant realm.

"Do you toy with me, Plant Man, or is this the best you can do?" he taunted.

"The infidel shall hold his tongue or find it ripped from his mouth!"

"Not before my axe has shorn your roots and cut them from your trunk!"

Charging Plant Man, Khalam-Sharru ducked to miss his sword-swinging and, kneeling low, he swung with all his strength, slicing his enemy's ankles, felling him with a single blow. Falling backwards, Plant Man lay like a recumbent beast brought low by huntsman's deadly arrow. He stared at Khalam-Sharru with horror as the priest stepped onto his chest and raised his axe to give the death-blow.

"For Asharru!" he cried as he made ready to drop the axe upon his enemy's neck.

As the axe-head swung down, Plant Man's face changed from shock and horror to a grimace of deceit, while his arms swung together and grabbed hold, vice-like, onto the axe's haft, pulling it from the priest's grasp.

"As King Ishmael once said of his Biknog foes, 'so always do the faithless fail'!" he quipped as the priest's axe now swung round and suck deep into Khalam-Sharru's thigh, slicing through muscle and vein, and unleashing torrents of blood upon the plaza stones.

Reattaching his feet like shoes, Plant Man rose to his feet, unnaturally, like a catapult, and sunk another axe-blow into the priest's belly.

"*Khaffshik* bastard!" were the priest's words as he spat blood and bile.

The pagan fell prostrate upon the ground, which was soaked in his blood.

"Ifunka!" he cried.

"Any last requests?"

"Keep Arwa safe…" he coughed.

"Very well. Say hello to Afflish the Accursed!"

One final swing of the axe and Khalam-Sharru's head was severed from his body.

"Praise the Great Spirit!" Plant Man cried, his eyes like those of an enraged *yeshka*.

"*Khan Vabakh yôsh min-ish* (Praise the Great Spirit)!" echoed the crowd in Shaffi.

"March on, Shaffu; the day of reckoning is nigh-at-hand!" Plant Man proclaimed.

Throwing aside his weapons and suspending himself upon his vine-appendages, he glided back towards the slain priest's house. How could he now face his wife?

~

Ushwan, Ffen and Shem sat within the parlour of the house while Arwa rested alone in her room, gathering her thoughts. Meyla served them tea—*gveg*-leaf tea with *sheff*-cinnamon. This was presented on a tray, along with white-powdered biscuits called *shilab*s in Tremni—*ab* being the name for 'powdered sugar' and *shil* meaning 'biscuit'. These rather resembled marbles and they proved exceedingly difficult to dip in tea, without becoming lost at the bottom of the tea-cup, that is. This fate befell Shem, who lost his *shilab*, sinking as it did with a 'plop', while Ushwan munched gaily away, sipping his tea profusely. He had endured days and weeks of suffering and privations while imprisoned in the dungeon, so now he enjoyed whatever pleasures were offered to him. Ffen was preoccupied with his thoughts. Ever since his early days as a monk, he had been somewhat of an extremist in disposition and he recognized himself in Plant Man—his own passion and radical bent. Would he not make the same choices, the same decisions, if he were in Ifunka's shoes? Would he not use force to eliminate the infidels and cleanse the world of the wretched Theocracy?

"I say, old boy!" Ushwan interrupted this train of thought. "How did you get here? Shem tells me you were forcibly married to three sisters and prevented from leaving Ffash Valley by its lord, what was his name? Is that right, old chum?"

"Lord Tem Ffash is his name. Yes, well, I told it to him straight: 'I love your daughters, Reshga, Yimga and Mashga, and I swear upon my life that I will return, but I must save my friends from danger'. I could feel it in my bones. I knew you were all in trouble. I left two days after Ifunka and Shem and have been catching up ever since."

"You didn't bring that wretched *meish* then?"

"What, Shig?" he laughed. "No, he's looking after the three ladies—God, they are beautiful!"

"Sowing your wild oats, my boy? Good on you, mate, good on you. I myself am no stranger to the ladies, though they thought me so. Foolish bastards! Oops, sorry for the language."

"In any case, everything has changed now. There's no going back to our old lives."

"Ifunka's gone mad. Whatever this Verdant Coin is, we've got to free him from it before he ruins himself and our whole world," Shem interrupted them.

He looked sullen and depressed, his eyes weighed down by a great weariness born of life's suffering combined with a heart-wrenching journey.

"Cheer up, old boy; I'm sure he'll be fine soon."

"And what of the blood—the streets running with blood? All is lost; there's no going back from such violence!"

"Come now, Shem," Ushwan consoled him. "There is always room for forgiveness. As long as we are breathing, and hearts beat within our chests, we can repent of misdeeds and turn to the Almighty Great Spirit for forgiveness. He is Merciful and Compassionate! Forgive Ifunka and pray that he repents and is forgiven by the Almighty Forgiver."

"You know," said Ffen. "I'm not sure he's wrong."

He had been debating whether to broach his ideas with Shem and Ushwan for the last few hours but now he decided that the time had come.

"What do you mean, brother?" asked Shem, worried.

"There really is no other way to prevent Asharru from rematerializing other than killing all of his worshippers."

"Are you justifying Ifunka's actions?"

"I'm saying that he has a valid reason. Do we not glorify Ishmael the Great, who slaughtered countless Biknogs?"

"I see your point, brother," acknowledged Ushwan. "But Ifunka is not Ishmael. He's a monk of non-noble stock with no authority given by man or God, nor any lawful right of descent."

"I'm not so sure about that," Ffen continued. "His mother is from Clan Bishkwa of the Tribe of Avis, which descend from Votsku, our Great Seer. If he descends from Votsku on his mother's side, what about his father? We don't even know who *he* was."

"Kandaspu, I believe," said Ushwan.

"I mean—that's what we've been told, but who was Kandaspu and where did he come from?"

"Are you suggesting that Ifunka Kaffa—the abandoned child—is a descendant of the royal house?" asked Shem.

"I'm saying that we do not know and cannot assume that he is not of noble stock when he might well be."

"Assuming that to be true," Ushwan continued. "Why should he be king of all Tremn? Is that not a heinous and self-serving pretension?"

"Would you call Kubba Gven—our first emperor—pretentious?"

"No, he was a great leader," Ushwan replied. "But I fear that Ifunka is driven by a lust for power—something is burning within him: rage, vengeance, desire; it's like he has forsaken everything we stand for in order to feed these base passions."

"Well, I am open-minded on this issue," Ffen persisted. "Will you not at least consider supporting him?"

"It sounds as if your mind is already made up," Ushwan observed. "As for me, I am still a monk, come what may."

"We could be on the verge of a new epoch," Ffen continued. "It's all coming to shape in my mind. Can you imagine? Ifunka is now possessed of such power that he could conceivably deal a death-blow to the Holy Theocracy of Tremn and usher in a new kingdom. The conspiracy which has kept the Theocracy in place is crumbling as the Shaffu are now entirely under his spell."

"Maybe," said Shem. "But I can only go so far. I also want the corrupt theocracy to crumble—don't get me wrong—but I want to do so on a morally-sound basis. Does Ifunka look alright to you, Ffen?"

"I admit he seems different," said Ffen. "But let's give him time. He must get used to his new powers."

At that moment, there was a knock on the door. Whoever it was did not wait for an answer, but stormed in and began climbing the stairs.

"See who it is," urged Ushwan.

"I will," said Ffen as he rushed to find Plant Man reaching the landing.

"My friend," Plant Man greeted him. "My hands are drenched in blood."

He said this despite the fact that his hands were clean. He walked into the parlour and stood before them. Meyla bowed while the others stared in perplexity, still unused to seeing his plant-like exterior and vine-locks, his unnatural eyes and superhuman body. He was powerful, confident—yet his yes betrayed a certain sorrow and worry, as if he carried a terrible burden. He raised his hands, as if to show Ffen the blood that he imagined to be upon them.

"Where is my heart?" he asked enigmatically.

"Ifunka… what do you mean?" asked Ffen.

"My beloved Arwa."

"She's in her room."

"I must go to her—there is something terrible I must tell her."

"Are you sure that is wise?"

"Wise? Is it wise to slay your father-in-law?"

"No, I should think not, but, are you sure you wouldn't rather sit down to have a cup of tea first? Tea soothes the soul, as they say."

"No, if I delay the wound shall only grow deeper."

He buried his face in his hands.

"Why was the old fool so stubborn? If he hadn't betrayed us…"

"I'm sure you did what you had to," Ffen assured him.

"Indeed, but women don't think as coldly as men. They're not as logical. They are driven more by emotion."

"True, brother. Speak softly. I believe they like it when men speak softly."

"I shall try."

He slowly moved to Arwa's room where, not long before, he had consummated his marriage and lost his virginity. There his wife awaited him, cloistered away as if she knew doom was coming. He knocked on the door. She opened it.

"My darling," she said as she embraced him. "Is this how you shall stay?"

She referred to his new appearance.

"Your Tremni improves by the minute, my dear," he replied. "I think I can remove it."

She stood back as he focused all his energies on removing the coin. Gradually, the covering—the plant-like shell over his body—began to recede, until it coalesced into a cylindrical coin. Another cylinder, the strange device he had found in the Inner Sanctum, fell to the floor. He was stark naked, his clothes having somehow been consumed by the energy of the coin

"Darling!" she exclaimed.

He bent and picked up the cylinder, placing both that and the coin on a small wooden table at the edge of the room.

"What need is there for clothes between us?" he said with aplomb.

"There is no need!" she said with evident delight.

Though restored as the man she first knew, his body was enhanced—more muscular, more refined, as if his thin, monastic form had been refashioned—a statue chiselled finely out of a single block of green marble, if such marble exists.

"You are even more handsome," she said.

"And you are ever fresh and beautiful, like a violet *vinsh*-flower, wet with crystal-pure dew, bathed in the morning light."

"Come, then, precious husband—for I am wet with dew."

He moved to embrace her again but stopped himself, hesitating. He bowed his head and held his palms upward, as if in prayer.

"Will my hands ever be clean?" he asked rhetorically.

"They are clean. If not, I shall wash them, for I serve you, this life and next."

"You see with the eyes of the present. I see with the eyes of the past."

"How can you see the past?"

"The present is only motion—like the movement of a river. The future is where the river has not yet coursed, but the past is etched in the lay of the land; it is written in the banks of the river. It cannot be changed or erased. The bodies cannot be remade; the blood cannot be gathered up. It is all spent—cast along the river banks like so much dust!"

He fell to his knees and held his face again within his palms. She knelt down and wrapped him in her arms.

"All the past will be forgotten," she said. "Love washes away the dust."

"Will you forgive me?"

"I fear what you are to say!" she replied, jerking backwards. "Do not say it is so!"

"It is so," he replied. "Your father is dead."

"Why…?" she fell back against the bed. "You *knew* I loved him."

"I had no choice—he challenged me! What was I to do?"

She stared at him with wild eyes, unsure of what to do or say.

"And that coin—the Verdant Coin—it makes me someone else. I feel hungry—hungry for power and vengeance. The world is not enough! I want Tremn and I want more than Tremn!"

She was silent, neither crying nor displaying emotions of any sort. She merely regarded him with eyes which concealed a universe of pain.

"Say something!" he pleaded with her. "Or I swear I shall kill myself and end this madness once and for all!"

"No!" she stared, her senses recovered. "You are all that I have now!"

Her eyes welled with tears, her voice choked as she tried to continue speaking, and she began to sob.

"I'm so sorry," he said. "So, so sorry!"

"No," she replied. "It was my father… he was wrong. He did not understand my love for you. He would not see that he was wrong. I have you now. I have the Great Spirit now. Nothing else matters."

"Then you forgive me?"

"I forgive you always, because I love you like my own heart. We are like one tree with two branches. Our children shall be twigs, stems and offshoots of that tree."

"Then I am healed by your love, Arwa," he said, his own voice choked with emotion. "Your love washes the stain from my heart."

He embraced her tightly and they kissed passionately. Overcome with emotion, frustration and passion, she bit his shoulder and he tugged at her hair with his strong hands. She pulled off her dress and they made love on the carpet as the night waxed on and cast its shadow over the ill-deeds and bloody acts of the day.

As a new day dawned, Meyla knocked on her mistress's door and came in, only to find the two lovers wrapped in a blanket on the floor, locked within each other's arms and legs like the tangled vines which spilled over the roofs and balconies of Khanshaff. She quickly backed out of the room.

Morning broke over the blood-soaked stones and gutters of the ancient city—the black pearl hidden within the deepest depths of the gargantuan forest of Ffushkar. Its inhabitants were either arrayed in the garb of watchmen or lay dead on its streets, save only for women, children, the elderly and the infirm, who watched stoically as the newly-minted soldiers of Plant Man's army gathered up the bestrewn corpses of their compatriots and heaved them onto wooden carts pulled by *biffbaffs* to be burned as infidels in a mass bonfire at the heart of the city. Boys, the youngest of the new recruits, gathered water in buckets and washed the pavement—almost a task in vain, as the blood seeped deeper into the cracks and crevices that formed the veins and arteries of its stone and cement surface. Merchants exempted from conscription began to set up their stalls—business does not shy away from war; nay, it flour-ishes as war proliferates. All seemed well; no voice of opposition arose, no rebellion against the solid authority of the new self-proclaimed king, because he had used the time-old, time-proven, method of silencing opposition—a complete purge of all disconsenting voices.

A clean sweep had been performed, cleansing the city of anyone who claimed loyalty to Asharru. His images were effaced, his psalm-books and liturgies shredded and burned. Everywhere, Tesh-Khan raised the cry of 'Praise the Great Spirit!' or *'Khan Vabakh yôsh min-ish!'* in Shaffi. The revolution had taken on a life of its own, independent of its instigator and fashioner. Tesh-Khan, who had once been a simple and unimportant watchman had, for his linguistic ability and loyalty, become empowered and inspired with a new vision—the vision of one king to rule all of Tremn, Tremna and Shaffu alike, from the Sea of Matvakakan to the Sea of Sogyishifa, from the *Pfetishe Kodffile Ditvagayeng* ('the Isles of the Twelve Seas') to the *Pfetishe Kodffile Gatvayeng* ('the Isles of the Twenty Seas'), from the Great Forest of Nor to the great and untamed desert of Yatvegab; one king, one God, and one mighty army to overturn the existing world order in a flash of violence and terrible retribution. Such a vision inspired him to carry the revolution to its logical conclusion: that loyalty must be absolute and all traces of past beliefs wiped out. It was he that commanded the army as Plant Man slept in Khalam-Sharru's house. It was he that ordered images of Asharru to be eliminated and the bodies of the infidels burned. He went so far as to burn all small shrines, all priestly garments, every trace of the old religion, as the great temple, the Ffâna, smoked and collapsed under its own weight. The water which flowed over the streets cleansed the unclean blood of the disbelievers. The cries of loyalty to the king and of submission to the Great Spirit cleansed the hearts of those who had so recently been captive to a belief-system of deceit and impurity. The Shaffu, once distinguished and infamous for their rapacity and manipulation would now be renowned for their loyalty to the true religion and the true king of all Tremn. Such thoughts motivated Tesh-Khan as he held sway over the city in the absence of his somnolent lord.

Ifunka Kaffa awoke in the arms of his beloved Arwa, who was already awake, her chin on his breast. Her soft, black hair lay gently on his muscular torso. Her eyes, sweet and innocent as a *tvung*-faun, were like deep wells of mystery which drew him into their profoundest depths. She smiled widely, her teeth like white pearls, sweet dimples in her cheeks, her face a brilliant rose, refulgent in the early morning light.

He grabbed her tousled hair and planted a kiss on her soft and fulsome lips.

"Good morning," she said. "Shall we get up?"

"When I have had you once within my arms; is it ever enough?"

"So you don't want to get up then?"

"If you give me another taste of your sweet beauty."

When they had finished thus expressing their love, Ifunka arose from the bed. Arwa led him to the bathroom where she bathed and dressed him in the manner of an obedient Tremna wife. They performed their *kashroim* prayers and, after Ifunka had placed the Verdant Coin in his pocket, they went to the parlour where Ffen, Shem and Ushwan were already eating breakfast served by Meyla—*wish*-root cakes with *bauff*-bee honey, hot *gveg*-leaf tea and *ffentbaff*-cheese.

"Ifunka!" they exclaimed. "You're back!"

"Greetings, brothers," he said amicably. "I have removed the Verdant Coin in order to show you that I am still myself. The coin enhances my power but I *am* myself."

"Dear brother," said Ushwan. "We had thought you driven mad through that coin."

"What you see as madness, I see as necessity," replied Ifunka. "Even as we speak, every living person in this city is a believer in the Great Spirit. Proper conversion to the Right Religion must follow, of course, but behold—not a follower of Asharru remains, and I am the acknowledged king."

"That's just the thing, old boy," said Ushwan. "It is one thing to promote true religion but why have you so aggrandized yourself?"

"Amon-Ra told me that I have a great ancestry," he explained. "He did not give me further information, but that is enough for me to know for now. Look, Ushwan, the Theocracy is an oppressive mockery of the Tamitvar's teachings. Under the emperors and, before them, the High-Kings of Tremn, from Ishmael down to Gven Dakit, and from Emperors Kubba Gven to Kishton, Tremn was a vast and peaceful realm. I want to bring that back so that our children and our children's children may enjoy untold prosperity and happiness, free from oppression and tyranny."

"I agree with you, Ifunka," said Ffen, embracing his friend's proposal. "I have thought a lot about it and I am with you to the end."

"Excellent," Ifunka rejoiced. "Then you shall be my High Steward and Chancellor. You and your wives shall enjoy great prosperity for your loyalty to me. Shem, what think you?"

"I do not condone what you are proposing as it is likely to lead to civil war and untold bloodshed."

"You have spilt blood, brother, and you've enjoyed it."

"How dare you!" Shem burst out in an unusual display of rage.

"Calm yourself!" commanded Arwa. "Do not speak to my husband with disrespect."

"The woman speaks—in a gathering of men!" said Ushwan, half with amusement and half with distaste.

"She is not an ordinary woman, Ushwan," Ifunka defended her. "She is the Queen—remember that! No one may challenge her—even my Steward, Ffen, and my General, Tesh-Khan, must bow the knee before Arwa."

"I speak Tremni slowly and with an accent," Arwa continued. "But I have a voice! I am the servant of my king but you are my servants. I wash his feet but you must wash the floor beneath my feet."

"Prideful nonsense!" Ushwan exclaimed. "Are we to endure such codswallop, old boy?"

"Hold your tongue, Ushwan!" Ifunka commanded in regal tone. "I am your king! I will not punish you but it is evident that we must part ways for now. You may follow my army's progress and we shall speak again when you have humbled yourselves. Come, Steward, let's speak to Tesh-Khan."

"Yes, your Majesty," said Ffen.

Ushwan and Shem stared in disbelief as Ffen, Ifunka and Arwa left the room.

"So much for brotherhood!" said Ushwan.

"So much, indeed!" said Shem, who sighed.

He beckoned Meyla over, who embraced and comforted the sensitive monk.

Before leaving the house, Ifunka took the coin in hand and

transformed into Plant Man, the rough green skin and viny hair taking over his body. Arwa looked at him in wonder, this being the first time she had seen him transform into the being. Outside the door, she found two guards posted, evidently at the command of Tesh-Khan. Ffen followed behind.

"Who ordered this?" asked Plant Man.

"By order of General Tesh-Khan, milord," replied one of the guards in a thick Shaffi accent.

"You shall address me from here on as 'your Majesty'," Plant Man ordered.

"I apologise, your Majesty," replied the guard, abashed.

"This *Tesh-Khan* has assumed power," Ffen remarked.

"For now," said Plant Man. "But he must answer to you, Ffen, as you are my High Steward and Chancellor."

As he departed from the house, the two guards followed behind them. They passed through the streets of Khanshaff to the cries and cheers of its denizens, who greeted their conqueror with great jubilation. He observed that the stones were clean of blood, the bodies of the slaughters having been carried away. The fire no longer burned in the ruined temple and the great *ffaika*'s body had been cut up into chunks and disposed of.

"*Yish lekht-ôn shffu min-ish* (long live the king)!" the citizens cried in Shaffi as he passed.

"Steward—make note: the people of Shaffnâ shall be taught Tremni in schools to be established through the Royal Treasury."

"Noted," said Ffen, even though he had neither pen nor parchment to hand.

His memory was at least as good as any other monk, and monks were trained to memorise numerous *shiffgatv*s of the Tamitvar and other documents. Ffen had memorised about half of the total of Votsku's revelations. As they reached the central plaza of Khanshaff, they saw a vast army which choked the entire width and span of the area, and the surrounding thoroughfares—more than ten thousand soldiers kitted out in the garb of watchmen, carrying swords and axes. More than half, some six thousand, were mounted (three apiece) on large *ffentbaffs*, there being two thousand of these, while the other four thousand sat on the back of baggage and personnel carts pulled by another five hundred baggage *ffentbaffs* carrying eight soldiers apiece. These were smaller, adolescent *ffentbaffs* unsuited for the heat of battle. In addition, a large number of *biffbaffs* carried small loads of baggage, including extra food, tools, tents, and bedding.

"They've already massed, your Majesty!" Ffen exclaimed.

"Indeed, ready for their king to lead them!"

"Make way for the king!" Ffen cried.

Soldiers turned and bowed, the *ffentbaffs* groaning as they were brought to their knees. Tesh-Khan, at the centre of the mass rushed forward to meet his liege lord while *beig*-trumps, curled bronze instruments, sounded at his approach, and *diffka*-drums thundered. These were thin, round marching band drums used by the watchmen during their marches and drills. Tesh-Khan bowed on one knee as he came near.

"All hail His Royal Majesty!" he cried.

"All hail the king!" the army cried in Tremni.

"I taught them that," he said as Plant Man bade him rise.

"You have done much in my absence," said Plant Man.

"Only in line with your commands, my lord," replied Tesh-Khan, in awe of his master.

"Very well, but be it known that I am the ultimate authority on this planet and, after me, Queen Arwa, and then my High Steward and Chancellor, Ffen of Ffash Valley."

"Understood, Your Majesty," acknowledged Tesh-Khan with a bow. "I shall serve them both and obey their orders."

"As you should," said Plant Man with a glance of authority. "I shall now address the crowd. You may translate."

"As you wish, my lord."

Plant Man, Arwa and Ffen walked with dignity and aplomb as they approached the newly-repaired platform at the centre of the army. They ascended to address the crowd. The army cheered until, with his hands raised, they hushed to silence.

"The entire city and all the villages of Shaffnâ are taken," said Tesh-Khan.

"Very good," replied Plant Man. "Now I shall speak to the crowd."

As he raised his voice so that it could be heard and echo across the plaza, all were silent and attendant.

"This is the beginning," he began. "Of a new age—an age of kings, an age of piety, an age of justice!"

"Fto ffônt-go... yundâ khelet-eym-ish–khelet yish-zen-eym, khelet nayat-go-yeym, khelet ffîl-go-yeym!" Tesh-Khan translated.

"This is the beginning of a conquest that shall make the priests of Kubbawa shake with fear!"

"Fto ffônt-go sift-go-yeym-ish kel deisht-ôn nash-ifft-îff predh-bara-zen Khubbâva-yeym khon-ish!"

"We shall not stop; we shall not falter, until the whole of Tremnad falls before the march of this army—the Army of Plant Man!"

"Ffâsh-ôn ftâkh kha khon-ish; baidh-ôn ftâkh kha khon-ish, dhô velôff-ôn akhav Temnâ-yeym dhôm-go makhô-fto-yeym-vôn-ish–Makhô Reym-Shaff-eym!"

The crowd roared and then fell silent as he raised his hands to bequiet them.

"Ignorance shall be swept away! Knowledge, science, technology and industry shall flourish!"

"Shkhâ-yîm yoyn khakhôr-go khon-ish! Amutî-yôn khôr-go ffi khôrkhû ffi ftînâ ffi hultâ khon-ish."

"Theocrats shall be put to the sword and one king shall reign over all the land."

"Khufftemîff-îm teshleyân-paft-zen khon-ish ffi ardhê-yôn akhav nâ-reffû dhi yish khon-ish."

"This is the true glory of Tremn, which is one world under one sun—mighty Vukt—with one religion and one God—the Great Spirit."

"Fto yashffâ guft Tem-eym-ish, kel dhi areft dhi âma–haman Vûkht–dhi ralîshva-yifft ffi dhi Tesh-ifft–Khan Vabakh."

"Today, at noon, we shall begin our march through the density of Ffushkar, to Ffantplain, and then Ritvator, and finally Kubbawa itself—the heart of the theocracy."

"Khulfto, khulfaftîn, ftâkh-an dhôm ffônt-ôn khûzeff-go Shaffu-Meftadhnâ-fferâ-yeym ftâkh khon-ish, Ffamlayn-im ffi Riftator-im, ffi dakhtê, Khubbâva-mônî–ffamsh teshleyân-eym-shivt."

"There, we shall defeat the army of the High-Priest, Shawaku, destroy the theocratic government and I shall be crowned High-King of all Tremn! Praise the Great Spirit and all hail the King!"

"Loft, makhô Ffeshû-Predh-bara-yeym, Shavâkhu, khôney-ôn ftâkh khon-ish ffi teshleyân yûgîff-ôn ffi Ffeshû-Yish akhav Tem-eym zelânîff-îm okh khon-ish! Khan Vabakh yôsh min-ish ffi akhav Yish hey min-ish!"

The soldiers repeated his refrain with a roar so loud that it deafened the ears of all who heard it: *"Khan Vabakh yôsh min-ish ffi akhav Yish hey min-ish* (Praise the Great Spirit and all hail the King)!"

Such an army, massed in one place, determined for victory and conquest, had not been seen in countless millennia upon the face of Tremnad. What existed on the smaller, unexplored continents of the planet, no one in the civilized world knew, but even these Plant Man intended to discover, colonise and subdue (or subdue and colonise, as the case may be). These may have been observed from above during the scientific heyday of *Klet Patsipatveyeng* ('the Age of Emperors'), but they had never been visited or explored by the people of Tremnad, in line with imperial decree. So also had the wild tribes been allowed to proliferate across the east and extreme west of Tremnad—far too long for Plant Man's liking. Beyond the *Varome Sintva* (the 'White Mountains') lay the realm of Nor within the Great Forest of Nor, itself sparsely populated and only vaguely within the authority of the theocracy, ruled over by the Great Lady of Nor, having in its midst the holy Tower of Inta and, beyond Nor, wild tribes of wandering nomads with strange languages, customs, and rituals, moving across rolling plains, perhaps even peopling the oases which are scattered across Matvakakan—the Great Emptiness that stretches from the Sea of Matvakakan to the River Metvura (called *Methura* in Vocatae) and south towards the southern border of Nor and the Isles of the Twenty Seas. Further north, the mysterious Isle of Offlising (*Singoplic* in Vocatae), lay silent to the world and outside the pale of theocratic dominion. The southern islands, those of the Twenty Seas to the southwest and the Twelve Seas to the southeast below Yatvegab, paid nominal tribute to the theocracy, while the scattered tribes in the extreme north of the Old Central Kingdom, bordering on *Kodffil Lehiffavt* (the 'Frozen Sea'), and west beyond the provinces of Kraina and Yalaniuntva, on the Sea of Sogyishifa, roamed free, causing recurrent but slight annoyance and trouble to the Patriarchs of those provinces. Further south, the

Great Desert of Yatvegab stretched on for hundreds of *kobotv*s, sparsely inhabited by exotic tribes of Bedouins who raided and plundered and traded from remote outposts and cities hidden within a realm of sand dunes, blasting heat and pounding sandstorms which had defied even the most ambitious conqueror; their peoples, shrouded in the mists of myth and legend, were far beyond the theocracy's grasp. Yet Ifunka Kaffa's imagination encompassed all of these lands and dominions; his ambition knew no limit and his vision no boundaries. One world, of the many worlds of the Great Spirit, under one king and, after him, his descendants, who would rule a kingdom that would stretch on and endure for eons, until such time as the Lord of the Worlds would wrap up Tremn like a scroll and burn the mountains to dust with exceeding heat, and the oceans dry up, and all be consumed in the fiery wrath of Vukt, the sun of his world.

As he beheld his army amassed before him, he felt powerful, triumphant. All the humiliations of his life, all his pain and loss, faded away before this horde of brutal warriors, all armed and ready to hack and maim their enemies. He raised his arms to calm them and bestill their raging enthusiasm. Tesh-Khan then took over, preparing them for their imminent march—a march that would need to end in the conquest of all that came in their path. Plant Man turned to his wife as they walked through the crowd towards an emerald-green tent that had been put aside for him and his companions at the edge of the plaza.

"Have you ever seen your people so enthused?" he asked her.

"Never, my love. We have been as if in a dream, but you have woken us up!"

"Your Majesty," Ffen thus addressed him. "How shall our armies match up against the Theocracy?"

"The Theocracy is weak; soft with much complaisance. What does their army fight—wild tribesmen on the frontiers of Kraina and Yalaniuntva? We have a mission—a goal. What do they have?"

"I estimate that the Theocracy has about twelve thousand regular troops, based on what I have read. But each city has a city guard proportionate to its size, and the Theocracy could raise a hundred thousand troops if it so wishes. Ffantplain is a city of about twenty-five thousand inhabitants. As such, it must have a guard of around one thousand and perhaps twice as many reserves."

"Once we have conquered the city," Plant Man replied. "We shall enlist its men, just as we have enlisted these Shaffu. We shall be unstoppable."

"Very well," said Ffen. "And what shall we do with Shem and Ushwan?"

"They may follow us to Kubbawa. I imagine they'll have changed their minds once the Theocracy has toppled to dust."

Tesh-Khan entered the tent.

"All the preparations are underway, your Majesty," he reported. "We will be ready to march on schedule."

"Excellent," replied Plant Man. "Ffen, I have a special task for you. You are to go with the General and meet with his commanders—you have selected commanders and lieutenants, haven't you"—Tesh-Khan nodded—"And teach them the Testimony of Faith. They will then teach it to their subordinates and so on. I want the whole army to embrace the Right Religion before we march; otherwise, their souls shall be imperilled should any of them die in battle."

"Very well, your Majesty," said Ffen as the two of them left the tent.

Plant Man remained alone with Arwa; he sat on a polished wooden chair with a rattan back while she sat on one beside him. He held her hand gently and she squeezed his.

"The others don't see your eyes," she said. He turned to her.

"My eyes?"

"You're sad."

"Sad?" He frowned.

"You still feel the pain of your uncle and your aunt's death."

"I do feel it," he replied. "It is always with me; all the pain and tribulation of my life is with me. That you see it surprises me; I have bottled it all up deep within my soul."

"You cannot bottle up such fierce emotion. It will bleed out and then explode."

"Whatever wrath you see me evince," he reassured her. "It shall never be directed at you, my sweet *gebnav*-rose. You are more precious to me than my own self. I desire to see a crown on your head more than I do on my own. Great Spirit be praised! You are the greatest bounty in my life. Without you, I would only see blackness and despair on every horizon. You are my inspiration—my hope!"

"You have given me something to love and to dream for," she replied in kind. "For whatever you do, my heart belongs to you."

He kissed her.

An hour before noon, Plant Man's army began to take formation for the march. He had ordered that the remainder of the Temple be demolished thoroughly. The work was well under way as Ffen, along with a staff of clerks he had gathered—seven in number—who formed his permanent retinue, took an accounting of the Treasury, made note of and valued the coins (mostly *patsims*, *patsimad*s, gold *zelana*s, silver *zitv*s, and bronze *ffitsa*s), all the gold, diamonds, rubies, sapphires, amethysts, and gems, platinum, silver, precious weapons and armour, plates and cutlery (porcelain and bone china). He estimated the total value as one hundred and twenty-nine million *patsimad*s, of which Plant Man allowed fifty million to remain as the city treasury, and seventy-nine million to be carted off in the supply wagons in order to fund his military campaign and build his new empire. When all was set and ready, Plant Man summoned his friends, Ushwan, Shem and Meyla, and offered for them to share his howdah—a carriage which is positioned on the back of a *ffentbaff*, which they politely declined to do. He therefore gave them a similar howdah behind the royal one. Called a *ffentwa* in Tremni, the howdah contained scarlet-red plush leather seats (two rows), covered with a canvas roof situated upon a thick, finely-embroidered rug to protect the *ffentbaff*'s back, called a *gilba*, while a driver sat on the beast's enormous neck. The leather seats on Plant Man's *ffentwa* were emerald green, as was the canvas roof, at the pinnacle of which there was hoisted a royal flag.

"Do you like it?" asked Ffen.

"Magnificent!" Plant Man rejoiced.

"How did you make it?"

"I found the best embroiderer in Khanshaff. It took them only two hours but it came out beautifully. I've had them make a standard as well."

This was carried by a sturdy warrior, seven-foot tall, with angular features and hawk-like eyes.

"What the Great Spirit wills!" he uttered.

Both the flag and standard were light-green with a brown *kay*-owl in the centre. Its wings were outspread, its head face on, beak open, claws extended. Two runes were visible, one in either of the top corners: Minwa (*Manu* in Vocatae), which represents the i or y sounds, and Latis (*Latus* in Vocatae), which represents the c or k sound. Together, these initials stood for Ifunka Kaffa. Minwa has the shape of an angular backwards-facing R while Latis is the reverse, such that they formed a perfect symmetry.

Mounting the *ffentwa* with Arwa and Ffen (who sat in the back row), Ifunka stood on the *ffentbaff*'s neck behind the driver and gave the signal to proceed.

"To destiny, to the conquest of Tremn and the overthrow of the Theocracy!"

He unsheathed his sword and held it aloft.

"To the one true King of Tremn! In the Name of the Great Spirit, ride! Ride! Ride!"

"Akhav Yish hey min-ish! Akhav Khan Vabakh yôsh min-ish (All hail the King! All praise the Great Spirit)!" they echoed in Shaffi.

The royal *ffentbaff* was an enormous beast, four *okshas* high and six long, with a great woolly mane, legs like trunks, a long wispy tail, huge eyes buttressed by sharp cheekbones, wide nostrils and huge, mashing teeth. Its thick trunk, like a fifth limb, curled upwards to emit a loud, thunderous bellow, while its pearl-white curled tusks shone in the midday sun. Such a sight, two thousand mounted *ffentbaffs* and five hundred in train, carrying an army of thousands more, had not been seen since the end of the Empire of Tremn and the beginning of the Holy Theocracy, marked by the final great battle, the Battle of the Three Kings. At that battle, in the open plains of Nubrak in a place called Ardesi (meaning 'three kings'), the mighty army of Kishton, the last Emperor of Tremn, faced the armies of Kraina and Ritvator, who had come out in aid of the Pretender, Prince Ush—the emperor's full-brother. This foolhardy and self-obsessed prince had styled himself with the presumptuous title of 'Emperor Kletush the Second'. He was supported by King Pamitffta of Kraina, known to his enemies as *Entva Kveffi* (the 'Evil One'), as well as King Shegwa of Ritvator and Kvel, Head of the House of Kven. When all the armies had assembled, the Emperor's troops numbered some six hundred thousand, facing off against two hundred and eighty thousand Biknogs of Kraina, two hundred thousand of Ritvator and a hundred thousand from the House of Kven, aided by fifty thousand wild tribesmen—thus more than six hundred and twenty thousand soldiers—one million, two hundred thousand Tremna in all. Each side had a cavalry of at least eight thousand mounted *ffentbaffs*. In addition to the *biffbaffs* of the baggage trains, the forces of the Pretender had more than a thousand mounted *sheshkabaffs*—tall desert beasts of burden—and a dozen huge *meshtobishbaffs* with twelve-legs each and fierce horns, fangs and tails.

Ffen recounted the tale of the battle as they approached the southern gate of Khanshaff, recalling, in vivid detail, how the two armies amassed, with the principal protagonists at each head armoured and arrayed in unprecedented splendour and majesty. Kishton, with his golden helm and breast-plate, his hair long black and smooth, with great mustachios and tuft of beard waving in the gentle breeze, his ancient spear, *Mitvul Kubara* (the 'Holy Sceptre'), held aloft, while his brown-haired son Prince *Ishmael Ffendongarikipatv* (the 'People's Defender') carried *Mitviksa Tsilelyeng*, the Spear of the House of Tsilel; Prince Kish carried the sword, Prince Kubba the mace, Prince Trel the bow and arrow, and Prince Ushwan the long-sword. Glorious and long as this battle was, its results were all too tragic, with the two armies, equally matched, both annihilated, and all the best blood and the finest fruits of manhood the world had ever seen utterly spent. So much blood soaked into the soil that it is said that 'the grass grows greenest on the plain of Ardesi'. With the Pretender and his allies killed and Kishton's army wasted, and his body badly wounded, his daughter Revna, who had taken the Pretender's bastard son Kabanik as her spouse, had fled to *Pash Shiwev* (i.e. 'Greenleaf'), a small monastic village in Ritvator Province. Having burnt down the monastery and all its monks within, Kishton found that his daughter had fled further afield, along with her child, Kabanik's heir, and the seven original copies of the first four chapters of the Holy Tamitvar, which had been kept safe within the monastery since the time of Votsku. When he eventually found his daughter in the Great Forest of Ffushkar, Kishton sliced off her head and was going to impale his grandson, when a beam of light blinded him, and he heard the voice of Amon-Ra, who warned him not to slay the babe and banished the House of Tsilel "until the end, when Ishmael shall return". Together with his five sons, the Emperor Kishton boarded a great sky-ship and sailed away into the stars—or so the legend goes.

"What do you think became of Revna's child?" asked Plant Man.

"I don't know," said Ffen. "Perhaps you are of his line?"

"I should hope not," he replied. "For that would make me the heir of Kabanik, who was the bastard son of Prince Ush. Ush was of the House of Tsilel which was exiled by Amon-Ra. As such, I cannot be of the line of Tsilel or it would invalidate my kingship."

"You could be a descendent of King Ishmael the Great, though," Ffen continued. "Through another line. And who knows if the babe of Revna was a boy. It could have been a girl and you a descendant nonetheless, as a house is defined by its male line."

"An interesting theory," said Plant Man. "But Amon-Ra's wisdom is quite inscrutable to me. Perhaps he will reveal my true lineage in good time."

The army marched north over the drawbridge, across the moat and into the Great Forest of Ffushkar. As they entered the tight-knit woods, the ground rumbled as *ffaika* emerged to prey upon them. Hundreds of soldiers cast lances into the beasts, slaying them as they marched onwards, their oozy blood leaking across the forest floor. The *beig*-trumps sounded, the *diffka*-drums beat incessantly, the massive formation progressed, tightly-formed and well-aware of the dangers of worms, *shan*, clay men and *yeshka*s, shaking the ground and toppling saplings and even grown trees under the crushing weight and pounding footsteps of the *ffentbaff*s. *Meish* and *wigwaff*s, *ffig*s and *ffubish*es fled and dispersed, *tvung*-deer scattered and *ffentwash*-bishon hid themselves from its juggernaut like progression. They crushed globule-thrusters underfoot while the *shan* themselves avoided the immense force of arms. At some distance, on a small hill, there stood two figures, unnaturally resplendent and refulgent, arrayed in wondrous flowing robes and a halo of light. Their exact figures and faces were obscured by the glow, but they were not *shan* nor, in fact, were they creatures of Tremn at all.

"*Cumi, ves tuobuin aerbon maituictae avaraso* (Him, what thinkest thou of the coin-bearer)?" said one.

"*Sohrhab daiamiccum le, Ramaen* (he is full of rage, Worrier)," replied the other.

"*Aquan iout Niato Ramoslegionoic ca leso* (is it not time for the Holy Theocracy to fall)?"

"*Isva, avium phantosisin Temic vaeroncacum vaiascon. Aersilai Silelciu deanatmon phespha bav celphic arretap lis* (perhaps, but he shall bathe the cities of Tremn in blood. We banished the heirs of Tsilel to give this world peace)."

"*Celphic pretel Solis elenmon le vesutam. Cansaphuscumcum bahaemon cub Mirad Maitucumapcum lison. Cum deatovut Aerd Maelic phelic initog nibaint lemon ca leso* (Amon-Ra hath chosen this monk for a purpose. He guided him to Khanshaff and gave him the Verdant Coin. Is he not the return of Ishmael, whose coming was prophesied)?"

"*Celph Maraquineam bobo le. Solisciuhrhon Aerd pheum iumcumhrhon bobogai Maraquinecimcum cuint hrhuba* (that is for the Legion Council to decide. Amon-Ra is our king but he must explain his decisions to the Council)."

"*Leci cadu Iphunca Capha phada Candaspu boboint lecon* (then shall the fate of Ifunka Kaffa, Son of Kandaspu, be decided)."

"*Raval, Ramaen—raval* (even so, Worrier—even so)."

Plant Man thought he could see a faint glow on the hilltop, but it vanished as he gazed upon it. 'A trick of the eye', he said to himself as his *ffentbaff* grunted, grabbing a tree bole with its mighty trunk, ripping it from the ground and tossing it aside like a mere twig. After a short while, they approached the woods of Jyoff. An arrow burst through the air and lodged itself in Plant Man's shoulder. Unfazed and unhurt, he ripped the arrow out and challenged the assailant.

"Who dares attack the King of all Tremn?"

"Bastard Shaffu!" screamed a voice. "Ye've come to take me at last! Come on, then! I'll kill you all!"

It was Jyoff Wagva himself, unaware that Ifunka and Shem had returned.

"Death to the Shaffu!" he cried.

Arrows flew left and right, killing Shaffu warriors, knocking them from their *ffentwa*s. Plant Man hid Arwa behind him. As the army retaliated, Plant Man cried "Stop!" and they ceased.

"You too, forest man!" he ordered.

"Why should I?" Jyoff cried.

"For it is I, Ifunka Kaffa, returned!"

∼୬

CHAPTER XXII.

The Forest March

~

"Ifunka!" Jyoff cried.

The bedraggled recluse emerged from behind a tree bole.

"Do not harm him!" Plant Man commanded. "Behold, I entered Khanshaff, slew its rulers, banished the false god Asharru and was blessed by Amon-Ra with suzerainty over the plant kingdom. I have slain all the followers of Asharru and converted the remaining Shaffu to the Right Religion. This is my army; I am heading to Kubbawa to crush the Theocracy."

"Inta's beard!" the hermit cried. "Art thou speaking true? Such a revolution of events is scarce credible. I would fancy thee mad if I were not beholding this self-same army with my very eyes. Ifunka the monk, a conqueror of men! How the weak are exalted and the proud fallen, as the Tamitvar says!"

"The followers of the Tamitvar are never weak," replied Plant Man. "Come, Jyoff; these are not the Shaffu you remember. These are the Army of Plant Man. We are an army of God under one king, with one goal: the overthrow of the theocracy and the unification of all Tremn. Is that not a lofty goal?"

"Thou wantest me to join thee? By thunder!" the man stomped as he spoke, as if he were the living embodiment of a *ffentbaff* paw. "And give up my forest home—my freedom?"

"No man has freedom as long as the oppressive clerics reign over Tremn. Thou canst liberate all of Tremn if thou join me."

"Join thee and those Shaffu scum?" He pointed widely at the army.

"Soldiers of the good cause," Plant Man corrected him. "Look, Jyoff, an army moves like a river. Join us now or we shall pass on by, as shall glory and honour. Live in peace here in the forest depths and die alone, or, come with us and be forever immortalized in the annals of Tremn."

Jyoff pondered the proposition for a few moments and then nodded to himself.

"The Theocracy," he muttered. "Is like a cancer on the face of this land. I will join you."

Plant Man signalled for his *ffentbaff* to be lowered while Jyoff, carrying on the clothes on his back and his bow, arrow and quiver, climbed aboard the *ffentwa* and sat beside Ffen. The *ffentbaff* grunted as it rose again.

"Where's Shem?" asked Jyoff.

"He's a bit further back," Plant Man replied matter-of-factly. "He and Brother Ushwan do not support our war because they feel I am mad with power."

"All conquerors are mad with power," Jyoff opined. "But that doesn't mean they're not justified. Ishmael the Great was justified; Kubba Gven was justified; Kishton was justified."

"Even though Amon-Ra exiled him from the world?"

"So they say," replied Jyoff. "But he was only translated to another place. There are worlds out there, suspended in the sky. Every star is a sun, like Vukt, my father told me, and each one has its planets, just like Tremn. Somewhere out there the heirs of Tsilel can be found."

"Who was Tsilel?" asked Arwa in her distinctive accent.

"A woman!" exclaimed Jyoff. "And a Shaffu one at that! Long has it been seen I have gazed upon the feminine type."

"Be careful, Jyoff; this is my queen, Arwa."

"Very pleased to meet thee," he greeted her.

"The pleasure is mine," she replied politely.

"My wife is the ruler of Tremn in my absence," Plant Man clarified. "So treat her with the utmost deference and respect."

"And what of my question?" she persisted.

"Ah, yes," Plant Man began. "I have read something of the history of the Age of Kings and its origins. Tsilel was the eldest of the sons of Ishmael the Great and his wife, Queen Gwel. The people greatly rejoiced at his birth, calling him *Tvam Ayalatsa* ('Rejoice for him') but, when he grew up, he proved to be power-hungry, capricious and cruel, so Ishmael chose his youngest son, Prince Mael, whose mother was another wife, Queen Rel, to be his heir, because he was loyal, hard-working and humble. When he became High-King at the age of two hundred and fifty, he assumed the regnal name of Ishmael *Gan* ('Ishmael the Second'), though many called him *Tsabt* ('the Short'). Prince Tsilel, on the other hand, was made Duke of Wafftayunda, which title passed to all of his heirs until his descendant Kubba became Kubba Gven, the first Emperor of Tremn, but that's another story."

"So, two families have ruled Tremn?" asked Arwa.

"The heirs of Ishmael *Gan* ruled as kings until Gven *Dakit* ('Gven the Last') and then the heirs of Tsilel ruled until Kishton, but now the High-Priests hold power—and these are the descendants of the Seer, Votsku. Baku son of Ffal was the first High-Priest to bear the title of *amlegyanoshai* (i.e. 'Head of the Theocracy') while the current, Shawaku son of Ffen, is the eleventh Head. The High-Priests are descendants of the royal and imperial families, however, through female lines. It is well known as the Princess Mana, a daughter of Kishton, married Baku while his great-grandfather, Wawaku, married Princess Kvaid, who was the youngest granddaughter of Kubba Gven. Likewise, the High-Priest Ushwan, three generations earlier, married Princess Yimash, a daughter of King Gwel *Amta*."

"Your memory is almost as capacious as mine, your Majesty," Ffen remarked.

"Thank you, Steward."

"The descendants of Ishmael the Great are numerous," added Jyoff. "How many there be only the Great Spirit knows, but the total number must be in the thousands, at least in the direct male line."

"Indeed," agreed Plant Man. "The Age of Kings, if I remember correctly, lasted one thousand, one hundred and fifty-five years, from the reign of Ishmael the Great until the end of King Gven's reign. There was an interregnum of about one hundred and seven years, followed by the beginning of the Age of Emperors, when Kubba Gven took up the throne. There were four emperors: Kubba Gven, Gavidron, Kletush and Kishton, with the last of these going into exile in the fifty-ninth century from *Kultvum Dian* (the 'First Day'). How long is that Ffen?"

"The Age of Emperors lasted one thousand and ninety-four years, your Majesty. Kishton was exiled in the year five thousand, eight hundred and eighteen from *Kultvum Dian*. It is now the year seven thousand, nine hundred and ninety-nine, so roughly two thousand, one hundred and thirty-one years have passed since the end of the empire and four thousand, four hundred and eighty-seven since the beginning of the reign of King Ishmael the Great."

"You see?" observed Plant Man. "The year eight thousand is well-nigh upon us. That is the year that Kubbawa shall fall and the theocracy perish. Then shall the new Age of Kings dawn."

"Indeed," said Ffen. "It's now the month of Taryam, if I haven't lost count of time. We are nearing the end of *Gilwa* season ('late autumn'), with *Leffwa* ('winter') beginning in only a few short days. That leaves five months—less than eighty days—until the new year."

"Excellent," Plant Man remarked. "Then we shall endeavour to conquer the three cities within that time."

The planet Tremn circles Vukt in an orbit which lasts three hundred and seventy-five days, roughly ten more than earth's own orbit. The inhabitants of Tremnad divide this year into five seasons of seventy-five days each: *Raimwa* (apring), *Ashwa* (summer), *Ffalwa* (cool/mild season), *Gilwa* (late autumn) and *Leffwa* (winter). Each of these is, in turn, divided into five months, with a total of twenty-five months in the year, and each month consisting of fifteen days. Each month has a name, as does each day of the month, while a Tremna week consists of five days (there being three weeks in each month). The days of the week are numbered according to the ordinal numbers (first, second, third, fourth, and fifth respectively). The years are counted from the *Kultvum Dian*—the First Day—which is the traditional date of the beginning of the world or, rather, when Inta (i.e. the 'Him') first set foot on Tremn, along with the Seven Fathers of Tremn and the Seven Mothers of Tremn, who were the traditional ancestors of the entire Tremna population. The veracity of this story and how the years were calculated, no man knew for certain—only that the ancestors told the story of Inta and that the Tower of Inta could be found in the depths of the Great Forest of Nor. For official documents, royal and imperial decrees, and the diktats of the theocracy, the name of the ruler (whether it be the king, emperor or head of the theocracy) and the year of his reign were used. Thus, the present year was Shawaku CCVII, it being the two hundred and seventh year of Shawaku's reign as High-Priest, Archbishop of Kubbawa and Head of the Theocracy.

"It's time for *kashatvin* (the midday prayer), your majesty," observed Ffen.

"We will stop at Lake Ffush and there perform it, along with the *kashashom* (afternoon prayer) and other missed prayers," replied Plant Man.

The army marched relentlessly, without pause, for another seven hours. Day gave way to night and the *ffentbaff*-drivers lit torches to guide the way. The *shan* could be seen occasionally glimmering in the pitch blackness of the surrounding woods but they dared not attack the massive force. They continued on till midnight and, even then, they had not reached the water's edge. Scouts went ahead and reported that they were now less than a *tvinshaff* distant from the lake's edge. Two hours would suffice to cover the distance, so they pressed on, finally reaching the lake at around the third hour after midnight. They halted, gathered water for ablutions and performed the prayers they had missed, including the *kashofftishatvin* (the midnight prayer), facing the far-distant Tower of Inta in the west. Then they set up campfires to cook a meal of *pengiffmi* with *brakshogim* bread and hot, sweet *gveg*-leaf tea, while several thousand soldiers took axe to bole and hewed down hundreds and hundreds of trees, split them in half and bound them together with rope to form rafts and barges in order to transport the army to the opposite side of the lake. This task took upwards of four hours, with soldiers in rotation, some eating and resting while others hacked, hewed, split and bound the rafts together. Plant Man surveyed the troops, walking among them and observing their operations. He watched them sing old songs of Khanshaff's ancient past in Shaffi, while talented bards among them composed new odes to the king of all

179

Tremn and his mighty army which marched over the whole face of the land. He walked with Arwa hand-in-hand, followed by Ffen, and then Jyoff, who sighed at the decimation of the surrounding forest—but he said nothing, as he knew that loyalty to the new king was a matter of life and death. Shem, Ushwan and Meyla stayed close together, gazing out upon the moon-glittering waters of the lake, which shone and glowed with the subtle brilliance of the twin primary moons of Tremn, Ffash and Tvash, and the lesser moon, Obish, recounted their encounter with the lake-worm and wondered how Ffen had survived the crossing.

"I expect he used a small boat and moved slowly," Ushwan opined. "In my case, the Shaffu took a longer route along the lake's edge, but that is impractical for such a huge army."

"We'll be reaching the village of Ffush soon," said Shem. "That's where Tvem lives. He taught us the nine-fold path and informed us about the *mimra*, the force which surrounds and embraces all things, like a blanket."

"Yes, or a field," said Ushwan. "I have heard something about it, actually, in the forbidden section of the Great Library of Kubbawa."

"Forbidden section?"

"Yes, where they store books deemed inappropriate or subversive."

"How did you access it?"

"I had my connections," he explained. "After all, I do belong to the gentry—that middling class betwixt the aristocracy and the common plebeians. My father, Sir Gven Potvek, was a Knight of Inta, the holy order which protects and defends the theocratic government. He was also a descendant of the Dukes of Tremael, through numerous genera-tions, but we are not even closely related to the current Protector."

"What have you learnt from the library?" asked Shem.

"From the forbidden section? Much that they would not have people know: incidents of corruption, nepotism and intrigue, stories of suppression and persecution of monarchists (imperial or otherwise), tales of pretenders to the throne who were silenced or executed in the most gruesome manner—even the *shegbash*."

When the barges and rafts had been constructed, the army embarked upon their voyage, floating across the cool waters of the lake. Already the air was cool and crisp, like the beginning of winter. The army looked uneasily at the surface, aware that, at any moment, a lake-worm could emerge and attack them. Though Shem and Ifunka had managed to slay the lake worm that had attacked them, there were usually more than one in each lake. About midway across the water, there was a bulge in the distance—an enormous head and neck lifting out of the water, only to come crashing down again in an explosion of foam and bubbles. Waves ripped across the lake-face, knocking several of the smaller *ffent-baff*s and *biffbaff*s into the cold depths below. The drivers cried out in confusion while some of the troops, being strapped into their saddles, were pulled down by their beasts' weight to their watery graves below.

"Hold fast!" Tesh-Khan ordered.

"Steady!" cried Plant Man. "She's trying to confuse us—knock us off guard!"

Even as he spoke these words, the worm burst from the water behind them and nearly toppled the royal *ffentbaff*. Quickly reacting to the situation, he shot scores of vines onto the barge, holding it in place and preventing its passengers from falling out. The worm flailed to and fro, knocking *ffentbaff*s while arrows and spears bounced off its thick, scaly hide. The serpent's mouth fixed upon a large *ffentbaff*-cow, sunk its teeth deep into the beast's muscle and bone and, while it bellowed pitifully, dragged it into the lake depths.

"Calm yourselves!" Plant Man commanded as the troops continued to fling spears and lances into the water to no end.

Climbing onto the *ffentbaff*'s neck, he leapt into the water below. Spurting forth tentacle-like vines, he glided through the water like a graceful jellyfish, using the vines to push the water behind him and propel forwards. The serpent whirled round and surged towards him in a vicious attack, mouth wide open and razor-sharp teeth and gums visible. Rushing into the vile creature, its jaws extending wide to take him in, Plant Man grabbed hold of its neck and latched on, wrapping it in a coil of vines—sharp with flesh-piercing and muscle-rending thorns. Clouds of blood engulfed the beast as it struggled, throwing its neck to and fro in the lake-water, trying to break free from its pursuer's iron hold—but he held fast, undeterred, implacable, undaunted, digging in deeper and deeper—yet the thick, muscular neck of the monster would not break, nor would it bleed out due to its immense proportions and humongous vital system. Its head burst through the water, lifting Plant

Man up into the brisk night air, revealing itself to the onfloating army, exposing itself to a hail of arrows and javelins which dug into its thick and scaly hide, unable to hit any of its vital organs.

Focusing his mental energy on the surrounding *mimra*, Plant Man sensed some *woksh*-trees firmly rooted into the lake-bed. These were large trees, more than ten to fifty *oksha*s in height with roots buried as deep as a *kobotv* into the beds of seas, lakes and oceans; *woksha*s could even be found in the depths of great rivers such as the Sogyishifa, absorbing nutrients from their rich deposits. Mostly white with light-green leaves, these have thick bark and wide boles, flexible branches with thorny twigs, which support vast and unusual underwater ecosystems. Dead *woksh*-trees become the basis of coral reefs and provide shelter for numerous underwater herbivores, as well as many predators, including vicious water spiders—*binkvish*-spiders—which have a white hue, enabling them to blend in with the *woksh*-trees' bark, despite their enormous size (some grow to an *oksha* or more in length). Summoning a particularly wide and large bole from the lake-bed, it grew tall and yet even thicker, shooting up like a rocket and hitting the serpent in its belly. Its hands (branches and twigs) wrapped around the fat girth of the monster and pulled it down to the lake-bottom, some one hundred *oksha*s below. Squeezed to death, its innards burst out, its ribs cracked and its flesh ripped apart. Plant Man emerged from the water triumphant—his army breathing a sigh of relief as they helped him up and back onto his *ffentbaff*.

"The serpent is dead!" he cried, to the lustrous roar of his soldiers.

"I was worried," said Arwa, her eyes tender with love and concern.

"Worry not! I am made of strength," he replied.

Soon they reached the other shore, with Tvem's manor in view. Disembarking in vast numbers, the Lord of the Manor emerged and stood before them. Carrying his staff in hand, he approached the thronging masses with a proprietorial mien and a booming voice.

"What brings these savages to my house!" he cried. "I am Tvem Hiff, Lord of this lake and this Manor."

"It is I," Plant Man responded, leaping off his *ffentbaff* and standing before him. "Ifunka Kaffa. I have returned, by the grace of the Great Spirit."

"Ifunka?" he was astonished.

"Indeed!" cried Jyoff. "I have not seen thee for ages."

"Jyoff Wagva?" exclaimed Tvem. "But thou art an inveterate enemy of the Shaffu, as art thou, Ifunka."

"Much has changed," Plant Man continued. "These are not the same Shaffu who have ravaged the land aforetime. These are the Army of Plant Man, who bear aloft my standard and march in my name. I pray thee, Lord Tvem, let us camp near thy manor."

"I taught thee to follow the nine-fold path, not to raise an army and conquer enemies."

"I have not forgotten thy wisdom," he replied. "Rather, I honour it. Behold, I have cleansed Khanshaff of evil, banished the false god, Asharru, and have been honoured by Amon-Ra with the power to control the plant kingdom through the agency of the Verdant Coin."

"Amon-Ra rarely interferes in the affairs of men," Tvem observed. "Not since Kishton's exile has he directly intervened in our world. Some have taken it as a sign that the Legion favours the Holy Theocracy; others have said the opposite. If he has given thee such power, then truly no force shall be able to withstand thee."

"What sayest thou, then, lord?"

"Dost thou seek vengeance or justice?"

"I have slaughtered many in the name of the Right Religion, but I seek only justice and righteousness."

"I fear your words are as light as a *ffubish*," Tvem replied. "I shall not join you, but you may camp here."

Plant Man signalled to Tesh-Khan, who ordered the army to make camp. Thousands of *ffentbaffs* grunted in a cacophony of sound, *biffbaffs* brayed, soldiers loudly called commands, arranged supplies, set up tents, formed temporary defences out of the wooden planks and beams of the rafts and barges, started campfires, began cooking vegetable stews, boiling pots of tea, quick-bread—thin, unleavened round loaves called *ragsh*, *pengiffmi* and dried fruits. Camp songs reverberated, the *mimgeff*-lute sounded, and the hum of chatter extended across three *kobotv*s of field, to the edge of the forest. There, guards were on patrol, ready for any *yeshka*, clay-man or *shan* that might approach the camp. The Lord of Ffush invited Plant Man, Arwa, Meyla, Shem, Ushwan and General Tesh-Khan, to his manor, where they sat around the hearth, eyeing one another uncertainly. Shem, Ushwan and Meyla sat on one side while Plant Man, Ffen, Tesh-Khan and Arwa sat on the other—two opposing factions which regarded one another with awkwardness. Tvem sat at the head, observing both parties silently, while Jyoff sat opposite him.

"Are ye all well?" Tvem asked.

"Yes," replied Plant Man, while the others nodded.

"Then what's this? There's no harmony."

"Harmony?" asked Shem. "We desire peace and spirituality whilst those—" he pointed to the opposing party. "Will bring Tremn to civil war and destruction."

"I bring the world unity and abiding peace under the reign of one king," Plant Man declared.

"Question not the glorious majesty of the true king of all Tremn!" Tesh-Khan cried.

"Calm yourselves!" Tvem command. "Positive will is essential—only by opposing negativity can true results be obtained. As the eighth teaching states: 'All negative energy can be opposed and overcome by positive energy, which is stronger and more effective'."

"Which of us is right?" asked Ushwan. "Is it right to use force of arms to destroy the theocracy and assert kingship?"

"Truth must prevail over falsehood," replied Tvem cryptically.

"What does that mean?" asked Shem. "*Who* is right?"

"What is the seventh teaching?" he asked them.

"Sacrifice and determination are the foundations of success and attainment," Shem replied.

"Even so," continued Tvem. "Without sacrifice, success is unattainable. When blood is spilt, great forces are unleashed into the world; not the blood of the enemy, but the blood of the seeker in attainment of his goal. To achieve that which is higher, we must shed that which is lower."

"But what of the innocents who shall die in the oncoming war?" asked Ushwan. "They do not choose to sacrifice themselves."

"The *Ontva Navein*—the nine-fold path—is not partisan. It does not pertain to one party or one cause. It simply holds that, as the eighth teaching states, 'all negative energy can be opposed and overcome by positive energy'. If Ifunka's energy be positive, it will overcome the forces of negativity. If he be truly supported by Amon-Ra, the King of the Legion, who watches over the affairs of Tremn and many other worlds, then perhaps he is right. If he seeks vengeance, however, and mastery over others, that is negative and the *mimra* shall not be in his favour. As the fourth teaching states, 'light, energy and will are of one essence'. Rememberest thou the practical implication of this teaching, Shem?"

"That, if we have will, we can succeed," Shem repeated.

"Indeed. All things belong to one substance which exists within the field which encompasses reality—the *mimra*. Everything we see in existence is the result of interactions within the *mimra*—the effects of positive and negative will, with the positive overcoming and nullifying the negative. Positive will can, furthermore, transform reality by effecting positive results."

"I seek kingship because it has been thrust upon me," argued Plant Man. "It is positive to uphold one's duty—one's mission in life."

"That makes no sense," Ushwan protested. "You cannot seek what is given to you."

"Amon-Ra gave me the Verdant Coin. I have been chosen for a mission: to free Tremn from tyranny and oppression, to destroy falsehood and superstition, to annihilate the Theocracy and re-establish the natural order of the world and cleanse the Right Religion from hypocrisy and deceit! If there is to be a king, who else should it be?"

"Calm yourselves, brothers—and sisters," Tvem urged, though the two women were silent. "The ninth teaching is this: 'there is no power and no force greater than that of unity, and unity springs from loving-kindness'. Are ye not friends? Shem and Ifunka, ye twain did come to me in search of Brother Ushwan, whom ye love as ye love your own selves. Ffen, I met thee on thy way to rescue Ifunka and Shem. Love is the greatest force in existence; it bestirs the inner depths of the soul; it radiates through the medium of the *mimra*; it burns away the veils of delusion and idle fancy; it unifies opposing elements, heals the wounds of discord and strife, cements the bonds of fraternity and camaraderie and binds all divergent paths into one path. A kingdom founded upon hatred and disunity cannot long endure. One founded upon love and unity is everlasting. Heal your divisions, resolve your differences, and no force on Tremn shall be able to stop you."

These words stirred their consciences and bestilled their antagonism.

"Ifunka," said Shem. "I shall follow you, if you truly seek justice."

"As will I," said Ushwan.

"Meyla?" Arwa called her.

"I follow," she replied.

"I forgive you all," said Plant Man. "I promise you that I am not mad with power—I seek to unify Tremn for the greater good."

"Very well," said Ushwan. "Tvem's wise words have dispelled my doubts. I am with you."

"Roaring *yeshka*s!" exclaimed Jyoff—his interjections could mean anything, so the companions eyed him curiously as he spoke. "That is very well, isn't it? We could hardly hope to bring the blasted theocrats to their knees if we were ourselves wobbly in disposition."

"Jyoff, son of Jyem," Tvem addressed him. "You're as obscure in your verbiage as a *shan* is opaque."

"I pride myself in confoundment," he chuckled. "But dost thou aver, my lord, that we have right on our side?"

The two had not met for many years but the forest folk knew one another well, as they were few in number and dependent on cooperation for trade in goods and arms. Long ago, the people of Tvak, Ffush and Ffash had exchanged women exogamously, and travelled to one another's villages for commerce, festivals and general social intercourse. Depopulated due to the Shaffu, they had a common animosity against both them and the Theocracy. With the Shaffu now tamed, only one common enemy remained—the Theocracy. Tvem had long staved off the clay men and Shaffu raiders, even as Jyoff had thinned them out in the purlieus of Khanshaff. Now, his furrowed brow evinced an intensity of concentration as he pondered upon the subject.

"I can only declare," said Tvem at last. "That the issue is undecided. Unless the true heir of Ishmael is made known, I cannot support a revolution. The heirs of Tsilel have been banished, so only the heir of Ishmael Gan, the second High-King, can rule. Who is thy father, Ifunka?"

"All I know is the name: Kandaspu."

"Of which House—of which clan?"

"I'm afraid I do not know."

"*Kanda spu*, the 'long nose'," Tvem pondered. "An uncommon name in this region. What of thy mother?"

"Her name was Sapya of Clan Bishkwa, of the line of Votsku. She abandoned me as a child, leaving me with my uncle, Matuka Wobga."

"The House of Avis," Tvem observed. "Strange, indeed, that a descendant of the priestly line should wish to overthrow the Theocracy."

"Whatever my ancestry," he replied. "Amon-Ra chose me for the Verdant Coin and told me that my pedigree is great."

"That could mean anything," said Ushwan. "You could be the heir of Kabanik, or even of a line of chiefs from the Isle of Offlising, descended from their ancient king, Iasata. We won't know for certain unless we find out who Kandaspu was and where he came from."

"The Great Spirit knows," said Tvem. "So, as I said before, I cannot endorse your struggle. I can only warn you not to seek vengeance and hatred, but only justice and righteousness. Follow the nine-fold path and ye shall achieve true victory. The Right Religion is a message of compassion, not of force and compulsion. Therefore, ye must act carefully and not go beyond the limits of moderation."

"Very well," said Plant Man. "I thank thee for thy consideration and shall be sure to reward thee when I achieve my kingdom. These woods shall be populated again, the people of Tvak shall be numerous once more, and Ffush shall flourish under your heirs, Lord Tvem."

"Heirs? At my age?" he baulked.

"Yes, so it shall be," declared Plant Man. "Numerous wives shall ye both have, thou and Jyoff, and colonists to build up your lands. Ffash Valley, also, shall chime again with the murmur of souls, and Ffushkar shall prosper immensely."

"A beautiful vision," said Tvem. "I hope you achieve it."

"There is something I must show you," said Plant Man, reaching into his viny flesh and producing the cylinder which he had removed from Asharru's throne in Khanshaff.

"This comes from the Inner Sanctum of the Ffâna in Khanshaff."

He handed it to Tvem, who examined it diligently. He was fascinated, in particular, by the cursive script on its face. He turned it over, tossed it from hand to hand, and held it to the hearth-light.

"Most peculiar," he said in a curious tone. "This is not from Tremn."

"Not from Tremn!" Ushwan gasped. "Then what, by Fox, is it?"

"The script is ancient," Tvem explained. "Representing a language used by early star explorers."

"Star explorers!" Shem exclaimed. "No man can fly, let along sail across the star dome!"

"It's not a dome," Tvem corrected him. "During the Age of Emperors, we first made contact with the Nyzorlians, from Nyza, which circles round Vukt."

"Vukt circles round Tremn," Plant Man asserted. "We can see it with our very eyes!"

"That's what the theocracy would have you believe," said Tvem as the others gasped. "We are but one of seven major planets circling Vukt like balls extended on strings from a central sphere, much larger than the rest. Vukt appears small because it is far distant, but it is, in reality, much larger than Tremn. There is a force which holds these planets in orbit, called gravity, which is one of the many forces projected from the *mimra*. The energies of the *mimra*, when they enter the realm of realization, are diversified. Smaller bodies circle round larger bodies, which is why Tvash, Ffush and Obish circle round Tremn, because they are smaller than Tremn."

"Tremn, thou sayest, is close to Nyza?" asked Ushwan.

"Not by our standards," he said. "But yes. The nearest planet to Vukt is Kavukh, followed by Ashkabra; then Tremn and Nyza, which are both peopled by men; and then Tvugman, Potvekya and Shifan; each of these has their own moons. Beyond our system, there are many other star systems with which we used to trade and hold intercourse, each of which consists of a star like Vukt, circled by a host of planets. After Kishton's exile, the Theocracy disbanded our space fleet, dismantled all electronic devices and hid their knowledge from the population."

"Is this cylinder Nyzorlian, then?" asked Plant Man.

"No, it seems to be more ancient. Perhaps it belongs to Asharru's own craft, which brought him to our world. I cannot say."

"Is there no perfidy which the Theocracy has not committed!" Ushwan cried.

"Do you see, now, brothers?" Ffen addressed them. "They've kept us ignorant like sheep, while all the while we could have been sailing between planets and exploring all the material worlds of the Great Spirit?"

"Why have the Nyzorlians abandoned us?" asked Shem.

"Perhaps they have their own troubles," Tvem suggested. "As for other races—it may be more the work of Amon-Ra. In any case, we have been isolated for too long. This cylinder may be a key to unlocking a space ship which can revolutionise our fortunes and bring us once again in touch with our neighbours on other worlds."

"Sailing through the stars!" said Arwa. "Can you imagine it, my darling?"

"One day, we shall fly through the sky—even to Nyza or above," Plant Man promised her. "The possibilities are endless."

"Even so," Tvem continued, bringing the conference to its conclusion. "Is there anything else I can do for you before ye depart?"

He tossed Plant Man the cylinder, which he deftly caught.

"No, my Lord of Ffush," he said. "We are wearied with our journey. We shall go to bed."

"But not to sleep," Arwa whispered to her husband, who smiled gaily.

As they left the manor and headed to the camp, they felt the brisk wintery air and heard the howl of wind through the encompassing forest branches. The moons shone overhead, providing subtle illumination, while the hustle and bustle of the soldiers breathed life into the stark remoteness of the place. Hand-in-hand, Plant Man and his wife approached the royal tent, seven *oksha*s long and three high, embroidered with the royal standard, while the others went to their respective tents. Shem and Meyla eyed one another with love and affection, eager to disrobe and enjoy the pleasures of married life. Ffen looked out towards Ffash Valley, pining after his beloved wives who awaited him—so near and yet so far. He was sharing a tent with Jyoff, while Uswhan slept alone. Tesh-Khan, as a general, also had his own tent, replete with a table for spreading out maps and parchments used for drawing up plans of attack. Plant Man and Arwa retired to their capacious tent, lay upon the typically soft Shaffu bed, and made love until a few hours before dawn, when they finally slept, exhausted but fulfilled, both emotionally and physically.

When the *beig*-trumps sounded at dawn, they arose, washed—or, rather, she washed and dressed him, and then they performed the *kashroim*, along with all the troops. Three hours later, they had eaten and were ready to move. They bade farewell to Lord Tvem and set off into the forest depths. As they penetrated its thickness, they came upon clay men lairs. The Shaffu soldiers took balls of *ffentbaff*-fur mixed with twigs, parchment and *ffentwash*-oil, lit them, and cast them down the tunnels pouring smoke and fire into their labyrinthine fastness. As the desperate savages emerged, weapons in hand, they were easily shot or cut down, except for the queens, whom Tesh-Khan had ordered to be captured and bound. These were tied up and fastened to a *biffbaff*-cart at the rear of the army. Three queens in total were captured, Yaghla-Haz (the successor to the Washyag-Haz whom Ifunka, Shem and Shaff had previously defeated), Heigal-Shim and Kahitv-Kshaff (who had both previously captured Lord Tvem), leading to the complete annihilation of all their warrens or 'colonies'. Though, doubtless, many other such colonies existed throughout the wide expanse of Ffushkar, it was a severe blow to their fortunes. The fate of the queens would be decided by Plant Man in due course.

Eventually, they came to the edge of Ffash Valley and began their descent; *meish* scattered as they approached. Birds, snakes and mammals fled their crushing onslaught, as saplings were pulverized under the thunderous, lumbering weight of the massive beasts. It was not long before Tem Ffash, Lord of Ffash Valley, emerged with his pet *welg-meish*, Shig, on his shoulders and his three large *yeshka*s, Raff, Shed and Lash, growling and fierce at his side. He raised his hand in greeting and said, "Peace be to you!" to which Ffen, leaping off his *ffentbaff*, replied, "And upon thee peace!"

"Son!" Tem cried as he embraced him.

The *meish* grinned oddly and patted him on the head.

"My daughters have not slept a wink since thy departure. They love thee so," he said. "I thought thee utterly lost!"

"By the grace of the Great Spirit, I live," he said. "And so does our brother, Ushwan, and Shem and Ifunka. They are both married as well, Shem to Meyla and Ifunka to Arwa."

"One wife each? Hardly sufficient!" Tem opined. "Where is Ifunka that I may greet him?"

"He is there"—Ffen pointed—"On the royal *ffentbaff*."

"I see only a strange creature with the form of a plant," said Tem, perplexed. "And an army of demon-worshippers! I trust this bodes well and not badly?"

"It does, my father," Ffen reassured him.

"The army is under Ifunka's command, but he is now known as Plant Man, for he bears the Verdant Coin, which gives him mastery over the plant kingdom. He is the new king of all Tremn and we are marching for Kubbawa, in order to cleanse it of the pernicious theocracy and build our new kingdom. I am his High Steward and Chancellor. Tesh-Khan"—he pointed—"is his General. As thou canst well see, he has tamed the demon-worshippers, brought them into the Right Religion, and fashioned them into an indomitable force."

"The All-Highest be praised!" Tem exclaimed. "Come and greet your wives. The army may pass through in peace, secure."

"Thank you, Lord Tem," said Plant Man. "We are most grateful for your hospitality. We shan't be staying long as we intend to reach Ffantplain in all due haste, then Ritvator and Kubbawa. Perhaps you would like to accompany us?"

He thought for a moment and reached for his sword. He pulled it from its scabbard and swung it round, thrusting and swinging in the manner he had learnt as a boy.

"My father, Bem, always said," he spoke loudly. "That the theocracy would have its day and pass away in a blaze of wrath, a clash of armies more brutal and sudden than any previous war. I will join you, along with my daughters, who shall keep Ffen company. What man can fight while his loins are starved?"

He chuckled.

"Indeed," agreed Plant Man as he glanced at Arwa, who was smiling brightly.

As the army moved through the valley, three *ffentbaffs* abreast in order to avoid destroying all the vegetation of Ffash Valley, Ffen hurried ahead with Tem. As soon as they heard his approach, the three beauties, Reshga, Yimga and Meshga, burst from their long-house and embraced their beloved with a flurry of kisses, on cheek, eyes, nose and mouth— he was practically drowned in their love. They grabbed both his arms and pulled him, nay, yanked him, into the house.

"But I… but we!" he cried.

"Now!" ordered Yimga.

Tem stared blankly, his eyes practically popping out of their sockets as his daughters dragged away their prize.

"Heavens above!" he muttered to himself. "May the Great Spirit grant me such eager wives!"

"You shall have them!" called Plant Man as his *ffentbaff* drew near. "I intend to populate the forest regions."

"All the more reason for me to join you," Tem replied. "Let me gather some supplies."

"I'll send you some *biffbaffs* to load."

The command was sent back to the baggage train and two *biffbaffs* were hurriedly drawn ahead to supply his need. This took no more than a half hour, at which time Shem was sent to collect Ffen. He reluctantly emerged, hair dishevelled, face ruddy green and smelling of sweat and passion. His wives followed behind in a similar state of disarray. Ffen was given a separate *ffentbaff*, accompanied by his wives and Tem Ffash and little Shig and, as the *beig*-trumps sounded, the army set off. Tem's *yeshka*s were ordered to stay in order that his house be kept safe from invasion by clay-men or other malevolent forces during his absence. Before long, they were ascending the opposite rise of the valley until they were back into the density of Ffushkar.

Turning northwest, they began to take a different path from that which they had taken via Habka. Instead, they marched for five days (a full Tremna week), through dense and uninhabited forest, relying upon their ample supplies, good humour and joyous songs of battle and triumph. They had now reached the area of habitable forest surrounding Ffantplain and its villages. When they reached the edge of a large clearing, comprising farmland at the purlieus of a small hamlet, the army halted, and scouts were sent forth to survey the lay of the land. When they returned, it was reported that the hamlet was called

Taffgu, consisting of three farmhouses inhabited by unarmed farmers. Beyond this, at a distance of a *tvinshaff*, was the village of Shainba—one of thirty-seven villages and hamlets within the vicinity of the city. As the army waited, it began to snow, and a thin layer of the stuff dusted the ground until everything was covered in white. The treetops were similarly covered in the first evidence of winter's blessed coming. The soldiers were delighted, while the companions rejoiced that the season was upon them for, even though it betokened bitter cold, what must follow cold is warmth, what follows death is new life, and winter is the harbinger of spring, the new year, and all the blessings and fortune, the beauty and splendour, that that most felicitous of seasons manifests. The sun was midway above the horizon, the fallow fields where *braksh*-wheat grew, shone resplendently while in the sunlight, like so much lace laid out upon a table. *Wultva*-budgies chirped, *ffubish*es floated delightfully in the treetops, and all was peaceful, tranquil—the eye before the storm. There was a palpable tension among the troops, who were untried and untested in battle—few among them being trained and experienced watchmen or raiders.

"It's all or nothing, Tesh-Khan!" Plant Man called out to him. "We must take them unawares. If Ffantplain falls not, then all is lost. We march, and we march quickly!"

"We have no siege weapons, your Majesty," he replied.

"We *have* ladders," Ffen informed them. "And a battering ram. That should be sufficient. They're not prepared for war—there hasn't been a proper war in over two thousand years."

"Very well, then," said Plant Man. "For the King; for the Great Spirit; march!!!"

"*Dhôm-krâ* (march)!" Tesh-Khan commanded in Shaffi.

The *ffentbaff*s burst through the forest into the open, knocking trees to pieces as they did so, like so many frail twigs, the ground pounding with their footsteps, such that the farmer-folk of Taffgu rushed out of their homes to see what made it. They could be seen, staring it terror, their cries going up as they fled towards Shainba with all due haste. One of them mounted his own *ffentbaff* and began to flee.

"Take down the beast!" Tesh-Khan commanded.

A hail of arrows sliced through the air and hit their mark, piercing its muscular hide and delivering its quietus. The farmer was thrown off and into a nearby hedge. The army quickly overtook them, and they were swept up like beetles, tied and bound.

"What do you want with us?" cried one. "I'm a dad and I have a good lot of bairns."

"I'm but a 'poverished farmer," said another. "Poor I am, I swears it!"

"Fear not," said Plant Man. "We have only bound you as a precaution. We mean you no harm."

"Who are you, sir; are you man or beast?"

"I am Plant Man, and I am king of all Tremn. The Theocracy is finished—now, a new kingdom shall begin."

"The blasphemy!" said one coarse farmer with a rough, wide face and bulbous nose. His hair was shoulder-length and curly and he squinted as if half-blind. His *geltv*-hat was full of loose straw and holes and his overalls worn and soiled.

"Blasphemy is to presume to rule in the stead of the king," asserted Plant Man. "The Great Spirit has given sovereignty to kings, not priests or elected officials. Kings rule by divine right!"

"It don't seem right is all," said the farmer. "I han't heard nothing the like in my home nor any monk has taught me the like."

"I was a monk once," continued Plant Man. "Not so long ago, but Amon-Ra has favoured me with a tremendous power and now I am a king among men. What you have been taught is a packet of lies and untruths."

"My priest never done lie to me," insisted the man.

"Shall I cut out his tongue, your Majesty?" asked Tesh-Khan.

"No, he is merely ignorant," he replied, calming the general's zealous enthusiasm. "Ignorance is not a crime and, as for impertinence, he doesn't yet understand who I truly am."

"What's your name, farmer?" asked Ffen.

"Bosh Taffgu, son of Dosh."

"And you?" he pointed to the adjacent captive.

"Dosh Taffgu, son of Dosh, milord."

"You're *brothers*."

"Aye, milord."

"And you're Dosh son of Dosh?"

"Aye, milord."

"Inventive folk, these peasants, eh your Majesty?" Ffen commented.

"We are not from highborn families ourselves, are we?" Plant Man replied.

"You don't know your ancestry, Majesty," said Ffen. "As for mine, the Weshgas are a proud family."

"A proud family of what?"

"Bookbinders, your Majesty. My father was a bookbinder and his father before him, back to Weshga himself, our eponymous forebear."

"How many generations ago was that?"

"Five, I believe. We came from Ritvator originally, being descendants of a lesser noble or knight perhaps."

"Mayhap we can find your ancestor in the city archives."

"Perhaps, Majesty."

"Why trouble you much over forebears?" asked Bosh. "I only cares for my *ffentbaff*s, which ye done killed!—and my *braksh*-wheat… I drinks my ale and I does my missus, or she does me as the case may be, and I seeds her with my hearty seed. When all is said and done, I has lived my fill o' life and be done with it."

"Truth from the mouth of a simple farmer," said Plant Man, satisfied with Bosh's forthrightness. "But what of the Great Spirit?"

"The priests'll save my soul for Ganka."

"There you are wrong, my friend," advised Ffen. "It's the Great Spirit which saves the soul. It is adherence to the teachings of the Tamitvar which grants paradise to the true believer."

"I only know as I is taught. If I is taught faulty-like, then is as him what taught me as is should go to Gahimka to burn in flames."

"He and you both, I'm afraid," Ffen clarified. "All men are responsible for their own selves, according to the Tamitvar. Have you read it or at least heard it?"

"I can't as I say I done read it," replied Bosh. "As I ain't able for to read, but I has heard something like, though as to what meant it, I can't for to say. It's all written poetry-like for that we simple folk don't understand it not a whit. Methinks it's them high-folk what wants us commoners to wot little of it."

"I see," said Ffen, intrigued. "Education is essential, it seems, so that men's souls may be saved. As Chancellor, I shall make it a priority."

"You've proved us right, Bosh," said Plant Man, addressing him. "We seek to liberate every man from the shackles of ignorance. I guarantee you that all men shall be educated. None shall be excluded, not even your sons, Dosh. The priests want you to be unlettered; they want you to obey authority blindly. I tell you, theocracy is illegitimate; true authority comes from hereditary monarchy, which is a divine system, chosen by the Great Spirit. I am the true king of all Tremn and I shall give you peace, education and order under a just and honourable system."

"We has too much taxes," complained Bosh. "A quarter of all our harvest goes to the Theocracy, for God knows what."

"I shall lower taxes and ensure that everyone pays the same, from the lowest serf to the highest lord."

"Then I shall support you heartily," said Bosh.

"And I," agreed Dosh.

"Release them and their families," Plant Man ordered. "And give them each five silver *zitve* for their troubles."

"Most gracious, your Majesty!" they cheered as the *ffentbaffs* halted to let them down. "Long live the king!"

They continued on their march. Within a short time, they reached the outskirts of Shainba, which lay in the shadow of a mighty aqueduct. This immense construction, twenty *oksha*s high, stretched across the fields and through the villages until it reached Ffantplain. It originated far to the south, connecting with the mighty aqueduct ring which encompassed the entire Old Central Kingdom. Another connected with Ffantplain from the west and yet another to the east, stretching towards Ritvator, whence it extended north-east towards Kubbawa. As soon as the massive army became visible, an alarm was raised in the village, a small settlement of several hundred inhabitants. Men, women and children rushed out of their houses and, staring in alarm at the ranks of *ffentbaffs* massed together in a formation, juggernaut-like with inevitable progress, the like of which the Tremna call a *galad* (i.e. a military formation of a hundred or more *ffentbaff*s). The first to observe them was a young boy who ran to his mother, a milk-maid who swept up all her brood of children and threw them onto the back of a fat and lumbering *ffentbaff*.

"Run, run, run, you fast cow!" she screamed in shrill voice.

"What's going on?" asked the boy.

"It's the end of the world, son!" she cried. "Afflish the Accursed has raised an army of demons to murder us all!"

Others leapt onto *biffbaff*s or merely ran as fast as they could. The army swept past them and around the village, overtaking the fleeing villagers, some of whom were armed with scythes and pitchforks. They screamed and formed a circle as they were surrounded—kettled in.

"Fear not!" Plant Man called out to them. "We mean you no harm. I am Plant Man, the bearer of the Verdant Coin, given to me by Amon-Ra himself. My name is Ifunka Kaffa, son of Kandaspu, and I am the true king of all Tremn. Submit to me and ye shall not be harmed."

"As ye wish, my lord," said one elderly man who appeared to be the chieftain. "I am Wain Shainba, the chieftain of this village. On behalf of all of us, I relent. I am your humble servant."

"Very well," said Plant Man. "Do ye all so swear?"

"We swear it!" they shouted, in obedience to their chieftain.

"Then return to your village in peace," he commanded. "We seek Ffantplain, which shall open its doors to us or suffer the bitter consequences."

The villagers moved through the *galad* ranks and back to Shainba. At that moment, on the high walls of the city of Ritvator, a watchman stirred. He had been napping when a six-winged *dakral-ish*—a dragon-fly—bumped into his nose, waking him from his slumber. Blinking, he stretched and groaned. His companion, a boy of about eighteen, was fast asleep opposite him. He hissed and whistled, but the ill-featured lad kept sleeping on. His auburn hair hung over his plump bepocked cheeks and flat nose, his fingers like stubs and his leather armour hardly adequate to defend against a siege. At his side, there was a bow and arrow, which hardly looked much-used, being an ornament of his profession only. The boy was of a similar age, if not younger, his hair chestnut brown, his face thin with greyish, keen eyes and his bow and arrow evidenced of much use but diligent maintenance, each arrowhead shining with a fresh sheen.

"Psst," he called again. "Yobid—Yobid! Get up! We're s'posed to be on watch."

"On watch for what?" Yobid groaned. "Ain't nothing but villagers plompin' and stompin' in the fields, like."

"We can't sleep and laze about forever, you old numpkin."

"I has a right mind to thwump you, one of these fine days, I has. Let sleepin' rabbits sleep, as my old uncle says. Days are for sleepin'"

"What's nights for, you old piss puddle?"

"For sleepin' as well, o' course," he chuckled. "You take watch, Ffelka, you old *biffbaff*."

Ffelka stood and stretched, gazed out towards mighty Ffushkar and then, lowering his eyes upon the villages and hamlets dotted around the city, espied a train of *ffentbaff*s nearly three *kobotv*s long, thousands of soldiers armed to the teeth, a mass of supply animals, all holding aloft foreign banners and standards, indicating but one possibility—invasion. Panic-stricken, he could neither think nor move, and then he grabbed his *beig*-trump, which hung from a leather strap over his shoulder, and sounded it with all the breath he could muster. Yobid sprang to his feet perplexed and in shock.

"Have you gone daft, Ffelka?" he cried.

Again, he blew the trump, and a third time, alerting the watchmen to an invading army.

"*Heika!*" he cried. "Ffantplain ho! Ffantplain ho! *Heika!* Ffantplain ho!"

As Yobid stared out at the oncoming army, his eyes could not reconcile themselves with his raging mind.

"Impossible!" he screamed, his voice all-too-effeminate and cowardly.

"Who *are* they? Where have they come from?"

"Ready your bow, Yobid!" Ffelka ordered him. "War has begun!"

Five hundred *beig*-trumps sounded from the Shaffu ranks, *diffka*-drums beat like thunder, *ffentbaff*s bellowed and *biffbaff*s brayed. Plant Man cried: "*Ishein heikra!*" an archaic battle cry from the Age of Kings which means 'Hail the King!' while the reply, *"Ishein hei! Ishein hei! Ishein hei!"* resounded on thousands of tongues until every man, woman and child within the fast walls trembled.

"What is that sound?" asked the befuddled Ffesh, Bishop of Ffantplain.

"That, your Eminence," said his Lord Chamberlain. "Is the sound of doom."

⁓

CHAPTER XXIII.

The Siege of Ffantplain

~

Ffantplain, a major city located in the western part of Ritvator Province, was a round, walled metropolis of twenty-seven thousand inhabitants, mostly descendants of the Houses of Kven and Ril, spanning half a *tvinshaff* in diameter with walls of solid granite, twenty *oksha*s high and one and a half thick, presided over by the Head of the House of Kven, Kven the Fifth, fifteenth Lord of Ffantplain, whose title was purely ceremonial, while real power lay in the hands of His Eminence Ffesh, Bishop of Ffantplain and, after, him, the Ffantplain Council of Priests, of which he was the Chairman. His Lord Chamberlain, Dilwa, carried out his commands, while each district of the city was governed by a district priest who ensured that the Theocracy's laws were implemented, and dissent was punished. Lord Kven merely appeared at ceremonial functions and signed the Bishop's decrees in order to give them greater legitimacy. This was particularly necessary in Ffantplain, where the tribesmen of Kven had a strong bond of allegiance to their hereditary chief. While the House of Ril owed loyalty to a different chief, the *Datvelipatv* (or 'Protector') of Ritvator and Head of the House of Ril, Yiffwa the Second, they still regarded the Lord of Ffantplain as their liege lord to whom they owed military and other service. The Lord of Ffantplain also crowned each incumbent bishop with the *ffitv* (an episcopal hat)—the symbol of his authority—and bestowed upon him the rod and staff of office. The chiefs of Kven had had a troubled history, being the heirs and descendants of Lord Kval, who rebelled against Emperor Kishton in alliance with the Pretender Ush and King Shegwa of Ritvator. After the Battle of Ardesi, which decimated their people, the House of Kven resided mostly in Ffantplain itself and the surrounding towns, villages and hamlets, or in Tremael—the first city—which they settled along with the Houses of Kyeshob and Mael under the leadership of Vashab, Head of the House of Kyeshob, and was still ruled by his descendants.

Like most cities of the imperial period, the buildings of Ffantplain were made of large stone blocks, granite, marble or concrete, circular in construction, with slightly sloping roves, iron gutters, round pane-glass windows, curving streets and no right angles of any form or shape. The entire city was thus an exercise in Euclidean geometry, with every path and thoroughfare bending around the circumference of a smaller or larger *tvinshaff*, leading to the three centre-most cylindrical buildings: the Temple of the Great Spirit, the Manor of the Lord (a palatial complex), and the Episcopal Headquarters (large yet plain and bureaucratic in its interior). Several round parks, plentiful with *limbatv* and *kaptitv*-trees, *gebnav*-bushes and flower gardens, with large fountains in the centre and statues of historical figures deemed suitable and appropriate to the interests of the regime, such as the Seven Fathers and Seven Mothers of Tremn, the Seer Votsku, Baku (the first Head of the Theocracy), Ishmael the Great, Kubba Gven and Kven, 1st Lord of Ffantplain. Poets and litterateurs (e.g. the poet Hashpa and the orator Mogshiff), religious scholars (e.g. the theologian Wentva and the commentator Yishpa), and great bishops also dotted the city in an endeavour to legitimize the present system by harking back to a halcyon age of legend and great deeds, even though the present age bore little resemblance to the glories of the past. The River Shiv, flowing from its source in the *Varome Sintva*, entered the city through a water-gate at the west of the city and, flowing through a curved canal through its centre, issued out of another gate at the east and then across Shivka to Ritvator. In his office, on the third floor of the Headquarters, Bishop Ffesh paced back and forth while Dilwa shook his head in dismay.

"What are we to do?" he cried.

"Invasion, your Eminence. We are doomed. We can arm every man, woman and child!" Dilwa cried desperately.

"The watchmen are already moving to the wall, bows and arrows to hand, swords at their sides."

Dilwa was peering out the large round window at the south end of the office.

"We can't see who is invading from here. We must await word from a report."

"Blast the report! Bring me the Superintendent of City Defences, the watch commander and the Lord."

"The Lord, your Emimence?"

"He may be a figurehead but we need him to rally the city to its defence. Just go!"

Dilwa rushed out of the room, nearly tripping on his absurdly-long skirts. He was a short, pudgy man with an unfortunate girth, a stubby nose, squinty eyes, a near-bald head, except for short-cut tufts of light-brown at the sides, an impertinent chin, meaty jowls, stubby fingers and a mien of undeserved self-importance. He wore a long, silver robe and, around his neck, a round onyx pendant. He carried a tall crook, which he leaned upon to relieve his wearied toes of their too-heavy burden, making him appear to hop about like a *bitv*-frog which has eaten too many worms. In contrast, the bishop, wearing a *ffitv*, a bright crimson episcopal robe tied tightly at the waste with a knotted cincture, a gold pendant about his neck emblazoned with the *metvek*—the heraldic symbol of the Theocracy: a tree representing Melekraffu, the primeval tree, that same tree that Inta had sat under when he addressed the Seven Fathers of Tremn during *Kultvum Dian*, the First Day. Dilwa rushed orders to his stewards, who dashed about like mice, relaying messages and gathering information. The mere exercise of passing on these commands had Dilwa in a puff, causing him to bend down and rest his arms on his knees.

"Dreadful job; why did my mother talk me into this? 'Dilwa,' she said. 'Enter the service of the bishop. That's a good job, my son, and very little exercise or work involved.' If only she knew; if only she knew the work I do!!!"

A steward rushed back to inform him of his intelligence.

"My lord," he said.

"What *is* it?" Dilwa sighed. "Can't you see I am busy?"

He was busy doing nothing but resting on his knees.

"Sir…"

"Help me up! Can't you see I'm struggling?"

The steward lifted him up.

"Yes? Get on with it!" he bellowed. "There are about ten thousand soldiers armed with swords, axes, bows and arrows; at least half are mounted on *ffentbaffs*. They bear a green standard with the image of an owl and the letters *Minwa* and *Latis*. They are currently circling around the city, preparing ladders and a battering ram, though the main force remains near the southern gate."

"What???" the Chamberlain cried. "Open the armoury, arm the reserves and give daggers and slingshots to boys and men, of any age. Lock all gates, heat the pitch and load the catapult!"

"Sir!" saluted the steward as he rushed to pass on the orders.

Within minutes, the Superintendent of City Defences, Tvem Liksh, the Head of the Watch, Sfen Wuksh, and the Lord of Ffantplain, His Lordship Kven the Fifth, Son of Kval the Second, Chief of the House of Kven, arrived, and Dilwa led them into the office.

"Your Eminence, they have arrived," he said, bowing to the bishop.

"Yes, I can see that Dilwa."

"Your Eminence!" The three men bowed, even the Lord.

"My bishop, they carry swords and axes and are mounted on *ffentbaffs*, at least five thousand infantry and a greater number of *ffentbaff* cavalry in the *galad*."

"Swords and axes?" pondered Kven. "Who carries swords and axes but no shields?"

"Only the… impossible!" the bishop hesitated. "It cannot be they."

"They who?" asked the Lord.

"The demon-worshippers. No, we have an arrangement. They are a surety *against* revolution, not the means of it."

"Demon-worshippers?" asked Kven, perplexed. "Who are they?"

"My Lord of Ffantplain," said the bishop, addressing him. "All your airs of grace and authority notswithstanding, you have no idea."

"The secret is out now," Dilwa observed. "We might as well tell him, your Eminence."

"Tell me what exactly?" the lord burst out, angrily.

The bishop was unsure of how to proceed. He looked at Dilwa uncertainly while the two others stared.

"Sir," said the superintendent. "I do not wish to interrupt, but what is your command?"

Tvem Liksh was a man of about forty, young by Tremna standards as their race can live up to two or three hundred years, with dark brown hair, brown eyes, a round face, cleft chin and long nose with a bump in the middle, wearing a military uniform, i.e. black leather leggings and a white leather jerkin over a black cloth doublet, over which he wore a steel cuirass emblazoned with the emblem of Ffantplain: a small *kaptitv*-tree beneath three five-pointed stars with the runic letters *Latis* (an angular R) and *Yur* (an angular E) to the sides, which represent the 'k' and 'v' sounds respectively, standing for Kven (this being also the emblem of the House of Kven). His doublet extended into bases (a military skirt), also in black—a typical element of the theocratic uniform. Over his legs he wore plate armour, as on his arms, with his hands protected by metal gauntlets. Around his neck there was a gorget and he wore a y-shaped barbute on his head with a metal ridge along the back thereof.

The chief watchman, a perfunctory fellow with wispy blonde hair and an equally wispy nose, a large brow, pointy cheeks and chin, overly-small ears and blue eyes—the appearance of a man of duty for the sake of duty—duty to *zitv* and *zelana* at least. He was dressed in black leather trousers and a short black doublet, over which hung a hauberk with the insignia of the watch: a diagonal white cross like the Star of St. Andrew, and, on his head, he wore a visorless helm.

"Do… something!" Ffesh cried at both of them impatiently. "I'm sure you've already sent *some* instructions, Dilwa."

"Indeed, I have," replied the Lord Chamberlain.

"Very well, then," said the bishop. "Are you all still here? Defend the city!!!"

The two officers bowed and left, vacating the room with all the grace of two waddling *dish*-ducks.

"Well?" barked Kven, the imperious and self-important aristocrat.

While his House might have once held the balance of power during the Age of Emperors, the current lord was little more than a symbol of an institution which had long ago been usurped by theocratic authority. Kven was tall, after the Tremna type, seven-foot in height, with a high brow, dagger-like nose, keen brown eyes, jet-black hair dancing on his shoulders, long ears, a thin bony face and strong chin, seated upon a long thin neck and gaunt frame, rather like a depiction of death itself, his body draped in a white cloth doublet over a *woffgi*-silk shirt, tight trousers of the same hue and material as his doublet, over which he wore an outer robe, open in the middle, rather like an Arabian *bisht*—called a *sfal* in Tremni—lined with gold thread along its hem and embroidered with the emblem of his house, as on his doublet, such that there could be no doubt as to his identity. Around his neck he wore a thin gold torque, on his hands white leather gloves and white high-heeled boots of the same. Altogether, he was a fine example of a decadent and long-redundant aristocracy who had long since outgrown their usefulness. Rather, like an extra cog on a tightly-cogged wheel, he was frustrated and perpetually dissatisfied, yet too subdued by tradition to lift a finger against his tormenters. That did not stop him from speaking like a lord, even though he hardly befit the title.

"They must be demon-worshippers," Ffesh continued. "Though they call themselves the Shaffu. The children of Asharru, the demon servant of Afflish the Accursed, they have helped our government for thousands of years. We use them to silence our critics, remove dissent and keep the Theocracy in power. We pay them annually—protection money—a tribute, if you will and, in turn, they are our guarantee against rebellion. But to march in public—in the open—is unheard of! And they've come against us! How dare they!"

"Who is master of whom?" Kven asked, concerned at this revelation.

"We… well—we *pay* them."

"But who pulls *your* strings?"

"We have been on good terms with them for thousands of years. Something's wrong… but what?"

"Did someone forget to pay?" Kven said sarcastically.

"Why the seal of Amon-Ra? It just doesn't make any sense."

"Doesn't it?" asked Kven. "Who first spoke to Amon-Ra in a vision—at least in recorded history?"

"Ishmael the Great."

"So whose banner is it? The heir of Ishmael."

"The Protector of Ffantbav?"

"He's Saffik's heir," said Kven. "So, he's hardly the heir of Ishmael. It would have to be through Saffik's younger brother King Ishmael Gan, which leaves the Protector of Okayeshvi or Wadakit."

"Wadakit is already under the protectorship of Saffik's heir," Ffesh observed. "When Benad died, his son-in-law, Weshob the Second, Protector of Ffantbav and Duke of Tvimbal, who was married to Benad's daughter, Daffla, became the new protector."

"I know that, of course," Kven asserted. "But there must be other males in the line of Wadakit. In any case, it should be the heir to the lines of Wadakit or Okayeshvi. Saffik's line has never held the throne; the Duke of Yalaniuntva is of a non-royal line from the House of Mael, though next in line for the throne after the male heirs of Ishmael the Great, while the Protector of Wafftayunda and the Dukes of Melekaman are all of the line of Tsilel and hence excluded from the throne by Amon-Ra's ban. The Dukes of Tvimwush, Tvimnub and Yigvaltv are descendants of Tsilel's full-brothers."

"So Wadakit or Okayeshvi—allied with the Shaffu… it still makes no sense. No one even knows about the Shaffu, except for the bishops and patriarchs and their trusted advisors. No, none of this makes sense."

"I shall go to the wall," Kven said. He was fatalistically bound to his house and city. "And die in defence of Ffantplain if need be. Perhaps I shall suffer for Kval's sins."

"Go then and Godspeed," said the bishop. "I shall stay here and wait. I fear that the horde of infidels shall burst through our walls and murder us all."

"If the House of Kven shall fall this day, let it be said that we died fighting, sword in hand, and the Great Spirit was on our side. Farewell, Bishop."

He left the room in a hurry, ordered his manservant and squire to fetch his armour, shield and sword, and made ready to mount his *ffentbaff*. The squire fit his helm, breast-plate and sword-belt with sword and sheath; his *ffentbaff* was large and muscular, its wool died white and its body covered in bright steel plate-armour. The beast groaned loudly as he mounted it, followed by his squire and a dozen knights in train, each armed and mounted in the same manner as Tvem Liksh. Hundreds of watchmen rushed to and fro, mounting the wall and rushing to defend the city gates, led by Sfen Wuksh, while Tvem Liksh gathered the reserves, knights and squires, builders and other fit boys and men, arming them in haste, as the city's catapult was wheeled out by two large *ffentbaffs* and the defenders at the walls boiled pitch and collected shrapnel and other missiles to throw at their enemies.

"Commander, what news?" called Kven, addressing an officer of the watch on the wall.

"The invaders have stopped, milord," replied the stone-faced warrior. "Their army waits at the gates."

"Why do ye not attack?"

"We've received no orders to, milord."

"Open the gates! I will speak to them."

"My lord? The gate is our defence. They will swarm us!" Tvem Liksh warned him.

Sfen stood at his side with an expression of concern.

"Come Tvem, Sfen. Let's find out who leads this invasion. Are you two afraid of facing the enemy?"

Sfen grunted.

"Open the gates!" Tvem ordered.

A watchman turned the wheel, two *oksha*s high, and the great gate groaned and opened slowly, like a lumbering *kunug*—or 'giant'—its huge iron hinges firmly fixed in the thick stone walls. Made of *jyag*-wood, the hardest of trees from the Great Forest of Nor, it was a foot thick and four *oksha*s high, opening on one side. When it had opened fully, the three men rode forth atop their *ffentbaffs*, followed by the twelve knights. Kven's heart sank in his stomach as he saw the huge army facing him, countless mounted *ffentbaffs* with lofty *ffentwa*s atop, each carrying archers, cloaked infantry bearing brutal axes and swords—a barbarian horde thirsting after blood and conquest. Still, he was a lord and he maintained his dignity and poise as he approached the Shaffu forces.

"*Heika!*" he called. "How now?"

"*Heika!*" Plant Man called in reply.

As they looked up to behold the plant-like man atop the royal *ffentbaff*, their eyes betrayed fear and confusion.

"Who are ye?" he asked them, his tone imperious and his voice loud.

For a moment, Kven froze as his mind attempted to comprehend what his eyes were telling him.

"What manner of man art thou?" he asked.

"Are we slaves that we should be questioned so?" Plant Man thundered. "Speak, soldier. Who are ye?"

"I am Kven the Fifth, Lord of Ffantplain and Chief of the House of Kven, Guardian of Shivka Forest and Lord Martial of Shivka District. This is the Superintendent of City Defences, Tvem Liksh, and Head of the Watch, Sfen Wuksh, and these are the knights who form my personal guard. We demand to know who ye are and what your business in the Theocracy is."

Plant Man laughed, while Ffen and Arwa smiled.

"Is that all?" he asked sardonically. "I am called Ifunka Kaffa, son of Kandaspu, but I am now known as Plant Man. As ye can see, I am a being of immense power, the bearer of the Verdant Coin, a gift from Amon-Ra himself. I rule over the plant kingdom, controlling every blade of grass beneath your *ffentbaffs'* hooves. Behold!"

Stretching forth his arm, a ring of *kobotv*-trees sprung up from the ground as saplings, surrounding the lord and his retainers, quickly fattened and matured and reached four *okshas* high, walling them in. Alarmed, their *ffentbaffs* bellowed and tried to extricate themselves. Kven's white *ffentbaff* reared and threw him into the branches of one of the trees. Raising his arms again, the trees retreated into the ground and vanished. Kven struggled to his feet and tried to remount the *ffentbaff* which, instead, charged off into the distance, leaving him behind. Tvem pulled him up onto his own mount.

"I apologise," said Plant Man. "I did not mean to completely humiliate you—I only desired to put you in your place. You see, I am now the King of all Tremn and your pathetic Theocracy is about to come crashing to the ground in a blaze of chaos and destruction. Your options are these: renounce the Theocracy and swear allegiance to me as High-King of Tremn, and live—nay, even remain as the Lord of

Ffantplain—or maintain allegiance to the Theocracy and perish in a sea of bloodshed and terror. Where is your puppeteer, the Bishop Ffesh? He is your real leader, is he not? Thou art but a petty puppet, art thou not, Kven—a lord in name only? See how they even send you to me like a huntsman sends his cur! Go back to thy master and tell him what I've said."

"And who are these?" asked Kven when he had recovered his poise. Raised to be a lord, he would not cower before the fearsome aspect of his enemy. "Wild tribesmen? Demon-worshippers?"

"They were infidels from the depths of the forest, the assassins of the Theocracy, keeping your world in order. They were called Shaffu, from Shaffnâ; now they are all followers of the Right Religion, free from the domination of false priests; these are the Army of Plant Man! We shall scale your walls, burn your houses and annihilate the House of Kven— that most treacherous of houses, which betrayed Kishton and supported the usurper, Ush. Go to Bishop Ffesh and speak my words. Tell him that Brother Ifunka Kaffa of the Order of the Monks of Bishgva, from the Monastery of the Brown Owl, is here, with Brothers Ffen, Shem and Ushwan—yes, Ushwan—whom he sought to murder at the hands of the Shaffu. Tell him that we spared his life once but the time for reckoning is at hand! Go!"

Flushed and dismayed, the lord and his knights turned about and rushed back into the city, ordered the gate to be closed and rushed back to the Bishop's Headquarters. He approached the bishop with all due haste and repeated what Plant Man had told him. The bishop's face went pale green, as if all the blood had been drained out of him; his expression was one of grief, his eyes lost any spirit of hope and vivacity. He fell to his knees and bowed his head.

"*Waila, waila, waila!!!*" he yowled—the Tremni expression for extreme grief and despair.

"Your Eminence, there is no time for this!" Dilwa urged him. "We must act and act now!"

"How has this happened?" Ffesh cried. "The Shaffu have betrayed us! Where is the Sage, Shaffu-Nayakht-go? What of Asharru their Lord?"

"I saw no sign of them," said Kven, though he did not, indeed, know what either looked like.

"Send riders to Ritvator. We need reinforcements."

"To what end?" asked Ffesh. "He will rip down our walls with the very trees of Shivka!"

"We can hold them off at the walls," Kven advised. "They have only a battering ram and ladders. We can stave them off, keep them at bay, until Ritvator comes to our aid. By then, Kubbawa will have raised an army of tens of thousands to quash the rebellion."

"I agree, your Eminence," said Dilwa prudently. "Send the riders; call Ritvator to our aid."

"I myself shall go," Sfen volunteered.

Kven eyed him disapprovingly.

"Very well," said the bishop. "And send word to Okayeshvi in the north and Ffantbav in the south. This is a threat to the entire Theocracy. They may have surprised us but they shall not catch Ritvator and Kubbawa off-guard."

Sfen saluted and left the chamber; he left his deputy in charge of the watch, mounted his *ffentbaff* with two of his men and selected three other groups of riders to send word to Kubbawa, Okayeshvi and Ffantbav. Opening the back gate, they set off. Having anticipated this move, a battalion of mounted Shaffu engaged them. A hail of arrows struck the Ffantplain riders like pins in a cushion. Sfen's chest was punctured with a dozen shafts, blood pouring out from every wound, his mouth gurgling blood and bile, and then the fool fell headfirst off his mount.

"*Yônadh-im khû erim-krâ* (bring him to the General)," said an officer in Shaffi. "*Khashla-zen khashvavuff-krâ ffi miftîkhsha-zen-ffish ftôn gvînshuff-krâ. Ffêntaff-zen vâl-krâ ffi gâladh-im ftôn gayiff-krâ* (behead the others and stick them on spears. Harness the *ffentbaff*s and join them to the *galad*)."

They beheaded the other riders and dragged Sfen's corpse away. When they reached Tesh-Khan, he smiled.

"They've tried to warn the Theocracy," he said. "But they have failed, your Majesty."

"Excellent," said Plant Man. "They have given us their answer. Rain arrows upon their watchmen!"

"*Shân-paft-zen! Shân-zen atolsha-zen-reffû* (archers! Arrows over the wall)!"

Thousands of bows were drawn by myriad archers on *ffentwas*.

"*Lîffê-krâ* (fire)!"

Kven was in the Headquarters with the bishop and Dilwa as they heard the whining scream of thousands of arrows soaring into the air.

"It's begun," said Kven stoically as his eyes watched the jagged-edged arrows dotting the air above the city like streaks of black on a cyan-blue canvas.

The watchmen and citizens looked up in alarm as the missiles rained down upon them, piercing eyes, sticking throats, stabbing shoulders, backs and breasts, filling the streets with splatters of blood and bits of torn flesh. The jagged arrowheads sliced and pierced, ripping meat from bone, slaying watchmen, knights and bystanders alike. Women suckling babes, beggars on the curb, children-at-play; all fell dead or maimed at the first volley. Cries of anguish, shrieks of pain, desperate pleas for divine protection in their moments of agony, deafened the ears of all spectators, who watched in horror as their compatriots died and clutched at wounds all around them.

"Holy Votsku!" exclaimed the bishop. "What of our riders?"

"Dead, most likely," Kven supposed. "Our watchmen are all dead or maimed. We shall have to surrender."

"No!" Ffesh protested. "If they take us, they will conquer the next city, and the next! We must send out word to our friends."

"We have no messenger-*wultvas*."

"Is there no other way?" he pleaded.

Kven thought for a moment.

"My forebears built a tunnel. I am the only one who knows its location."

"Take me there," the bishop begged.

"Would you abandon your people?"

"These savages, this 'Plant Man' as he calls himself, will murder me."

"Why? What did you do to him—to his friend, Ushwan?"

"I didn't do anything. It was the Abbott. He asked the Shaffu to abduct the monk."

"Then this abbott has doomed us all. As for me, I must stay with my people, my clansmen. I will take you to the tunnel. We shall live or die as one people—the Children of Kven."

Fatalistic and determined to die an honourable death, the lord led the cowardly bishop to the underground tunnel. Located under the dungeon in a level accessed only through a drainage tunnel which led down into a narrow floor, one and a half *okshas* high, through which they, along with Dilwa, crawled with great difficulty. Squeezing through for some minutes, they reached the tunnel entrance. Carved through solid rock at least a thousand years ago, the tunnel led three *kobotv*s out to the edge of Shivka forest. Cramped, damp and confined, it was an arduous task to crawl through it, but Bishop Ffesh was willing to give it a try, especially as it meant the difference between life and death.

"I go to Ritvator," said the bishop.

"May the Great Spirit keep thee safe," said Kven as the richly-robed ecclesiastic crawled into the damp and dirty passage, followed by Dilwa, whose face displayed evident disgust.

Returning to the Headquarters, Kven called together Tvem Liksh and all the surviving watchmen and armed men, including Yobid and Ffelka, who had managed to avoid being hit by arrows by hugging against the crenels of the wall. They were three thousand strong, some as young as twelve and as old as two hundred, a motley gathering of weak and strong, the rich and destitute, the experienced and novice, the sure-handed and the clumsy. Children of Kven and some of Ril, they looked at their chief with eyes of expectation as the Shaffu army beat its drums and chanted *"Isheim hei! Isheim hei!"* He mounted his *ffentbaff* and stood upon its back at the centre of the crowd, his face a pattern of stoic resolve, of courage in the face of insurmountable odds and baronial dignity. He spoke to his people with words of inspiration, welling up from the depths of his soul.

"People of Ffantplain!" he thus addressed them. "The hour of deciding has come! This is the moment—one moment—when we rise or fall as a people. The tribesmen of Kven—my people—and the mixed host of Ril—ye are both joined together like clay and water and cannot be sundered. Yet now a hammer seeks to smash our bond of unity, to destroy your way of life. What is at stake are your lives and livelihoods, your families and babes, your homes and possessions. When these gates are breached, our lives shall be forfeit, our families—fodder for the sword and axe, and our homes shall be burnt to the ground. At this moment, let us stand as one people; let us steel our resolve and gird our loins. We shall fight as soldiers; we shall fight as never man has fought before; we shall fight as brothers-in-arms willing to die for one another. When their army ascends our walls, drop boiling pitch upon their skulls, slash at their arms and heads, send their ladders flying, smash them with our catapult and terrorise them so that it may said that Ffantplain did not shirk its duty, that Ffantplain did not cave in to evil, that Ffantplain did its darnedest! Go, men! Go!"

They mounted the walls just as the ladders were about to crash against the stones. The catapult rolled slowly along the main thoroughfare towards the gate, still embedded with scores of arrows, which stuck into its wooden beams like so many pins. At the moment that Kven finished his speech, Plant Man addressed Tesh-Khan.

"We have waited long enough and no surrender has come. Send in the ladders. It's time to enter the city!"

"*Deafful-zen* (ladders)!" Tesh-Khan cried. "*Ffam-im raffli-krâ* (enter the city)!"

"*Ishein heikra! Ishein hei!*" the soldiers boomed in unison.

Thousands of infantry began to mount the walls on all sides. The Ffantplain watchmen fired arrows, slingshot, rocks and stones. Pots of boiling pitch rained down on unfortunate Shaffu warriors. Yet no matter how many were killed or maimed, more ladders hit the wall and more siegers climbed up. Ladders knocked backwards were raised again. The catapult hurled great rocks at the *galad*, felling several beasts, but the army remained firm, neither alarmed nor dismayed by the counter-attack.

"Battering ram!" Plant Man commanded.

"*Mevtash* (battering ram)!" Tesh-Khan repeated.

A large *limbatv*-log, two feet wide and three *oksha*s long, with a *meb*-ram head, was pulled out by sixteen large and stout men who wheeled it to the gate. Suspended by metal chains, they swung it back and then, like a massive hammer, it pounded on the *jyag*-wood gate. Defenders rushed to hold it from the other side, but the ram knocked them flying with every blow.

"Aim for the ram!" Kven cried.

He was on the wall, engaged in swordfights with Shaffu warriors, here slaying and maiming one, ducking blows and severing arms from limbs of another.

"The battering ram!" he repeated.

"On it!" repeated Ffelka as he picked off the warriors operating the ram.

Yobid tried his best also, sometimes hitting a Shaffu warrior in the shoulder, sometimes in the leg and sometimes the ram itself. Ffelka turned suddenly to find a large Shaffu warrior bearing down upon him with axe and sword. Drawing his dagger, he stabbed the foeman in the groin. The man grasped downwards in agony, tripped and fell off the wall to his doom. More came at him.

"Retreat!" Kven cried. "The wall is taken!"

$\sim\!\!\!\circ$

CHAPTER XXIV.

The Hidden Heir

~

They rushed to the steps, fighting every inch of the way as their pursuers slashed and hacked at them. When they reached the ground, mounted knights rushed to their aid, helping the lord, as did Yobid and Ffelka who were fast behind. The knights cut down the warriors as they approached, the *ffentbaffs* struck them with their mighty tusks and tossed aside the dead ones.

Pound, pound, pound! The gate began to splinter and crack as the incessant blows of the ram beat upon it. While Shaffu troops swarmed about, slaying all who stood against them, the gate burst with a thunderous crack that sent splinters flying, the great door breaking free from its hinges and crashing down on half a dozen watchmen who were crushed to death like ants beneath a durdy leather heel. The *ffentbaffs* of the *galad* charged in, led by Plant Man himself. He had left the royal *ffentbaff* bearing his wife and charged through along with Tesh-Khan, Ffen and Jyoff. Kven, Ffelka, Yobid and Tvem Liksh readied themselves for one last stand against the enemy. As they rushed forward to meet their doom, Plan Man raised his hands and a grove of trees burst through the stones of the street and circled the remaining defenders. More than two thousand strong, they were utterly imprisoned and unable to resist.

Lifting himself into the air upon a tree throne which burst up beneath him, he addressed the encircled enemy.

"Ffantplain is fallen!" he said triumphantly. "This is your last chance, Kven. I shall spare thy people and thee if thou bend the knee before me and renounce the Theocracy. I am the true king of all Tremn. I am the new Ishmael—the new Kubba Gven. A new age is dawning. Submit to my command and all shall be well. If thou dost not do this, these very trees shall strangle the life out of you. What then of your tribe? The flower of its youth shall die here and now. Understood?"

"These are my people," replied Kven. "What good are we if we bow the knee to a tyrant?"

"Tyranny is that men should bow the knee to theocrats, who oppress the people through ignorance, who overtax the poor and rich alike, who usurp the rightful line of kings. Wouldst thou not prefer to be a lord in thine own right?"

"We are children of the Holy Theocracy of Tremn. We cannot change who we are," said Kven.

"Where is thy wife, Kven—thy children?"

"I have none. I have nothing; just these people you see around me. And I shall die to save any one of them."

"You!" Plant Man pointed to Yobid. "Do you wish to taste the cup of death?"

"No, my lord," said Yobid, terrified.

"I am sorry, boy. Death comes to us all."

The tree branches reached out and grabbed Yobid firmly, squeezing him, wrapping around his throat. He choked and coughed but could not resist the inevitable constriction which aimed to squeeze him to death.

"No!" Ffelka cried as he unsheathed his dagger and began to cut and slice the branches.

"Shall two taste death?" asked Plant Man as yet another tree wrapped itself around Ffelka and began to squeeze him until he felt his ribcage would burst and spill his innards like an over-ripe banana.

"Plant Man!" Kven screamed. "Cease this cruelty!"

"Very good!" said Plant Man. "Thou hast a moral backbone!"

"Release them and I shall submit."

"Very well."

The trees let go of their victims.

"I renounce the Holy Theocracy of Tremn forever and swear allegiance to thee, Ifunka Kaffa, son of Kandaspu, as my king and the King of all Tremn."

The others repeated in unison, even Ffelka and Yobid, who practically choked on the words, so filled were they with choler and indignation. With a sweep of his hand, the trees were swept away and Plant Man released the defenders.

"Tesh-Kan," he commanded. "Find the armoury; ensure each of these men is fully armed and then incorporate them into the *galad*. They shall march with us. A residual force of a thousand Shaffu shall remain here to ensure the city's subjugation, even in our absence."

"Is that really necessary?" asked Kven.

"It is not for you to question the king," said Tesh-Khan authoritatively.

"Take me to the bishop," Plant Man ordered him.

"The bishop?" Kven tried to postpone his reply as they both walked towards the Episcopal Headquarters.

"Yes," said Plant Man. "The bishop! Ffesh!"

"That will be a problem."

"Why?" asked Ffen, who accompanied them, along with Jyoff.

"The bishop has fled the city!"

"What?" exclaimed Ffen.

"I expected as much," said Plant Man. "The Theocracy is a nest of cowards. Bishops and priests are like *jyuk*-roaches. They scatter at the first sound of approaching steps. Where is he headed? Tell me truthfully, Kven, as your honour depends upon it."

"The tunnel is located under the Episcopal Headquarters. It goes north-east for three *kobotv*s, to the edge of Shivka, on the outskirts of a hamlet called Biffda. He will reach it before you can send a force to retrieve him and will then be able to procure a *ffentbaff* and ride for Ritvator. I doubt that you will reach him in time."

"No matter," Plant Man shrugged. "But we shall try. Ffen, tell

Tesh-Khan to send a detachment of five *ffentbaff* cavalry after the bishop."

"As you wish, Majesty," Ffen bowed.

"And then return with your clerks to survey the treasury. One third shall be taken for our campaign and loaded onto *biffbaffs*; another third shall be distributed to the citizens as tax relief and three thousand *zelana* shall be used to rebuild and repair the city. The rest shall remain as a surplus for Kven to use as he sees fit."

"For me?"

"Yes, Kven, you shall remain as Lord of Ffantplain, but now you shall be the sole ruler, in allegiance to me and my heirs. After me, all authority rests with my queen, Arwa, and then my Lord Chancellor, Ffen. Obey this chain of command. A thousand troops shall remain here to protect Ffantplain from any theocratic reprisals or any uprising in favour of the Theocracy. Nevertheless, ye are all free citizens of my new kingdom. All taxes shall be reduced to one tax—the fealty tax. Each villager or farmer shall give ten percent of his income or one tenth of his harvest to the local chieftain and each chieftain shall give ten percent or one tenth of all his earnings to the lord or duke of the city, as shall all the denizens of the city. Each lord or duke shall then give ten percent to the king of each province and each king shall give ten percent to the High-King of all Tremn. In this way, all citizens shall pay an equal tax and the High-King shall receive ten percent of all tax revenue, with the poor paying the least because they have little or no income and the rich paying the most because of the abundance of their income. Thus shall equity be maintained and justice established in all the realm."

"What about poor relief?" asked Kven.

"The poor who receive less than the cost of living, which may be set at two hundred *patsim* per year, shall receive however much they lack of that amount from the city treasury or the treasury of the nearest town, village or hamlet, as a negative tax."

Having relayed the orders, Ffen returned to his side.

"I have already explained all this to my Lord Chancellor. Now, the episcopal seats shall be burnt to the ground, all bishops and priests arrested until their loyalty can be guaranteed or, if not, they shall all be beheaded. All lands belonging to the episcopal sees shall be confiscated by the state and given to landless peasants."

"How will the church be run, then, your Majesty?" asked Kven.

"All believers are one assembly—one body. In each area, they shall select a council of presbyters who shall swear loyalty to the High-King before they take office. These shall not be paid but shall preside over all ceremonies. Monasteries shall remain untouched, for now. They are important for the transmission of learning and are the bedrock of rural communities. However, celibacy shall no longer be enforced and all abbots and assistant abbots, as well as all monks, shall swear an oath of loyalty to me and renounce the Theocracy. Any who fail to do so shall be rounded up with the priests and beheaded."

"Very well," said Kven, though he secretly felt that the bloodshed was unjustified. To protest, however, would have been tantamount to disloyalty, and disloyalty would bring only death to him and all others who followed him. It was a risk too great to take so, for his own sake and that of his House, he kept mum.

"Lord Kven," Plant Man addressed him. "You shall remain here, with your people, to maintain order in my absence. Tesh-Khan's lieutenant, Tesh-Mashda, shall watch over the city forces. Go to your people and explain the new situation, including the new rules regarding taxation and poor relief, even if you must speak to every guild and district, as I wander the city."

Kven bowed and left his company. Ffen headed for the treasury with his clerks. The royal *ffentbaff* approached and Arwa descended to accompany her husband. Jyoff, Ushwan and Shem, with Meyla at his side, also accompanied him. Tesh-Mashda approached his king.

"Tesh-Mashda," said Plant Man. "You are the commander of all my forces in Ffantplain and shall remain here. Round up the priests, let them swear loyalty to me and behead those who refuse. Burn the Episcopal Headquarters and silence all opposition with the edge of your sword. Is that understood?"

"Yes, your Majesty," he bowed.

"Very well, leave us!"

"Ifunka the Conqueror," said Ushwan, congratulating him. "Is that what they shall call you?"

"I do not know how historians shall appraise me," he replied. "Nor am I certain that I shall continue to use the name 'Ifunka Kaffa'. Do I honestly want to share a name with that brute, Ifunka Kunug? Come, let us see Ffantplain in all its glory."

Of the four men, only Ushwan had been to a theocratic city before. In fact, other than Khanshaff, Ifunka and Ffen had never entered a city of any kind, and Jyoff had only seen one from afar. They visited the market, where business continued as usual, even during the siege, as frightened citizens purchased pitchforks, knives, trowels and other garden implements to defend themselves—a boon for the garden supplies salesmen. All eyes were on them as they passed, overawed citizens bowing as they saw the victorious conqueror approach. They passed by the Episcopal Headquarters and saw Tesh-Mashda and his soldiers throwing torches through the windows of the *tvagshaff*, hacking at the stone with steel hammers and hitting its walls with the catapult which hurled large rocks against its solid walls.

"Was that really necessary?" asked Ushwan.

"It is a symbol," explained Plant Man. "Which must be destroyed so that the Theocracy dies in the consciousness of each individual. More powerful and lasting than bricks and mortar are ideas, and ideas die slowly. As long as the symbol exists, the idea can perpetuate. Remove the symbol and the idea shall fade away. Every trace of the 'Holy Theocracy' shall be effaced; every bishop defrocked or executed, all their statues of priests and theologians smashed, so that the idea dies with them."

"A wise man once said, 'the weed outlives the gardener'."

"That's why I shall incinerate the garden," replied Plant Man. "And kill every plant within it."

They passed through residential districts and wandered across parks lined with wooden benches, admiring the statues and fountains. Finally, they reached the alleyways and workshops of craftsmen and apprentices attached to the city guilds. Eventually, they passed by a humble stonemason's shop at the edge of the district: a small workshop manned by a grizzled old man with a grey moustache, deep blue eyes and grey, shoulder-length hair, his face wrinkled with deep lines, his body small and frail, his strong hands covered with scars and accumulated grit and dirt, grease and sweat. He wore a tattered old apron of *meb*-skin, thick with grease stains and stone dust. He was hammering away at a hunk of rock while his apprentice, a young man of no more than thirty, held it in place, his attire similarly tatty and appearance unkempt, with a misshapen nose—fat and bulbous at the end—like a deformed turnip, wearing the brown woollen tri-cornered hat of an apprentice, called a *wiksha*, and dusty besmirched overalls. Plant Man gave him a cursory glance and the boy let go of the stone in shock, fell to his knees, cowering before the conqueror, while the old man dropped his hammer on his foot, cried out in agony and the stone fell crashing to the ground, splitting in twain to form to uneven slabs of no value whatsoever. Looking up at the plant-like lord, he lowered his gaze.

"Hail the King!" said the young man, while the old man said only, "Welcome back!"

Plant Man paused.

"Didst thou just say, 'welcome back'?"

He was uncertain whether to laugh or be wroth with the man. "Dost thou mock the king?"

"He's only a poor peasant," urged Ushwan. "Let's leave him be. We have obviously startled them."

"Here is a silver *zitv* for your troubles," said Plant Man, handing him the coin.

The man looked up at him.

"One *zitv*?" he asked. "For all my services?"

"For all your services?" Plant Man eyed him suspiciously.

"I may be a forest-dweller," Jyoff remarked. "But I've never heard of such impertinence. Shall we cut off his head and feed it to the forest worm?"

"Kvelikutim alyaog kaikavtilei (haste leads to sin), as the Tamitvar says," Plant Man replied. "Tell me, old man. What is thy name?"

"I am called Yon Kaffa," he said. The companions were taken aback.

"How comedst thou by the name Kaffa?"

"It is my family name," replied Yon. "My father was Ben Kaffa and his father Wen Kaffa, all the way back to Kaffa himself."

"And do you know any others called Kaffa?" Plant Man was intrigued.

"We are the only ones of our line, I and this boy, Ken, who is my nephew, and thou of course, your Majesty, Ifunka Kaffa."

"And what of Kandaspu Kaffa?" he asked, pressing for more information.

"There was no Kandaspu Kaffa," the man replied. "Though there was a Lord Kandaspu what lived with us, with his wife, Sapya, some twenty years ago, or thereabouts. He came to us forty years before that, hiding his identity and such-like. Here he lived as my own son and worked as an apprentice stonemason, just like Ken does now, and I arranged a dowry for him such that he could marry Sapya Bishkwa, the youngest daughter of Effi Bishkwa, the local priest, himself the nephew of Bishop Waltva, the father of Bishop Ffesh, and son of Gutvku, who vied with Waltva for the episcopal see some eighty years back. In any case, they had a son called Ifunka Kaffa, whom I took as my own grandson. Kandaspu died when you were only a week old and your mother, fearing that you might be endangered, or your identity discovered, took you to a family in Shivka forest called the Wobgas who had no children of their own and they were sworn to secrecy, telling all the forest-folk that Matuka was her brother."

Plant Man grabbed the old man's shoulders and stared at him intensely.

"Where is my mother?" he asked, emotion flooding him.

"She died some years ago," he explained, sadly. "But I can take you to her grave."

Yon and Ken led them to the local cemetery where bodies were buried in mounds surrounded by *givzash*-trees, each containing verses from the Tamitvar. On one mound were found the words: 'Sapya Bishkwa, daughter of the Priest Effi Bishkwa, son of the Priest Gutvku Bishkwa, son of Bishop Tseim'. Plant Man fell to his knees and embraced the mound like it was a living person, tears raining down his cheeks. Arwa embraced him from behind and Shem patted him on the shoulder.

"She loved me!" he cried. "She loved me!"

"She truly did," said Yon. "In her dying breath, she cried 'Ifunka'. Her daughters wept much over her."

"Daughters!" he stood up abruptly, supported by Arwa who clung onto his arm. "My sisters?"

"Indeed," said Yon. "Two of them. They were born after you, so they are slightly younger, but they live with me. Come to my home. It is the home you were born in, after all."

They walked back to the workshop and then ascended a stairway leading into a large *tvagshaff* housing hundreds of workmen and their families. It belonged to the Guild of Stonemasons and Concrete-Workers of Ffantplain, where each workman paid a nominal fee for bed and board such that it were as if they all belonged to a single corporation. Indeed, the head of the guild worked to ensure that retired workers were taken care of and, when profits were low, distributed from its treasury to the impoverished among them. These bodies of co-operation and mutual welfare operated as the bedrock of civilized society on Tremn, ensuring that the extremes of poverty were avoided, in line with the ethical and moral framework of the Holy Tamitvar. On the fourth floor, they found one small flat accessed through a singular round wooden door which creaked on its hinges. Entering, they found Yon's wife, Magda—a shrivelled old woman with a grey headscarf and beady little eyes who was too old to speak. She merely croaked a greeting and pressed her palms to her breast and extended them towards the guests in a sign of peace and welcome.

"My daughters," Yon called.

Two beautiful young girls with green eyes and silky-smooth bright ginger hair emerged, bowed and greeted them.

"Is this the new king?" asked one. "Whom they call Plant Man?"

"Indeed, it is, my darling," said Yon. "This is Ifunka Kaffa, your brother, who is the true High-King of Tremn."

"Does that make me a princess?" asked the other. She giggled.

Their ponytails bobbed as they spoke with an air of delightfulness and charm, yet their accent was atrocious, having been raised as stonemason's daughters, lacking in refinement and good vocabulary.

"Ye are both my princesses," Plant Man answered them. "And I love you both."

He embraced his sisters with great affection and Arwa joined them.

"We are delighted, Majesty," said the one.

"Call me *sister*, please," said Arwa. "I am your sister-in-law, Queen Arwa."

"All right," they agreed.

"My name is Pumi Kaffa," said the first one and, "My name is Kelff Kaffa," said the other.

"We are pleased to meet you, your Highnesses," said Ushwan.

"Indeed, we are," said Shem. "We are friends of your brother."

"Highness!" Pumi exclaimed. "Imagine that! Ain't it posh-like?"

"My lace and garters!" Kelff yolped. "We are high-folk now. And to think I thought of marrying Tod, the anvil-maker's boy!"

"We'll have to work on your poise and diction," said Plant Man. "It does not befit a lady to speak so."

"Ladies are by blood," said Pumi. "I has had the gumph of a lady long before I knowed it that I be one."

"Charming," said Ushwan sardonically. "Tell me, good sir"—he addressed Yon—"Who was this Lord Kandaspu?"

"He told me," explained the man. "That his mother's name was Lady Welda, the daughter of Kventa the Second, Protector of Okayeshvi, and that she died in childbirth with him, such that he was her only child. Now this is the interesting bit: she was married secretly to her lover, the Protector of Wadakit, Benad. Benad's wife, Liyan, had borne him no son—only a daughter called Lady Daffla, and she was married off to Weshob II, Protector of Ffantbav, so when Benad died, Weshob took over Wadakit and his heirs are thus protectors of two provinces at once. Benad had loved Welda with all his heart, but he kept their affair a secret and the marriage was also performed in secret, but the priest drew up a certificate so that, in good time, any son born to Welda might claim to protectorate of Wadakit. When Welda died, he named their son Kandaspu, for that the boy had a long nose and, when he was ten years' old, sent him to Ffantplain, as far away from Wadakit as he dared send him. With Benad's death, the secret went with him and only this remains as proof."

He opened an old wooden chest and took out a parchment which bore the seal of the officiating priest as well as the Seal of the Protector of Wadakit, imprinted in wax. It was definitive; Benad and Welda had married. He also produced a birth certificate for Kandaspu, who is called 'Lord Kandaspu of Wadakit, Prince of the Royal House of Ishmael, son of His Grace Benad, Protector of Wadakit, Heir of King

Ishmael Gan, and Lady Welda of Okayeshvi, daughter of His Grace Kventa the Second, Protector of Okayeshvi, Prince of the Royal House of Ishmael, and Lady Pumi of Tremael'. Finally, he showed them the marriage certificate of Lord Kandaspu, who is called merely 'Kandaspu, son of Benad of Wadakit', and 'Sapya Bishkwa, daughter of the Priest Effi Bishkwa and Kelff Bishkwa, his cousin'.

"It's all clear now," said Ushwan as Plant Man inspected the documents. "You are the true King of Wadakit and the Kings of Wadakit descend in the male line from Prince Mael, the 1st Duke of Wadakit, who was the second son of King Sfetva, High-King of Tremn. The Dukes of Wadakit were given kingship during the reign of Kubba Gven, and then all the provincial kings were reduced to symbolic 'Protectors of the Realm' during the time of Baku, the first Head of the Theocracy. Now that the Age of the Theocracy is over, your kingship must be restored. You are the true King of Wadakit, Ifunka, and the King of Wadakit is the true heir of Ishmael Gan; thus you are the High-King of Tremn by right of blood."

"Kings are made by blood," Plant Man opined. "But they reign through force of arms. These documents shall legitimize my authority, but we shall only succeed when the Theocracy is overthrown; else, why did Benad not claim his crown, if he was the true heir? Yon—" he turned to the poor old man. "You shall be a noble and rich man. You and Ken are coming with us, as are Princesses Pumi and Kelff."

"Yes!" they rejoiced.

"Bring your wife as well. Our *galad* only has effectiveness so long as we hit hard and fast, before the Theocracy can arm and deploy a large army against us."

"Where are you going next?" asked Yon.

"Ritvator," he replied. "Shall feel the wrath of the High-King!"

Yon quickly gathered some things while Ifunka's sisters packed two leather bags with their belongings, ready to leave. Yon's wife, Magda, had few possessions of her own.

"Arwa," said Ifunka. "Please take my sisters and the Kaffa family to the *galad* and help them find an appropriate *ffentbaff*. I must show these documents to Lord Kven. You can join me for congregational prayer in the temple before the army departs."

"Yes, my heart," she replied.

"And do pick up some appropriate clothing for them at the market on your way."

They walked together until they reached the centre of the city where Lord Kven could be found observing the demolition of the Episcopal Headquarters. Arwa continued with the Kaffas to the army without.

"For thousands of years," said Kven. "We've had a bishop. Then, one day, it all comes crashing down like toy blocks."

"There's no need to wax lyrical, your lordship," said Plant Man. "But anyway. There's something important I must tell you. Have a look at these documents."

The lord examined the birth and marriage certificates attentively.

"Remarkable!" he exclaimed. "So you are indeed the true king, the real King of Wadakit even!"

"Indeed," said Plant Man. "What do you think? Does this change anything?"

"It changes everything," he replied in eager tones. "Don't you see? Your legitimacy is established! The line of Wadakit has the best claim to the throne, excluding the House of Tsilel, which was barred, and the line of Saffik, which has never held the high-kingship. If your father, Kandaspu, was the grandson of the Protector of Okayeshvi, that makes you the great-nephew of Tvak, the current Protector. His sister was Lady Welda, your grandmother."

"Will they support us?"

"I cannot guarantee it," said Kven. "But we should try. My clerk can copy these, along with a letter signed and sealed by me, declaring my allegiance to you as High-King and asking for his aid. If Tvak can raise an army large enough, the Theocracy shall splinter."

"What of Wadakit? I *am* its king."

"I do not know if Benad II will give up the protectorate so easily. He is the only lord to have symbolic authority over two provinces and he surely believes himself to be the true Protector of Wadakit. He may even believe himself entitled the role of High-King. After all, Ffantbav, of which he is the head, was the seat of the High-Kings from Ishmael the Great until Gven Dakit, and was also ruled by Princess Pumi, Gven's daughter, until she married Kubba Gven, the first emperor. If they prove antagonistic, we can use Okayeshvi to strike at Wadakit, unseat Benad and seize the throne."

"Who shall take the letter to Tvak? It is a dangerous mission which requires the utmost secrecy, as the bishop and patriarch of Okayeshvi must not know about it, until that same patriarch can be captured and executed."

"I will go," Kven volunteered. "As I know Tvak personally. I went to school with his son and heir, Lord Trel, in Kubbawa. I cannot bring any Shaffu with me as they will be suspect."

"Take Ushwan with you."

"Majesty?" said Ushwan, perplexed.

"You are a sophisticated gentleman, old friend," said Plant Man. "I hereby appoint you as my Lord Emissary to Okayeshvi. Lord Kven shall find you appropriate attire, I'm sure. Take your knights with you, Kven."

"I shall," Kven accepted. "But Ffantplain shall need a ruler in my absence."

"Shem!" he called his friend over. "You are hereby appointed as the Lieutenant-Governor of Ffantplain. Where is Ffen to make note of all these things?"

A bespectacled clerk addressed him.

"Your Majesty," he said. "He is in the treasury with the other clerks, surveying the finances."

"Very well. You may draw up the relevant documents. When they're ready, Kven shall affix his seal and mine. Also see that these are copied."

He handed him the certificates.

"Go with Ushwan, Shem and Lord Kven and make all the necessary arrangements. Also, send a message to the Lord Chancellor. Tell him to give each soldier, including the new recruits from Ffantplain, a silver *zitv* each, two loaves of bread and a supply of dried fruit and nuts. Is that understood?"

"Yes, your Majesty," said the clerk, who scurried off to find a messenger.

When Arwa returned, he and she entered the temple, along with Jyoff. Hundreds of citizens had already begun to assemble for the *kashatvin*—the midday prayer; but there was no priest, as they had all been rounded up and interrogated, so the king escorted Arwa and Jyoff to the lord's prayer-box, and himself proceeded to the head of the congregation, all of whom faced the direction of the Tower of Inta—the *tsula* as it is called—which is the common direction of prayer for all the followers of the Right Religion. Before long, soldiers, merchants and others filled up the massive building until there was a congregation ten thousand strong. Those who could not fit inside the building prayed in the smaller shrines dotted around the city while most of the *galad* prayed in the open field, led by Tesh-Khan. Demolition of the Episcopal Headquarters was paused. The markets closed, workmen ceased their labours and, for the duration of the prayer, the city was silent, save only for the hum of verses recited in melodious tones in praise of the one Creator and Sustainer of the entire universe, the Lord of all the worlds and Tremn.

The temple was a large, circular fane, with a central dome supported by eight massive columns, a glass oculus pouring light from the sun into the centre of the hall. The worshippers stood on a huge carpet woven from the finest *woffgi*-silk, with colourful geometric patterns in hues of deep blue, jade and cyan, indigo and pearl-white, while the ornate mosaics on the walls formed calligraphic representations of select verses from the Tamitvar in cursive script—the *ffogat*—designed for such ornamental purposes and often used in correspondence and dictation. Light streamed through the hundreds of stained-glass windows while, within the central prayer-hall itself, *givzash*-trees could be found, forming a ring at the periphery, stretching around the circumference of the hall, containing the entire Tamitvar, carved into the living bark. At the centre of the hall was a single *yeshmelek* ('root descendant'). As in all temples of the Right Religion, this was said to be an offshoot or descendant of *Melekraffu*, the Primal Tree from *Kultvum Dian*. When he had reached this tree, Plant Man gave the *kvaila*—the call to prayer—which was only used for the three prayers that are preferably said in congregation: the *kashatvin*, *kashashom*, and *kashammanaffob*, while the *kashroim* and *kashofftishatvin* are preferably said at home or in private. It went as follows:

"Tesayeim yoshkimmin! Wabak Kakaneim yoshkimmin! Kash ffonitavtilei, ay yikralishwazinya! Intvkrafi

kashemkrafi, ay yikralishwazinya! Ramut iosint lemin! Cacansa Vaba iosint lemin!"

(God be praised! Great Spirit be praised! The prayer is beginning, O faithful ones! Come and pray, O faithful ones! God be praised! Great Spirit be praised!)

He performed the prayer and all those assembled followed his movements. When they had finished, he turned and addressed the crowd.

"O my people!" he said. "Today, you are free! Today, the Theocracy has departed from this city. Your bishop has fled and abandoned you. His headquarters are being demolished. But you have nothing to fear! Kven is now the true Lord of Ffantplain and shall rule over you without any obstruction from priests or theocrats. Taxes have been lowered to one tenth, excess wealth in the treasury shall be distributed to all those that are impoverished. The gate shall be repaired, and our dead shall be buried in honour. I know some of you have lost loved ones, but grieve not, for they are in Ganka—the Paradise where death and old age, sickness and want, suffering and pain, have no place. Some of you must see me as a foreigner or a monster. But I am a man like you—" he removed the Verdant Coin and appeared once more as his own self, nude save for a loincloth. The congregants gasped, Jyoff quickly throwing his overcoat over Ifunka so that he could appear modest.

"And I tell you this," he continued. "Which I have only just discovered. I was born in Ffantplain, in the stonemason's district, to Kandaspu and Sapya. The former was the son and heir to the Protectorate of Wadakit and true heir to King Ishmael the Great, while the latter was a descendant of the Bishop of Ffantplain, of the line of our Seer, Votsku. So, I am one of you and I am the true King of Wadakit and the High-King of all Tremn. Lord Kven must depart on a special mission so I leave Shem Effga as your Lieutenant-Governror until he returns. My people, all shall be well. May the Great Spirit be with you all."

"God save the King!" one old man cried, while a thousand others took up the cry, "Long live the King!" and "All hail the King!"

The temple thundered with their cries—cries born of a new loyalty. The tax cuts and generosity, the mild manner of his tone, and his association with Ffantplain fuelled their enthusiasm, while his humble origins in obscurity fed their delight. It was like a fairy-tale; too good to be true. As the story and his speech were repeated throughout the city, loyalty to the new king was cemented. Soon it would spread to the surrounding villages, and then from town-to-town—even to Ritvator—where the unity and integrity of the theocratic system would begin to deteriorate. When the troops had had their midday meal, they made ready to depart, now a mixed host of Shaffu warriors and Ffantplain troops. This detachment of citizens had now, as a result of the speech, swollen by another three thousand, such that they had some six thousand new soldiers, armed with all manner of weapons—even pitchforks and sharpened trowels. Not counting the Shaffu forces who remained in Shaffnâ, the army was now fourteen-thousand strong, with six thousand mounted on *ffentbaff*s from Shaffnâ, and an additional four thousand mounted four abreast on a thousand *ffentbaff*s gathered from the lord's stables or purchased from surrounding *ffentbaff*-herders. The other two thousand new recruits were positioned on newly-purchased *biffbaff*-carts.

Ffens' clerks had finished making a full account of the treasury, divided the money, and loaded a large amount thereof on the baggage-train. They also hired a hundred blacksmiths to accompany them in order to make weapons during camp, when they should pause for eight hours or more. Shem was attired in robes of state and bade farewell to his friends as they left. Meyla was clad in a splendid *woffgi*-silk dress which she delighted over. Ushwan was dressed as an officer of state, in majestic flowing robes, and set off with Lord Kven and his twelve knights, a personal secretary to assist him, a dozen squires, and Yobid and Ffelka, who were made to drive the *biffbaff*-cart which held the supplies for their journey to Okayeshvi. Plant Man mounted his royal *ffentbaff*, along with Arwa and Jyoff and, with a last glance at the city of his birth, ordered the *galad* to ride on, with all haste, to Ritvator:

"March, my army; march for Ritvator!"

"*Dhôm-krâ* (march)!" cried Tesh-Khan. "*Shkhî-krâ* (ride on)!"

"God save the King!" his army cried, even the newly-minted soldiers of Ffantplain.

Plant Man turned to his wife.

"Soon the news of our conquest shall reach the ears of theocrat and peasant alike," he whispered. "Soon the Archbishop of Kubbawa shall tremble as the city of Ritvator falls!"

~

END OF *GREEN MONK OF TREMN, BOOK II: THE RISE OF PLANT MAN, LORD OF WAR, CONQUEST AND REVENGE*

Preview Of 'Green Monk of Tremn, Book III: Kings, Queens and Thrones'

⁓

"Hurry up, Dilwa, hurry up!" cried the bishop with bated breath.

"I'm only as fast as I am, your Eminence," replied Dilwa. "I'm afraid I'm just not as young as I used to be."

"Codswallop!" shouted Bishop Ffesh. "I'm older than you."

They neared the end of the tunnel. Already they could see the light of day. They had squeezed through *kobotvs*' worth of blackness, grime and stale air, losing all hope of escape, until they reached this last stretch, where sunlight illuminated the last few *okshas* of toilsome crawling, until that final push, with their last ounce of energy, and they reached the exit. They found themselves at the edge of Shivka Forest, in the midst of a heap of moss and lichen-covered boulders. They had to push through spider webs and vines to break free but, even then, when they stood and stretched their cramped and weary limbs, bruised and sore, they found that the exit was practically invisible. The passage was well-and-truly secret. After resting for a few moments, they made with all due haste for the small hamlet of Biffda, which consisted of no more than five farmhouses surrounded by fields of *meb*-goats, *kogabish*, tame *nimff-ish*-gazelles, and a few *ffentbaffs*, whose hirsute backs were dusted with an abundance of snow. They approached the hamlet with caution, their feet crunching gently in the thin layer of snow which blanketed the fields and the rooftops of every *tvagshaff*, *tvansh* and *tvamshaff*. Approaching one of these *tvamshaffs* ('farmhouses'), a stout farmer with a *geltv*-hat, thick overalls and a grimy face waddled out, his prodigious belly making ordinary perambulations difficult. He carried a large pitchfork, and, at his wide black leather belt, there hung a curved dagger—a variety of *ffut* called a *ffutaish*. He eyed the bishop suspiciously, one bushy brown eyebrow raised above the other while his frown displayed an evident mistrust. It was easy to see why—Dilwa appeared to be a mud-caked *gatviff* bear, minus the blue eyes and fluorescent green fur. Bishop Ffesh, also layered with mud, his clothes torn and his hair unkempt, appeared to be a grubby drifter, wild and uncivilized.

"Who be ye?" growled the farmer.

"Do you not recognize us, farmer?" asked the bishop in his most imperious tone.

"A question with a question," replied the farmer. "What manner of trick is this?"

"No trick, peasant," said the bishop angrily. "I am the bishop!"

"A dirty bishop thou beest! What, hast thou crawled through the ground like a worm?" he guffawed.

"I am your bishop!" Ffesh shouted. "Treat me as such!"

"I reckon the king'd like for to have thee captive."

"The king!" Ffesh baulked incredulously. "There is no king!"

"Ffantplain is fallen and there's a new king what gives low taxes. Ain't ye heard?"

"How could you possibly know a thing about it!" Ffesh cried. "You're *kobotv*s out from the city!"

"News travels fast among us country-folk," he replied. "King Ifunka'll be hearing of this. Marga, get the boys to take a message!"

"What is it, thou old numpkin?" asked Marga, the farmer's wife.

"Send Tom and Bom to Ffantplain with a message: we've captured the bishop and his horrendous fat lover-boy."

"Lover-boy!" Dilwa cried in a tone which only confirmed the farmer's suspicions.

"The king'll give us a ripe ransom for this, I'll wager!"

~

Other Books by the Author

Check these other great books by NJ Bridgewater!
SCIENCE FICTION / FANTASY

The book that started the legend…
Green Monk of Tremn Book I:
An Epic Journey of Mystery and Adventure

MINDFULNESS / MEDITATION / SELF-HELP

MONEY-MAKING / INVESTMENT

* Also, please make sure to subscribe to our mailing list for updates on future articles or publications, including any other books in the *Green Monk of Tremn Trilogy* and the *Coins of Amon-Ra* series, as well as any future novels by NJ Bridgewater.[2]

    * **Click on** this link **to join our mailing list and get your** FREE GIFT: https://forms.aweber.com/form/58/1616149758.htm

    * **You can also follow the author, NJ Bridgewater,** @Nicholas19 on Twitter, Facebook **and** YouTube.[3]

---

1 For a FREE COPY of *151 Amazing Money Secrets: What the Rich Know about Money and Their Secrets to Success & Prosperity*, see: https://151amazingmoneysecrets.com/
2 See: https://forms.aweber.com/form/58/1616149758.htm
3 See: https://twitter.com/Nicholas19 ; https://www.facebook.com/NJBridgewater/ & https://www.youtube.com/channel/UCcMdGAbxcBf_so1WbhLDwog/

FULL LIST OF BOOKS BY NJ BRIDGEWATER
Science Fiction / Fantasy:

NJ Bridgewater (2017) *Green Monk of Tremn, Part I: An Epic Journey of Mystery and Adventure (Coins of Amon-Ra Saga, Book 1)* (Abergavenny, UK: Jaha Publishing). Paperback. Published: January 31, 2017. URL: https://www.amazon.com/Green-Monk-Tremn-Book-Adventure/dp/0995736901/

Mindfulness / Meditation / Self-Help:

NJ Bridgewater (2017) *Mindfulness: Five Ways to Achieve Real Happiness, True Knowledge and Inner Peace (Five Ways to Be, Book 1)* (Abergavenny, UK: Jaha Publishing). Paperback. Published: February 23, 2017. URL: https://www.amazon.com/Mindfulness-Achieve-Happiness-Knowledge-Inner/dp/099573691X/

NJ Bridgewater (2018) *Meditation: Five Ways to Master your Mind, Body and Spirit (Five Ways to Be, Book 2)* (Abergavenny, UK: Jaha Publishing). Paperback. Published: July 20, 2018. (paperback). URL: https://www.amazon.com/dp/0995736928/

Money-Making / Investment:

NJ Bridgewater (2017) *Bitcoin: 10 Ways to Make Money Using Bitcoin (Business Mastery Secrets)* (Luxembourg: Amazon EU S.à.r.l.). Kindle Edition. Published: November 18, 2017. URL: https://www.amazon.com/Bitcoin-Money-Business-Mastery-Secrets-ebook/dp/B077M1WJR2/

NJ Bridgewater (2017) *Information Products: 10 Ways to Make Money Using Information Products (Business Mastery Secrets).* Published on Gumroad.com, 28 November 2017. URL: https://gumroad.com/l/vvHYL

NJ Bridgewater (2017) *Gold: 10 Ways to Make Money Using Gold (Business Mastery Secrets).* Published on Gumroad.com, 28 November 2017. URL: https://gumroad.com/l/eYACw

NJ Bridgewater (2017) *151 Amazing Money Secrets: What the Rich Know about Money and Their Secrets to Success & Prosperity (Business Mastery Secrets)* (Luxembourg: Amazon EU S.à.r.l.). Kindle Edition. Published: December 6, 2017. URL: https://www.amazon.com/151-Amazing-Money-Secrets-Prosperity-ebook/dp/B077Z2RG87/

Also available for FREE at: https://151amazingmoneysecrets.com/

About the Author

Nicholas James Bridgewater, also known as **Abú-Jalál**, is an epic science fiction writer, poet, EFL lecturer and expert on Middle Eastern history and religion. He is also the author of several books on spirituality and self-development, including *Mindfulness: Five Ways to Achieve Real Happiness, True Knowledge and Inner Peace* and *Meditation: Five Ways to Master your Mind, Body and Spirit*, as well as books on business, wealth creation and investment, including short information guides on how to make money using information products, investing in gold and Bitcoin.[4] For more information on Bitcoin, make sure to read his article entitled 'What is Bitcoin?'[5]

NJ Bridgewater has studied Middle Eastern languages, history and literature at university and has a postgraduate degree in linguistics. He is also a qualified teacher of English as a foreign language (EFL) with experience in curriculum development and design. He has lived, travelled and worked in many different countries and spends his time reading, writing and teaching. He also maintains a blog called Crossing the Bridge[6] and has created an online course called Business Mastery Secrets.[7] In addition to history, religion and languages, he also writes about cryptocurrencies and digital assets, including Bitcoin and Ethereum.[8] You can follow him on Twitter @Nicholas19.[9]

---

4 See: NJ Bridgewater (2017) *Bitcoin: 10 Ways to Make Money Using Bitcoin (Business Mastery Secrets)*. URL: https://bizmasterysecrets.com/bitcoininformationguide
5 See: NJ Bridgewater (2017) What is Bitcoin? *Crossing the Bridge*, 7 December 2017. URL: https://nicholasjames19.blogspot.com/2017/12/what-is-bitcoin.html
6 See: https://nicholasjames19.blogspot.com/
7 See: Business Mastery Secrets: How to Build a Business Mindset Today! URL: http://bizmasterysecrets.com/
8 See: NJ Bridgewater (2018) What is Ethereum? *Crossing the Bridge*, 29 April 2018. URL: https://nicholasjames19.blogspot.com/2018/04/what-is-ethereum.html
9 See: https://twitter.com/Nicholas19